BAD AIM

ALAN LEE

SPARKLE PRESS

Bad Aim

by Alan Lee

First Edition
Printed in USA
Paperback ISBN **9798691888847**

Cover by Sweet 'N Spicy
Formatting by Vellum

Sparkle Press

Created with Vellum

THE DETECTIVE

The detective must be a complete man and a common man and yet an unusual man. He must be, to use a rather weathered phrase, a man of honor. He talks as the man of his age talks, that is, with rude wit, a lively sense of the grotesque, a disgust for sham, and a contempt for pettiness.

- Raymond Chandler

1

If I had a peer—I *don't*—it would be Liz Ferguson.

Liz had graduated from Virginia Tech and the ROTC program when she was twenty-two with a double major in Criminal Justice and Math. She immediately went into the Army, left six years later as a First Lieutenant, and became one of the DEA's youngest agents. Along the way she married her college sweetheart, man named Tom.

Tom developed a brain tumor in his early forties. Surgery was successful but the side effects remained—confusion, anxiety, fatigue, seizures. His career as an electrical engineer ended quick. Liz, God bless her, arranged an early retirement from federal work. Not enough to pass the rest of their days in comfort, but it bought her flexibility. She came home to care for her husband and be her own boss, working part-time as a private detective in Roanoke.

Liz did both well, with pluck and a smile. I was sometimes called by attorneys only after Liz had turned them down.

She came into my office on a warm morning in early September.

I corrected my posture.

She had a few years on me and she was married to a man I liked and I was married to a woman I adored, but I had a platonic crush on Liz Ferguson. She knew and tolerated it.

Were married men allowed to have crushes? It was harmless, similar to my feelings for Tom Cruise. I'd sit up straighter if he came into the room too.

"Knock knock, Mack," said Liz. She rapped on the door frame.

"Hello Lizzy."

"Got a minute?"

I stood.

"Always."

"Only you and my mother call me Lizzy."

"Us two, we know you best."

"I don't look like a Lizzy."

"Would you prefer Fergie?"

"Ugh," she said. It was the general consensus that we, the city of Roanoke, liked her appearance. Her looks were in her strength, her fitness. With her good jaw and the tiny cleft in her chin and her army-strong shoulders, if she wasn't so pretty she'd almost look masculine—but she didn't. She was biracial and she had enough Black DNA that her skin looked smooth and young; she'd told me Black skin doesn't wrinkle, which I thought unfair. Her hair was straight and didn't reach her shoulders.

I wondered if she liked how I looked.

She'd never mentioned it. Poor woman, eyesight must be going.

"How's Tom?" I said.

"Do you know, Mack, somehow taking care of him is the most important thing I've ever done. Isn't that the damnedest thing. He's happy and I'm more content than I thought possible."

"Show off."

She grinned. "How about you? You look good," she said. I *knew* it. "Tan and healthy."

"We vacationed in Bermuda for two weeks. *Two*. What madness."

"I'd have lost my mind. What'd you do?" she said.

"Built a lot of sandcastles and drank a lot of rum."

"You, Veronica, and the boy?"

I nodded.

"Kix laid off the rum."

"Do you know how often I get asked about your romantic life? No one can figure you and Veronica out and they think I should know," said Liz.

"Cause you're a professional snoop?"

She sat. I sat. She wore tight Levis and a tank top with a thin leather jacket over it, the kind women wear that look a little too small but really that's just the style. Black Nike running shoes and no gun that I saw.

I wondered if she was enjoying my potpourri.

She said, "Speaking of snooping, let's talk shop. You're hired."

"*Heyo!*" I said.

"Heyo?"

"It's a goal of mine to display excitement and enthusiasm organically."

Liz said, "But I know you. You're neither excited nor enthusiastic. Nor was that organic."

"I'm trying. Ninety percent of success is showing up. *Heyo!*"

"Sheesh Mack."

"I'm worth it. Who wants to hire me?"

She pointed at herself. “Me, with Roland Wallace’s money. Big bucks. He hired me but the job’s cumbersome and I want you to help.”

“Sure.”

“Good. That was quick,” said Liz.

“It’s important to maintain collegial relationships.”

“I plan on asking Walter Lowe too.”

“What,” I said, “the hell.”

“You don’t like Walter.” She said it wearing a smile.

“You don’t either.”

“For a private eye, he’s okay.”

“Hmm,” I said.

“He suffices. For what I want done.”

“Hmm,” I said. “I’ll say no more. Just hmm.”

“You don’t talk poorly about people behind their back, do you.”

“Fortunately for Walter.”

“I don’t need much from him, just a warm body. It’s you I want for the heavy stuff,” she said.

I *knew* it.

I said, “What’s the job?”

“Are you still turning away mundane work?”

I did a shrug. A modest one. Fingers laced across my stomach.

“Some of it,” I said.

“So you can start immediately.”

“I’ll juggle some things. If the job’s interesting.”

“Someone’s trying to kill Roland Wallace. He hired me to prevent it and catch the culprit.”

“Ooo.”

“You’re interested,” she said.

“Murder stimulates me. Who’s Roland Wallace?”

"An old rich guy, lives in a palace near Ballyhack Golf Club."

"You're DEA. You can't catch a bad guy?"

"My client would like to remain alive. Keeping someone alive's damn impossible if the killer's dedicated. You know this. It's a big job. A full-time job. I can't commit full-time hours."

"You hire Lowe," I said, "then Roland Wallace is toast."

She grinned again. I thought it was great when she grinned. "Walter Lowe has more hours to burn than you or me. He'll be a deterrent to murder."

"Tell me how old man Roland knows someone wants to kill him."

She did a nod. Settled more comfortably in the chair. She had a direct way of maintaining eye contact, like she didn't know she was doing it. "Roland called me two days ago and told me the story. Said he noticed his water bottle had been tampered with. He's naturally suspicious so he poured it out into his front birdbath. Lo and behold, two birds died. Then his gun goes missing, and he calls me."

As I listened, I steepled my fingers and looked brilliant.

She said, "I listened to his story, decided he's paranoid, but I visited anyway. Before I get there, he discovered his medicine cabinet's been tampered with. He showed me. While we were talking, I took a look at the stuff already opened. His aspirin looked funny. I took it to a lab. Turns out, it's strychnine."

"Jiminy Christmas."

"I forgot how stupid you talk. But yes."

"Strychnine would do it. Or ruin your month. Someone's trying to kill Roland," I said.

"Or he wants me to think someone's trying to kill him."

"You called the police."

"Over his protests. He hates police. He did a sixty-day stint when he was younger and it was bad enough that he'll never forgive them. They questioned him. He wouldn't cooperate. They dusted for prints, came up empty, filed a report, blah blah."

"I'm on the case."

"Great news. I knew you would be. But here's a caveat. Roland wants to catch the culprit. Not scare him away. Or her," she said.

"Ah."

She agreed. "Ah."

"So we gotta do this without the killer finding out we're doing it. Because if the killer finds out, he or she will head for the hills."

"You got it."

"Any guesses?" I said.

"I have six guesses. I'll tell them to you when we meet with Walter Lowe," she said and I glowered. "Mack, there's only three private detectives in Roanoke worth a damn. Walter is one of them."

"Don't you think," I said, "I should count as more than one?"

She did not.

2

The next morning was a big morning.

A morning of significance and consequence. And tears.

It was Kix's first day at a Roanoke's finest Montessori school.

What did Montessori mean? I wasn't positive. Was Kix too young for it? Probably. Did it cost too much? Goodness gracious. Was the waiting list infinite? It was, but Ronnie had cleared the dean of accumulating traffic entanglements. So, pow, we were in.

Kix wore Sperry boat shoes and khaki pants and a blue collared shirt, emblazoned with the school's crest. He pulled at the collar.

Robbie.

"Robbie," said Kix.

Robbie, I cannot believe, he said, *how good I look. It is remarkable.*

Ronnie wiped at the tears running down her cheeks.

"I cannot get over," she said, "how handsome he looks. It hurts, Mackenzie. It causes me physical pain. Something inside me aches at how gorgeous he is."

I KNOW. And the collars are good to chew on, yes? There's no other reason for them.

My dog, *our* dog, Georgina Princess August, a handsome boxer, watched her with concern. Wondering at the crazy lady's emotion.

I set down my coffee. "Good parentage, is all."

"The best parentage."

Kix requested more banana. Ronnie acquiesced.

I said, "He's had too much."

"It's his first day and he's scared. He can have the moon if he asks."

Kix smiled. At me. *Hah. Thank you, Robbie.*

"I like that he calls me Robbie." She turned to the mirror near the rear staircase. Wiped her cheeks again. She wore jeans that highlighted the unique and shapely wonder that was her butt, and a sleeveless silky pink blouse. Which meant no court today and no new clients.

I liked jean days.

I also liked short skirt days.

In fact, since Darren Robbins died, all my days were halcyon. No one wanted to kill me. Or Ronnie. She was happy, I was happy, Kix was happy, everyone was happy.

Except for this very minute.

"I'm lucky I had waterproof mascara." She snatched a tissue and blew her nose and wiped her eyes. "Okay. Okay. I'm ready."

You are not, said Kix.

"We still have a minute."

"Good. I'm not ready." She lowered into a dining table chair. Her jeans were so snug around her strong hamstrings I thought the fabric might rip. She didn't seem to notice the snugness so I did it for her. "Is he ready? I mean, ready ready?"

"A couple days a week at the Montessori school should be a breeze for him," I said.

"No. He's not old enough. Is he. Look at him."

"Maybe not, but also he's immortal. I cannot remember life before him. How could he not be old enough if he's immortal."

"This is a good school," she said.

"It's not school. It's not even preschool. It's guided play. And he'll be great at it."

I already am. Honestly, you two. Quit being babies.

She nodded "He will be."

I replenished the coffee in my Yeti—the rare import Manny allowed—and set the lid on.

Ronnie said, "I shouldn't have talked you into this. But it's a good school. And he deserves it."

I totally do.

I picked him up. Grabbed the coffee.

She looked panicky.

"But! What if he—"

"Ronnie."

"Yes Mackenzie."

"It'll be good. Let's go."

She nodded. "Yes. Okay. I'm fine."

~

THE SCHOOL WAS SMALL, not as big as a standard elementary structure, built on the outskirts of Raleigh Court. But it was new and full of windows. The drive lasted four minutes. My Honda Accord expressed some sheepishness, parked between Mercedes SUVs.

On the first day of school, parents walked their children all the way to the classroom. Kix gripped my shirt, tight, watching the other children, many of whom were crying. Ronnie gripped my arm, tight, watching Kix.

The place looked like a college for babies, with dark oak paneled walls in as many spots as possible, and plaques on the paneled walls. The air smelled like diaper powder and Febreze and money.

Kix and I had come to meet the teacher last week. Nice woman named Mrs. Buchanan, permed hair showing the first hints of gray.

Kix saw her and gripped with greater strength.

I have concerns. What are we doing?

Mrs. Buchanan smiled and clapped her hands and made noises like preschool teachers should.

She said, "Now remind me, make sure I'm getting my boys correct. This is Kix?"

Dear heavens, she doesn't even know my name.

"This is Kix."

"Why *hello*, Kix! Are you ready for fun?"

Shut, said Kix, *up. Father, let's get out of here.*

"What an interesting name, Kix. Where does it come from?"

Around us, parents and toddlers flowed and wailed.

This was like baby college mixed with prison.

I said, "His mother selected the name. I was told it has significance in the world of country music."

"*Oh!*" She beamed at Ronnie and shook her hand. "You're a Brooks and Dunn fan, then! Me too, and I have been for twenty years."

Ronnie beamed back. Some of the traffic flowing around us slowed as she did.

"I'm not his mother, I'm Ronnie. And no, I only lean into country as far as Keith Urban."

"*Oh!*" Minor embarrassment at the motherhood faux

pas, quickly moving on. "A pleasure to meet you, Ronnie! You're Ronnie Summers, aren't you."

"I am. I'm obsessed with the August boys and I follow them around."

"*Oh!* Isn't that the sweetest!"

I think this lady's a terrorist. I HATE it here!

I took Kix into the classroom. There were two other kids. One was crying. The other thought cryers were sissies and he threw a car. I respected that.

Father! This is a mistake! Ronnie's right, I'm too young!

I set him on a calendar rug near a toy bin and pried his fingers off.

Father! Dad. Hey *Dad!*

"Alright, kiddo, have fun."

Is that a joke? Does this look fun? Dad!

He grabbed at me again. Got a good hold on my shirt.

Dad! Hey! Are you listening? I can go louder.

Ronnie, the traitor, refused to come help.

Mrs. Buchanan was welcoming another family.

Dad! Dad! DadDadDad!

I levered his hand free again. He got my pants instead, pulling himself up. Tried to climb.

I set him down and he took hold of my watch. A fierce clench.

That kid threw a toy at us. Kix expressed his dismay. The next family came in, their child whimpering.

Hell on earth.

Batman, I bet, never had to do this.

~

Back in the Honda Accord. Feeling like I'd lost a boxing match to Sugar Ray Leonard.

Ronnie took a shaky breath and smiled at me and touched my face. “He scratched you.”

“He handled that about as well as you did.”

Small laughter. “Sorry.”

“You could’ve helped. Now I’m the one he thinks hates him.”

“No he loves his dad, that’s why he kept calling for you.” She pulled down the mirror to check her makeup. “And I got the impression Mrs. Buchanan would rather I not enter.”

“Because you said you’re not his mother. You said you’re just Ronnie.”

“I didn’t know what to do.”

“We’re married. You could say that.”

“We’re only married a little.”

“That’s not a thing.”

“It wouldn’t be ideal. Those idiot moms in there already look at me weird, without you trying to explain it.”

“You don’t care what they think.” I gripped the wheel, willing my hands to settle.

Mackenzie August, über wimp.

“Their opinion means nothing to me. But also...” She put up the mirror. Took another deep breath. “But also I’m angry at them.”

“Angry. At the idiot women in the hallway?”

“Yes.”

“Do you know why?”

“I don’t. But now I have to go weep all over my paralegal.”

I started the car.

3

Liz Ferguson and I went to Walter Lowe's office. He had a room on the upper floor of a hundred-year-old building, once a stately downtown house, now chopped into offices. Other than Walter, the top floor was empty, because it wasn't tax season and the graphic designer was out.

Walter Lowe, where you could 'Get the Lowe Down on Roanoke.'

Dumb.

Lowe sat in one of his client chairs, sneakers untied and up on his coffee table. He was playing on his phone. He looked like a truck driver but not a good one. Wore a thin beard to help his jaw. Empty bag of Cheetos on the table.

He glanced at us, then back to his phone.

"Liz and Mack, whaddaya doin."

"Feeling better about myself," I said.

Liz grinned. "Hello Walter. You look like a man with a moment to talk."

"Sure, whatever. Look at us, the three best detectives in Roanoke, all in one room." Still on his phone, talking loud. "I'm third. I know you're thinking it."

Liz dusted Cheetos detritus off the second client chair and sat. I moved behind his desk and took the swivel chair.

"Don't look at my computer. I use it for porn," he said.

I stood up from the swivel chair. Leaned against the wall and crossed my arms.

"Come on, Mack, I'm just kidding, kinda." He clicked off his phone. Set it down. "Want coffee?"

Lis said, "Are you busy the next ten days?"

"Nah, usual shit. Divorce work, plaintiff work, taking photographs when I get around to it. Courts are still backed up from the pandemic."

"I'd like to hire you," she said.

"Just me?"

"Mackenzie already agreed."

He nodded my way, looking pleased. "Big Mack wants to work me with, eh. Can't blame him." He tried to get up. Tried again and it worked. Went to his shelf and held up a book by David Allen. "Got the book you sent. Meant to say thanks."

I said, "Read it?"

"Sure, look at me, getting all the things done. Nah, I didn't read it. I might. Not a big reader. What's the job?"

Liz was making eye contact with me. Having second thoughts. I sent her a wordless message with a sigh and an eyebrow raise—*perhaps we should hire a poodle instead.*

She got it. And she smiled.

She said, "A man's life is being threatened. He asked me to keep him alive and catch the culprit. I need your help."

"Yikes. No thanks."

"Lowe," I said.

"What? I don't catch killers."

"You don't do anything."

"That's hurtful, Mack. What's it pay?"

She told him what she'd pay per day. It was the equivalent of his hourly rate times three. Not a lot, but more than he usually made in twenty-four hours, I was sure.

"The rich guy is springing for all us?"

"Roland Wallace is his name, and yes," she said.

"What's Mack making?"

"More than you."

"Ouch."

She did a shrug. A cute one. "More than me, too."

"How's that fair?"

I said, "I'm a Veblen good."

"You know I don't know what that means."

"Means people prefer to pay more for luxury products or services. For a Veblen good, people *want* to be charged more."

"That's bull," he said.

"Like paying an extra ten grand for the Jaguar emblem on their sports car. They can't wait to brag to their friends how much they paid."

"So you're a Jaguar sports car."

"At minimum," I said.

"And I'm an old station wagon, I get it."

"It's a complicated concept. I regret bringing it up."

He said, "Yeah me too. But I don't catch killers."

"Tell me why," said Liz.

"They *kill* people. And I like living."

"You're not living," I said.

"Go ahead, give me the Braveheart speech. Go on."

"You need stressors in your life, Lowe."

"Mel Gibson didn't say that."

"You're soft and comfortable, and that's the enemy. You need a challenge," I said.

"That makes no sense. Who wants challenges. That's why we have electricity."

"A good football player lifts weights. He needs the hurt, needs the challenge."

"Huh? What's that go to do with anything?"

Liz was grinning. "Use smaller words, Mack."

I said, "Obstacles, good. Free time, bad. Get it?"

"I absolutely do not." He dropped the book back on his shelf. Dust blossomed. "You two, a former detective and a federal agent. Me, I got two-thirds of a Political Science degree and a background researching house titles. Now I photograph spouses screwing around. The hell will I catch a killer?"

"If it helps, apprehension wouldn't be your job," said Liz.

"Huh?"

She nodded at the chair next to her. "Sit back down. Hear me out."

"Mack isn't sitting."

"You insinuated that you masturbate in the chair," she said.

He grinned some. "Sounds gross when you say it."

He sat.

"Roland Wallace," said Liz, "was nearly poisoned by a water bottle that'd been tampered with. Then his gun vanished. He got spooked and called me and I discovered strychnine in his medicine cabinet."

"I don't know what strychnine is," he said.

"Highly toxic, used to kill rodents. It's odorless. He could've downed several and not known until it was too late."

"Well damn. Someone's trying to kill Roland. How'd I do, Mack, was that some high level investigating?"

"Be a shame, someone slipped strychnine into your Cheetos," I said.

"That's aggressive. So who's trying to kill him?"

"That's what Mackenzie will find out."

"What'll I do?" he said.

"While Mackenzie snoops, you deter future attempts at killing Roland."

"Throw myself in front of a bullet, you mean. No thanks."

I pinched the bridge of my nose with my finger and thumb. Better than pinching his windpipe closed. "Lowe, how would someone get into the medicine cabinet?"

"I don't know. How?"

"How would someone replace water bottles in his fridge?" I said.

"Am I supposed to know? Use the door, I guess? I don't get it."

"Not many people," I said, "have access to Roland's medicine cabinet. Or even know where it is. Whoever's doing it, he or she is a common visitor to the house."

"Okay."

"In other words, he or she isn't taking long range shots with a rifle. No need to leap in front of anyone."

"Sure. Got any suspects?"

"Six of them," said Liz.

"*Six?*"

"So far."

"Who are they?"

Liz held up six fingers, four and two, and ticked them off. "Roland's housekeeper. Roland's landscaper. His nephew. His finance guy. His nurse. And his best friend. They're all at the house several times a week. His nephew lives there."

I was hearing this for the first time.

"Who benefits from his will?" I said.

"I don't know. I signed on for this two days ago and spent most of yesterday at Roland's house, checking it out, during a break I came to see you, and today I'm here. After our conference, I'm heading straight to Roland's. I know very little."

"I can take photographs of those six," said Lowe.

"What I want you to do," said Liz, "is go undercover and move into Roland's house."

"Like hell. Why?"

"To deter violence, as I mentioned previously," she said. "Whoever is doing this will think twice with you around."

"Cause I'm so intimidating to look at." He said it with a snort.

"You'll pretend you're a distant relative who lost his job. Roland's taking you in. You hang around, keep your eyes open, talk to people, listen to people, maybe you'll crack this thing all by yourself, Walter."

"Yeah Walter, all by yourself."

"I don't like your tone, Mack," he said, talking too loud. "Did you think this up?"

I shook my head. "Lizzy's calling the shots."

"Lizzy? We can call her Lizzy?"

"No you may not," she said.

"Mack just did."

"He's a Veblen good."

Wow!

Calm down, Mackenzie, since when do you care about the opinion of others.

"While I'm in the house, Mack is investigating the suspects?"

"Correct," she said.

"I should get paid more if I'm working round the clock."

"His house is impressive, Walter. You should get paid less because your full-time lifestyle at Roland's will be a significant upgrade over eating chips and playing your phone all day in this office."

"You two are mean," he told her. "What are you doing, then?"

"I'm helping you both as often as I can. Several hours a day with you, several hours a day investigating suspects with Mackenzie."

"Your husband still laid up?"

Liz took a deep breath and kept her eyes fixed on Lowe. Her leg, crossed over the other, stopped bouncing. "Tom does better with help, yes. I have a nurse check in with him when I know I'll be out."

"Sorry, I sounded insensitive. I like Tom, you know."

"Thank you."

"I want a bonus if I catch the killer. Or killers. Could be multiple."

"Good point," I said. "Hickam's dictum."

"Hickam's what? Easy, Mack, with the potty talk, Lizzy's listening."

"It's the idea that there's often more than one cause to a problem when the—"

"*Boring*, I take it back, there's only one killer."

I said, "So Occam's razor, then. The theory that the simplest solution is—"

"Okay, seriously, I get it, you're smarter than me, shut up."

"Maybe the entrance exam to being a PI should be more stringent," I said.

"It should be heavily weighted toward how long you can sit on your ass in one place, watching boring people do boring things," said Liz. "Our current case being the exception."

"I'm better than Mack at sitting on my ass. I should get paid extra."

"Charge your clients more," I said. "See what happens."

"I don't get enough work as it is."

"Charge more. And then earn it."

"Nah. Sounds like work." He picked up his phone. Held it sideways for the video game. "Okay, whatever, I'll keep Roland alive. I'll pack and be there tonight. Send me the address."

"We'll go together, Walter. Tomorrow. I've got today covered."

"Sure, even better."

Liz and I shared another look. She was coming around to my point of view.

Roland, we thought, was toast.

4

I went by The Fresh Market and bought filets. What's a cool September evening for if not steaks. Also I purchased a six pack of Lagunitas Day Time IPA. Drove to our large foursquare craftsman on Windsor, home sweet sweet home.

Ronnie was already there. She'd picked Kix up from his first day at Montessori school. She was reclined on the couch, a blanket over her feet. Kix sat on her lap, cradled against her chest. Both of them asleep.

Growing up's exhausting.

Ronnie's right hand was scooped around Kix. Her left rested on top of Georgina Princess, lying next to the couch. Georgina Princess watched me like, *she isn't scratching me but don't worry because no will hurt them because I am here.*

I set the steaks out to thaw. I did so without sound. Then sat in the reading chair to catch up on reading The Atlantic.

After two articles I decided I was tired of the world being on fire. It burned everywhere except Chez August.

I stepped outside and watered the flower beds with a hose, and soaked dry patches of grass still recovering from the hot summer. Anything outside the shade of our maple and magnolia trees got baked.

When I judged I had an hour before grilling, I rubbed salt and pepper into the filets. Sent out a group text message asking who'd be joining for supper. Took yellow potatoes out of the pantry. Verified we had salad ready to mix. Poured beer into a glass.

Eat, drink, and be merry.

Kix made noises from the couch.

Ronnie stretched. Softly she said, "Mackenzie."

"Yes Ronnie."

"I love waking up to you."

"Here's looking at us, kid."

Kix yawned. Turned over. Did some toddler sounds.

Ronnie said, "When I picked him up, the lady at the front desk radioed for him. Do you know what she said? Kix's ride is here."

"That bitch."

I could hear the smile. "Do you understand? Not Kix's mom or Kix's babysitter or Kix's aunt. His *ride*. They don't know what to do with me."

"How about I explain we're married," I said.

"Not yet."

"Because?"

She yawned. "Because I have issues."

I turned on the Alexa speaker and played Dean Martin radio because Ronnie liked him.

Manny Martinez came home. My friend the federal marshal. He'd been in the gym a lot since the pandemic eased and his shirts were tighter through the shoulders and chest, the showoff.

Set his satchel near the door—an empty satchel, carried only to make his coworkers feel better about themselves—

and washed out a protein shake bottle. Loosened his tie and took Kix from the couch and they flew up and down the stairs.

I fired the grill on the back deck, set it to high. Poured olive oil into a pan. Chopped potatoes into cubes and slid the cubes into the hot pan. Sautéd them with paprika, parsley, onion power, and garlic. Set the steaks onto the grill and they sizzled immediately and I knew that life was worth it all. Turned off the heat under the potatoes. Dumped salad into a serving bowl so Ronnie could pour dressing and set croutons and other accoutrements on top. I flipped the steaks and set pads of butter melting on each. Poured the steaming potatoes into a bowl next to the salad.

Timothy August arrived next. He held the door for Sheriff Stackhouse, who was smiling. They could be a couple on a soap opera, where the guy looks respectable and wise, and the woman looks like sex and determination.

Ronnie transferred food from the kitchen counter to the dining table, and I silently gave thanks to the merciful Lord for blue jean day.

The steaks came off the grill, maybe a minute more into medium than I wished.

Stackhouse and my old man were laughing about something at the front stairs, their foreheads touching, and I thought them indecent and hoped the laughter wasn't about their lurid lunch date; I also hoped they wouldn't explain themselves.

Ronnie retrieved white wine from the fridge and red wine from the pantry. Manny set Kix into the highchair, cut up fruit for him, and poured food into GPA's bowl.

I set cans of cold beer onto the table and all of us sat. We didn't have a dining room but we had a big table that sat in a space between the kitchen and the leather couches. The table had its own space but Manny said dining rooms were passé so we never called it a dining room. Besides, there were no walls, the whole floor was open, and who would've guessed Manny understood the definition of passé.

I said grace and meant every word of it, going a little misty with gratitude. It's stupid, I recognize it's stupid, but sometimes the planet slowed for me, where my life and the lives of those around were held in a crystalline drop of time, and I knew for certain the moment was a holy one, and that the hard work and the tears and sweat were a tiny price to pay, and raw existence was sweet, so sweet and pure it hurt.

The others felt it too, around the dining table. A reverence, an awareness our community was more than the sum of its parts, that we added up to something near the ideal. We couldn't discuss it, the thing being too fragile, a bubble that would pop when touched. But often we held hands longer than necessary after grace, because it seemed to matter.

And it did.

Or maybe, on the other hand, maybe I was becoming an old softy.

We tucked in with zeal.

The steaks, as it turned out, were correct.

As the cook, I had the honor of taking lead and relaying the highlights of my new case. My congregation responded with an appropriate amount of respect and interest.

Halfway through our meal, Stackhouse pointed at Manny with the hand holding her wine. "Heard about your partner, babe."

Manny leaned back in his chair and wiped his mouth with a napkin. Made it look cool. "You hear what happened to the guy who did it?"

"I heard you ran him over," said Stackhouse.

"I did. Then I backed up."

Ronnie said, "Fill us in. What happened to Noelle?"

"Collin Parks and me, we're serving a warrant. Big ugly white guy with a long mustache, calls himself Nathan the Ninja. *Ay caramba*. We knock on his door. Beck is in the car. Noelle Beck. Beck sees Nathan the Ninja jump out the back of the building into the alley. She draws her gun. Tells the ninja *pendejo* to lay down. He's wearing a robe. He gets down on his knees, hands up. Before I can get there, he draws a sword, a *sword*, one of those cut bananas."

"Katanas, maybe," I offered.

"What I said. He draws a *katana* from his back. Slices Beck across the stomach. Cut her wide open."

Ronnie made a gasp. I nearly did.

"She's okay, though?"

"She's sewed up now. They'll let her go home tomorrow. *Ay, venga*, I was so worried."

"You ran the ninja over?" I said.

"He cut her and ran. So I drove him over and backed up and that's letting him off easy."

I nodded. "Agreed. Maybe should be an eye-for-an-eye situation."

"I cuffed him to a lamp post and Collin drove us to the hospital. I held Beck's stomach closed on the way." Manny checked his watch—a Pelton watch, made in America he told me, and I didn't care much. He said, "About time for me to go. The mean nurses kicked me out, told me she had to rest. I said I'd be back in four hours but really I'm only giving them three."

Timothy set his wine down. "I always win at central office when the principals share about our families. Mine are the best stories. They keep asking about the crazy people I live with but they barely believe the stories."

"We'll send Noelle flowers," said Ronnie.

"She works in the marshal's office. No need for flowers. Send her a knife-proof vest." Manny drained his beer. Stood and retrieved Kix, who'd fallen asleep again without anyone noticing. He laid Kix's head onto his shoulder and said, "Big day. Taking him to bed before I go," and went upstairs.

Stackhouse muttered into her wine, "I swear, anytime that man picks up the baby my ovaries act funny."

5

Roland Wallace lived in a secluded neighborhood fifteen minutes outside Roanoke City, halfway between Ballyhack Golf Club and Horseshoe Creed Stables, with a view of both. In 2012, a real estate baron had shaved the dome of a wide hill and built a neighborhood at the peak. The neighborhood only contained eight houses, but each could be its own plantation. I looked them up on Zillow and the least expensive residence was valued at a million and a half.

The lone road leading into the enclave had an unmanned guardhouse and I drove through to the long loop beyond. The houses branched off a shared meadow. Roland's long driveway curled through a row of pine trees, beyond which were wide vistas of the Blue Ridge Mountains. His house was a modern sprawling manor, technically a craftsman with strong geometry and good lines. Over five thousand square feet, and another two thousand worth of porches. Three-car garage. I braked at the front steps and Walter Lowe parked his Jeep Cherokee behind me.

I got out. The view was even more remarkable at the

house, mountain ridges for eternity. Great trees throughout the neighborhood. I could see five of his neighbors from here. A landscaper was riding a mower near a distant fence.

Liz was already here, sitting in a rocking chair on the front porch next to Roland, under a ceiling fan.

She stood. "Welcome, guys. Mackenzie, Walter, I'd like you to meet Roland—"

"You." Roland pointed at me. "You're Mackenzie August. Recognize you."

"Breathtaking, isn't it." I came up the stairs.

"Bigger than I thought. She asked me if she could hire you. I said yes. Because I was intrigued." Roland looked like late seventies and he was beginning to slow. He stood up, carefully, with a minor stoop. Easy to see he'd been a stud most his life. Strong jaw, lots of silver hair. He said, "You know why? I wanted to get a look. You killed my brother."

Mackenzie August, caught off guard.

Killed his brother.

Liz looked she was trying to swallow a baseball. Behind me, Lowe made a snickering sound.

"Did I," I said.

"Mr. Wallace, are...are you sure?" said Liz. "You never mentioned..."

I put some pieces together. Wallace.

"You're Rob Wallace's brother," I said. "There's some resemblance."

"That's right." Snapped a nod. "He was my younger brother."

"I'm sorry about his death. I didn't shoot him but I was involved."

He nodded again, watching me, interested, suspicious. "What the newspaper said. That you were there, but a fucking cop pulled the trigger. Didn't trust the story."

"That's how it went down."

"What?" said Liz. "When was this?"

"Couple years ago. In an underground woodshed."

"That's right." Lowe snapped his fingers. "That thing. The missing kids. I forgot about that thing."

"My little brother, the religious nut. We hadn't spoke in years. Sit down, August, tell an old man what happened."

"Story's pretty accurate in the paper," I said.

Roland lowered into his rocking chair again. The front porch was deep and wide and populated with chairs. He nodded at the one adjacent. "Sit. Tell me. From your own eyes."

I sat. Liz did too. Lowe stuck hands into his pockets and wandered the porch, close enough to listen.

"It's not fun. Might be wise to remember him as you do now."

"I do not recall him in a good light, August. We parted years ago, over that damned church. Tell me how he died."

"I was hired to investigate a priest at All Saints. Louis Lindsey. He was a sexual predator and I proved it. I didn't realize your brother was involved, a supporter of Lindsey. He ambushed us in the bunker."

Roland held up a hand. "Us?"

"Me, Lindsey, and Hugh Pratt."

"Hugh Pratt."

"You know him?" I said.

"Remember him. Another zealot. Keep going."

"Your brother surprised us at the top of the stairs. Threw us down, took my gun. He dislocated Hugh's right shoulder and nearly cut his left hand off with an ax. Said he was doing it all for the good of the church."

Roland nodded. His eyes looked watery. "Sounds like the bastard, my brother. He took your gun?"

"He did. Fortunately a marshal showed up in time."

"Saved everyone's life? Rob would've killed you three?"

"Maybe not Louis."

"If you had kept your gun, would you've shot my brother?" said Roland.

"In a heartbeat."

"You ever killed a man?"

I nodded. "I have."

"I know you have. I read about them. The North murders in Los Angeles. And you killed a teacher, down in South Hill, shot your colleague." He sat back in his chair and sighed, taking his eyes off me. Like some part of him was sated, talking about it. "You helped Ulysses, too. Ulysses Steinbeck, married his housekeeper."

"That's right. Friend of yours?"

"Before his accident," said Roland.

"He's still the same guy."

"Gets uncomfortable for me. He can't remember."

"Imagine how he feels," I said.

In the distance, the guy on the mower finished with the field and moved on to another.

"I'm glad you're here, August. I wanted a man unafraid to pull a trigger. I know that Liz's never shot a man. I wanted someone who's done it."

"Given the chance, she'd do it well. I imagine she'd do it better than me," I said.

"How's that?"

"Look at her, she's nasty," I said.

"Hah," said Roland, and Liz smiled.

Liz was *not* nasty.

"What about it, Ms. Ferguson?" said Roland. "Are you willing to kill a man?"

"I'd rather not. But I'm trained for it."

"How're Liz and I gonna kill anyone if Mack shoots everybody first?" said Lowe. "I mean, save some for the rest of us, right?"

Roland ignored Walter. He asked Liz, "What do you carry?"

"A Glock 22."

"Holds fifteen rounds, shoots the .40 Smith and Wesson."

She nodded. "Eleven rounds for me. That's right."

"And you, August?" Pointed at the holster on my hip.

"Kimber 1911."

He seemed pleased. "I carry a 1911. SIG."

"Thought yours was stolen?" I said.

"Got a new one. Didn't feel right, unarmed. You shoot 9mm?"

".45."

"Good. That'll put a man down. I despise watching videos of a 9mm doing nothing, the guy just keeps coming," he said.

"You watch videos of people getting shot?" said Lowe.

"I do."

I said, "Mr. Wallace, you have a background in firearms? Military?"

"Vietnam. But more importantly I'm an American. So I bear arms."

"Your SIG shoots .45?"

"Damn right it does," he said.

"Have you fired it?"

"I have not."

Liz and I did our best not to glance at the other. A .45 was powerful, and it kicked and he hadn't practiced.

"Now that you're here, August, is Ms. Ferguson still running the show?" he said.

"She is."

"Suits me fine. But let me hear your ideas, August. Someone's trying to kill me."

"My ideas don't matter, I guess," said Lowe.

And somehow, intrinsically, Roland knew they didn't.

I said, "Liz told me about the six folks in and out of your home on a daily basis, or close to it. It's almost certainly one of them. You want this over quick, we can scare the heck out of them and see who runs. Then we have our answer."

He made a grumbling noise in his throat. Displeased with me. "I don't want them beyond my reach."

"Your reach?"

"*My* reach. Vengeance must be pursued."

"Must it."

"Revenge is a moral obligation." He pounded a hand on the rocking chair hand rest with each word. "I don't shirk my duties."

"Then Liz's plan seems wise. We leave Walter Lowe with you while Liz and I investigate. He'll keep you alive until we catch the culprit."

Roland twisted to inspect Lowe. "What do you carry?"

"I don't usually. It's nothing special, a revolver."

"You don't usually? Why not?"

"Not in a lot of gun fights," said Lowe.

"What kind of revolver?"

"A Ruger."

"A Ruger revolver. Why?"

"Why not?" Lowe shrugged, hands in his pockets.

"Single action?"

"I don't know."

"Double action," I said. "I saw it."

Lowe said, "What's double mean?"

"Means you don't pull the hammer back with your thumb."

"Where is it?" said Roland. "Your gun."

Another shrug. "In the car."

"Lots of damn good it's doing there, Lowe," said Roland, and Liz and I smiled at each other.

"I don't need it yet. Mack's here and he kills everyone."

Roland twisted back to look at Liz. "You want him to pretend to be my nephew?"

"Maybe your third cousin would be better."

"And you think he'll stop a killer," said Lowe.

"I think he'll always be around, watching, acting like a pain in the ass third cousin, and he'll be a significant deterrent. The person trying to kill you is being sneaky. Hard to sneak around if Lowe is staring at them."

Lowe said, "I can stare. Stare better than Mack, probably."

Roland shook his head and for a moment stared at his boots. Then, "Fine. Move in upstairs next to the master. My nephew Barry has already taken the main level bedroom." Lowered his voice. "And to be honest I doubt the stupid bastard will ever move out."

I pointed at the guy on the mower. "That's your landscaper?"

"That's him. Zeus. Short for *Jesus*. A Mexican name. Nice fellow, like him a lot."

"Zeus here full time?"

"Yes, though I share him with two neighbors. He's here every day working for one of us," said Roland.

"He comes inside the house?"

"Of course. Man has to use a restroom sometimes,

doesn't he? And he keeps some things in my fridge. I don't mind. Or I didn't, before someone tried to kill me."

"And Barry, your nephew, he's here full time," I said.

"Hardly leaves."

"And your nurse?"

"Yakira. She's Asian. Once or twice a day," he said.

"And your housekeeper?"

"Angelina. Pretty girl, she's Mexican, like Zeus. But no, she's some other country. Different accents. Costa Rican? She's my cook too. Comes every other day."

"Your finance guy?"

"Alan Anderson. Comes twice a week to talk money."

"Is that everyone?"

Liz said, "His friend, Johnny. They both served during the Vietnam War. He comes several times a week to chat."

"You served in Vietnam?"

"Yes. I did. Well...yes."

"You seem unconvinced," I said.

"I... Starting in '72, I built roads and bridges in fire-free zones in South Vietnam and Cambodia. Johnny, ah, he fought more than me."

I nodded, watching Zeus.

Those were our suspects so far.

Barry - the nephew, lived here full time.

Yakira - the nurse, came once or twice a day.

Angelina - housekeeper and cook, every other day.

Jesus - landscaper and gardener, here often.

Alan Anderson - money guy, twice a week.

Johnny - buddy from Vietnam, here often.

Liz told me, "Angelina is inside, cleaning or cooking, I'm not sure which. She arrived an hour ago. Zeus arrives with the sun each day. I haven't seen Barry yet. He watches a lot of Netflix in his room."

Roland made an unhappy noise in his throat. "My niece's kid. She's feeble and she left that oaf with me. Shouldn't say that. Something's not right in his head."

Lowe said, "Now I live here, I figure I'll poke around." He opened the screen door.

"Remember. You're Roland's third cousin," said Liz. "We'll figure out the details in a minute. You lost your job because of the pandemic. Only staying here until you're back on your feet. Right?"

"Sure, right, sounds good." Lowe wandered inside, the screen door closing behind him. We heard him say, "*Wow*."

"Maybe I'll make that one try my food first," grumbled Roland. "Be some good that way."

I nodded with approval. "Excellent idea."

"You, August, I can tell you disagree about the necessity for revenge," said Roland.

"I think it would be a pyrrhic victory. Maybe victory isn't the right word. A pyrrhic attempt at victory."

"Because you can't catch him? Or her?"

"I can catch him or her. Liz and me. But administering punishment often hurts the punisher more than the recipient."

"Plus it would be illegal for you to handle the punishment yourself," said Liz.

He smacked his hand on the hand rest. "I won't lay down and die!"

"You said you wanted vengeance. You didn't mention security. Nor justice," I said.

"Vengeance *is* justice. To keep it from happening to someone else."

"So you want the culprit behind bars."

"I want to kill him! Or her."

Liz said, "Mr. Wallace, that's not part of the deal. We'll

keep you alive and determine who tried to poison you. *That's* the deal."

"Keep me alive. And give me a name."

"We won't help you kill someone," she said.

He hit the hand rest again, trembling. "Good. I want to pull the damn trigger myself."

~

Liz and I sat in my car after Roland went inside.

"What do you think?" she said.

"I wonder, if he dies, can we get his house for cheap."

She smiled. Because I was hilarious and unpredictable and charming.

"He's a mess. Seems like a nice guy though, long as you're on his good side."

"Gonna shoot his own foot off," I said.

"No kidding. It could be the Wild West in there soon."

"Where's his money come from?"

"He was an engineer and he patented a type of wooden construction beam. For a while, he worked with his brother, who owned a lumber company. Roland neglected to tell me his brother had been murdered and you were there," said Liz.

"I wouldn't call it murder. More like executed in the nick of time."

She glanced at her watch. "I'm heading home to check on Tom. You good?"

"I'll poke around the internet for a while, learn about the suspects. I don't suppose Roland has security cameras inside?"

She shook her head. "None."

"I'd like to get Lowe some nanny cams to distribute. The

house is big. Nurses or cooks or friends or nephews could do anywhere."

"Good idea, Mackenzie."

"Thanks, Lizzy. It's because I shot so many people, that's what gives me the ideas."

6

I laid in bed that night reading Nassim Taleb because Manny was making me—he said their world views complimented one another—and I was wondering if I was fragile or not. I hoped I never met Taleb; he might skewer me in a book because I tried to control the uncertainty and randomness in my life, and he seemed punchy.

Ronnie finished emailing clients and she closed her laptop. She stepped into the closet and undressed. Then pulled the white nightie over her head and tugged it into place. The red one meant she was feeling frisky. The white one, less so. Most of her clothing was still at her apartment, where she occasionally slept.

She stopped at the mirror to undo her earrings—she wore four—and I told her she was damn good-looking.

She smiled at me in the mirror. "Is that a quote?"

"Hemingway."

"Who was he describing?"

"A woman. Can't remember who. The highest praise he ever gave a woman's appearance, damn good-looking."

She took a pin out of her hair and the rest cascaded down. She shook it and ran fingers through. The way she looked at herself, it wasn't positive. Some inner conflict.

I was a student of Ronnie Summers. Studied her, learned, memorized, admired. She was no longer in much mortal danger, but the absence of physical distress was allowing emotional trauma to surface. The human body could handle only so many crises at once, it seemed, and hers was bringing the most urgent to her attention as soon as she could spare the energy.

"I figured it out," she said.

"Ah *hah*."

"Do you already know what I figured out?"

"No. But I want to be supportive," I said. Although I had a guess.

I'd picked up Kix from school earlier. The lady at the front desk had smiled warmly and radioed that Kix's father was here. Not his ride. Ronnie's intuitions might be correct. I hadn't told her, but I could tell the thing loomed in her mind.

She said, "Do you remember when I said I was mad at the idiot moms at the preschool?"

"I do."

"I figured that out. It's because they see Kix as a boy with no mother. Like he's incomplete. *That* makes me mad."

"Do you see him as a boy with no mother?" I said.

She blinked and a beautiful tear spilled out. She wiped it away and sat on the corner of her bed. The perfect posture surrendered a few degrees.

I closed my book.

Mackenzie August, sensitive gentleman.

"For his sake," she said, "I wish his mother hadn't died."

"Me too."

"Mackenzie, I don't know why this is messing with me." She accepted the box of tissues I held out. Set it beside her. "She must have been gorgeous, his mom."

"She was no Ronnie Summers. But she did okay."

"Being the guardian of another human is...challenging. Not only do I care about Kix, I care about Kix's opinion. I care about what others think of Kix. I care what they think of you, because of Kix. I care what his pediatrician thinks."

I said, "What do you mean, his opinion?"

"One day he might look at me the way those idiot women do. Like he's not sure what I'm doing here."

"Kix is mad about you."

Another tear. She snatched a tissue. "I hope so. I spoil him to tip the scales."

"I do the same with Manny."

She laughed.

Sniffed. Said, "They're not idiot women, though. I think I'm jealous and it's as simple as that."

"Jealous they got to use their birthing canals?"

"I'm sure there must be better phrasing. But maybe." She turned to crawl onto the bed. Came halfway up and laid with her head on my stomach. Entwined her leg between mine and she sighed.

"You never wanted to be a mom," I said.

"I still don't. I just want Kix."

"You got him."

"Until he realizes I'm screwing him up."

"That's what I do all day long."

"I'm not mom material." She raised up on her elbow and said, "Do you know what drives me nuts, Mackenzie? Is that you don't care about his school. Roanoke City Montessori. I can tell you don't. And I know why. Because you know you'll do a good job raising him no matter which school he attends. Just now, I'm certain you were about to joke that you're not dad material, but that's absurd. You don't care about the school the way I do, because I'm desperate for it to cover my deficiencies, whereas you don't have any. Because you know, you *know*, you'll raise him up to become the man he should be."

I did a little shrug and nod. A modest one. "It's true, I think the school matters less than you think it does."

"Because you're the best dad I've ever been around. And you know it."

"How do you know? What makes me a good dad?"

She shook her head. Patted my stomach. "Nope. I'm not playing that game. I know you're setting a trap."

"Answer the question, you stinker."

"Mackenzie. No. No because you'll turn it around, but I'm emotionally drained." With the hand on my stomach, she pushed my shirt up. She kissed my stomach. I liked it when she kissed my stomach. "Instead of talking, would you care to have sex?"

"I would like that very much, yes."

"With me, I hope."

"My preference," I said.

"I'm the luckiest." She raised and slipped the straps of her nightie over her shoulders. Paused. "Is Manny sleeping here tonight?"

"I don't know. But please continue. This is my favorite part."

"Wait." She tiptoed to the door. Extinguished the light and went into the hall. Soft footfalls. She came back and her eyes were watering again. She closed the door and took another tissue. “Manny’s asleep on Kix’s floor. Isn’t that the sweetest?”

“The sweetest. Get over here.”

“Noelle’s family must be in town, otherwise Manny would be at her place, taking care of her injuries. Oh my heart. It hurts. Kix will be okay without his birth mom. So many people love him. And sleep on his floor, for heaven’s sake.” She wiped her eyes. “I have this crazy need for Kix to be happy. And I think he is. Right?”

“He has everything he needs to be successful and content and happy.”

“He does.” She slid into bed. The nightie remained in place, the traitor. “Can we postpone marital bliss until tomorrow night? I’m a disaster.”

“Of course.”

“Are you frustrated with undue prurience?”

“I’m...in love with a woman who makes me prurient. But I can wait until tomorrow.”

"I don’t want you sad or angry.”

“It’s less blissful when coerced.”

She put her hand on my stomach again. “I’ll make it up to you tomorrow. Twice.”

I placed my hand on top of hers. “Deal.”

“You can wait?”

“For you I’ll wait forever. We have a lifetime of tomorrows ahead.”

“Oh.”

“What?”

“I like that line. You’ll wait forever. A lifetime of tomorrows.” A big smile in the dark. Her eyes were round and bright. “Never mind.”

“Never mind what?”

She drew her face close. "Forget what I said about waiting until tomorrow. Your sweetness has seduced me."

"That was quick."

"Like I said. I'm a mess. I want you now, Mackenzie, if you're still interested."

And I was.

7

Roland Wallace's closest neighbor was Jettie Frizzell.

I *know*—what a name.

Jettie was a widow who'd made a fortune selling Mary Kay for thirty years. She had *two* pink cars in her drive, but she was globetrotting in Europe at the moment. I knew because her Instagram told me, so I took the liberty of parking in Jettie Frizzell's driveway with a set of binoculars.

I arrived at 5:45 in the morning, before the sunrise.

Atta boy, Mackenzie. Early bird and all that.

When the sun finally rose, the indolent woolgatherer, it was 6:30 and the landscaper arrived. Zeus. He parked a Ford pickup in Roland's garage, the third bay, and walked to the shed behind Roland's house. He extracted a wheelbarrow full of gardening equipment—nice stuff, black and orange Fiskars, a shovel and rake and sheers, and I wanted it all—and pushed the wheelbarrow to the front. Turned on sprinklers. Cut down some black-eyed Susans and sunflowers. Trimmed the boxwoods. Collected the refuse and dumped it into his pickup bed. Weeded flowerbeds near the porch.

Spread bags of compost around young trees on the northern lawn.

All this before nine. By then Zeus judged it was safe to operate the gasoline-powered weed eater. He slid on safety glasses and donned a straw cowboy hat.

I watched him through my binoculars and researched him online and found absolutely nothing, and wondered who was working harder, me or him.

Something wrong in our world, considering how much more I got paid.

As I watched him, I learned more about the house. Roland had a stone fire pit behind the house, in the western lawn. And an outdoor stone grill. Photovoltaic panels on the rear side of the roof. Rainwater collection barrels. Two outdoor eating areas in the back, one indoor, one out, both had televisions. I was charmed.

The nurse—Yakira Chen—arrived at 9:30. She drove a red Nissan Sentra. Her hair was dark and thick and healthy and just long enough to be held back in a ponytail. She was dressed in pink and blue scrubs, and she wore white New Balance running shoes. Carried a satchel and went through the front door.

I found her online. Youngish, apparently single, she'd uploaded a handful of photos on Instagram and Facebook, none of them smiling, her at a zoo, her at a restaurant with a friend, the usual stuff. People wished her happy birthday and a few months ago she posted about how wearing a mask was important, and a few months before that she'd expressed concern for Hong Kong, where her relatives lived —those were the only posts in twelve months. She appeared unhappy or so serious that she refused to smile. She was Chinese, or at least had Chinese ancestry. She'd attended nursing school at Jefferson College and now she contracted with At Home Nursing.

While Yakira was inside, the housekeeper arrived.

Angelina Rivera, housekeeper *and* cook. She came three times a week. If Yakira was serious, Angelina was stunning. Found her on Instagram. Had she been on other social media sites, like Snapchat or TikTok (whatever the hell that was), I'd never know because I *refused*. Angelina was proudly Costa Rican, buxom with striking features, rich brown hair, and her photos at the beach were not timid or modest. Unlike Yakira, the nurse, Angelina wore makeup. Sometimes a lot of it. She was married. To a white American guy. He had married up, but she seemed crazy about him. Must be funny. Or rich. Or both, like me.

Soon after Angelina arrived, Yakira the nurse left.

I made a note—find out what Yakira did during her visit. I assumed she helped Roland exercise and stretch and that she checked his vitals and his medications.

I was doing research on Angelina, not looking at her beach photos or the photo where she was wearing only a Costa Rican flag, when Walter Lowe came outside. He strolled the front porch and front lawn, smoking a cigarette. Like all ace detectives, Lowe wasn't keeping an eye on the guy paying him to prevent his murder.

I texted him.

How's it going?

Through my binoculars, I watched him check his phone.

>> fine

>> u wouldn't believe the women this guy has

>> hot girls come massage him and cook for him

>> being rick ain't bad mack

>> *rich sorry typo

>> doesn't have to leave his house, girls come here

Keep your eyes peeled. They could be trying to kill him.

>> **doubt it they seem nice**

You think the killer will act like one beforehand?

>> **fine okay ill stare at the hot women**

Stop smoking, you asshat, and get inside.

Lowe lowered the phone and turned in a circle. Looked every direction by mine, two hundred yards away.

I'm in my car, you moron. You've seen the car before.

>> **where the hell r u**

I didn't respond.

He dropped his cigarette into the grass and went in.

AT NOON, a guy I didn't recognize emerged from the front door and sat on a rocking chair. He set a plate of food on his knees and a glass of tea on the little table next to him.

Roland's nephew, Barry. He was pale and thin. Short dark hair. Wore his polo shirt buttoned all the way to the top.

Context clues from Liz and Roland led me to believe he had some form of Autism, maybe Asperger's.

He was still there eating lunch when a blue Acura sedan pulled up the drive. Busy day, here on the hill. I focused the binoculars on the man closing his car door, Alan Anderson, Roland's financial manager. He wore a shirt and tie, and stupid cheap sunglasses, the kind meant to protect your eyes and hurt your sex appeal. He looked like he did well in math class and everything else that required patience and precision. Probably played the piano. He carried a laptop case. Stopped to speak with Barry on the porch and disappeared within.

I found Alan Anderson's office online. Emailed, asking for an appointment. His office manager quickly replied, asking if tomorrow worked.

Why yes. Yes it did. See you tomorrow.

Zeus the landscaper took a break for lunch. He went inside for food, came back out and ate on the rear porch, alone. I wondered if the cook prepared his food too.

My phone rang. A call from Liz Ferguson, the second best private eye in Roanoke.

"Good morning, Lizzy."

She smiled. I heard it.

"Call me Liz. Lizzy is a little girl's name."

"But you're tiny."

"Only compared to you."

"I cannot imagine a reason," I said, "for you compare yourself to anyone else."

"I'm at the courthouse looking through old records on our guy. Guess what I found."

"Nudes."

"No, not nudes. Thank God. I found a certificate of divorce."

"The heck you say. He never mentioned a divorce," I said.

"All my clients are reticent, it seems."

"That file should be sealed."

"It was. But I know people and I'm cute," she said.

"How recent is the divorce?"

"Forty-five years."

"Oh."

"Oh?" she said.

"That's less exciting."

"But still, it's good to know. Perhaps it's germane and perhaps not."

"There's no marriage certificate?" I said.

"No. I'm still looking."

"Look harder, Lizzy."

She didn't answer. She hung up. Which, I thought, was rude.

An hour later, Angelina the cook and housekeeper left Roland's house, followed closely by Alan the finance guy, their jobs done.

Zeus got back to work, now weed-eating around Jettie Frizzell's lawn, not far from my car. If he noticed me, he didn't care. When he wasn't looking, I got out of my Honda and used the bathroom in the bushes.

Private detectives, a classy bunch.

But no! I was wrong about Angelina, her work wasn't done. She came back with groceries. Barry helped her haul them through the front door.

Soon after, Roland himself appeared on the front porch. He wore a pistol on his hip. Eased into a chair near his nephew, Barry. From what I could see, they didn't speak. Lowe came out too. Sat nearby and played on his phone.

Thrilling, thrilling stuff.

I could make out enough facial details to determine Roland was angry. Or stressed or anxious, or in some deleterious emotional state. He stared straight ahead, gripping the arm rails, his lips curled in, jaw flexing. I couldn't blame him, sitting like bait, surrounded by people he suspected of plotting his demise. One of these people, most likely, was out to kill him. And he knew it. And he wanted that person found, and then he wanted to shoot that person. The stress load, good grief—his house was full of persons he'd like to execute; he just didn't know which one it was yet.

Ronnie and I sent a flurry text messages. She was in the court house today but promised to send a risqué selfie if an opportunity presented. That would make my hours in the car better.

Manny picked Kix up from school. Texted me to say that Kix had a good day and he looked like a healthy and proud American. I wondered what the lady with the radio said. Kix's...uncle was here for him? A gorgeous Hispanic Uber driver?

Zeus called it a day in early afternoon, when the sun was baking and bleaching the world. I didn't blame him. That's why Zeus came so early, so he could get his work done in time to escape the heat. He changed shirts at the truck and motored away and I liked him.

I was hoping to see Roland's Vietnam buddy, and the man didn't disappoint. Johnny Stokes arrived in an old Toyota pickup at four. He looked younger than Roland and in fact he was, in his late sixties. A short guy but fit. His back was still strong, his arms sinewy and they bore ancient, faded blue tattoos. Had most of his hair, and he wore better shades than Alan Anderson. He put out a cigarette under his boot heel and he joined Roland on the porch. They spoke. He also spoke to Walter Lowe, who rocked nearby. Johnny went inside and came out with a bottle of beer and a chess set. He set the chess set on a table between him and Roland, and they played. Walter was close enough to listen —although he might be too stupid to do so—playing the video game on his phone.

I stretched in my car. Squirmed. Yawned. Turned the AC on again. Checked the radio for sports. Didn't find anything good. Employed some mild curse words.

Angelina called the men for dinner. I heard her through my open window. Barry the nephew, Roland the wealthy home owner, Walter the lackadaisical private eye, and Johnny the Vietnam vet filed inside. Through the home's many many windows, I could see part of the dining room. Angelina sat down with the men to eat. If she was trying to poison Roland, she clearly wouldn't do it over dinner she just cooked. I made a note to ask Walter what everyone talked about over dinner, and also a note to install a nanny cam in the dining room. And to find out if Roland had an alarm system.

I ate my peanut butter and jelly sandwich. Drank a final bottle of water. Got out to use the bushes again.

Dinner concluded, mine and theirs. Angelina and Walter cleared the table and washed dishes. Way to go, Walter! Look at you, contributing. I bet Angelina's tight shirt had tipped the scales.

Angelina left soon after. I bet the guys hated it when she left.

Sometimes Yakira the nurse returned in the evening, but not tonight. What necessitated an evening visit from her? Roland's pain or discomfort, no doubt. Having concierge medical care seemed indulgent, though I might feel differently in my seventies. I made a note to find out how many nights Yakira came over.

Johnny drank another beer on the porch and they finished the game of chess. Johnny cleaned up and departed in the old rattling truck. Barry the nephew went to bed first, on the main floor. Roland watched television until nine and he moved throughout the house, locking doors. His bedroom was located on the top floor, and into it he disappeared. I bet in a year or two he'd tire of the steps and move onto the main level, perhaps trading spots with Barry.

I got out of my car and walked around it, stretching. It'd been a long day, sitting in the driver's seat. But it'd been a good one, providing me with an opportunity to study every suspect. Had I learned anything? Maybe. Maybe not. Us brilliant detectives never know anything for sure.

A vivid purple night had fallen, and Roland's neighborhood was cheery with porch sconces and lawn lanterns. I liked it here. Maybe I should be rich.

Time to leave. I could review my notes at home.

Took a final look at Walter through the window. He'd fallen asleep in a recliner, asleep with his mouth open, phone in hand.

Because of course he had.

8

Alan Anderson's offices were located on the fourth floor of Coulter Business Center. I arrived there in blue jeans, a pale chambray shirt with the sleeves rolled up, and a baseball hat.

Incognito.

I had a situation to navigate through. Roland didn't want our investigation revealed to the suspects, not yet. Alan Anderson was one of them. But he was the keeper of Roland's financial records, which I wanted access to. Thus my impervious disguise, that of Roland's great nephew, Clayton Wallace, a guy who lived in Texas. I'd looked him up online. We didn't look alike, but we didn't not look alike, and in the Instagram photos he always wore a baseball hat. So I'd put one on.

Raw talent. You can't teach that.

Alan Anderson's receptionist Holly greeted me with a pleasant, "Hello there!" and buzzed for Alan. He shared the receptionist and a conference room with three other small offices—all financial companies. The whole area, most of the fourth floor, felt sterile and hard and cheap. Alan

Anderson appeared, looking like a guy who was good at math and not much else, certainly not football. He also looked like a guy who should be wearing reading glasses but he wasn't. I gave him a handshake at five percent and he waved me into his office.

I sat. "I'm here to look over Roland's affairs. He called me last week and asked."

Alan was halfway into his chair and paused. "Roland? Roland *Wallace*?"

"Yessir, that's him." I smiled politely like a Texan would.

"Roland Wallace asked you to look into his *affairs*?"

"That's right. I was coming to town anyhow. I figured, shoot, why not."

Alan sat all the way now. His excitement had dimmed; I wasn't a potential source of income. "I wonder why he didn't mention it to me. Not to be rude, but how are you involved?"

I gave him *aw shucks*.

"I'm Clayton. Natasha is my mother," I said.

He gave me back a blank look. "Can you be more specific, Clayton?"

"Oh sure, my apologies. I'm Clayton *Wallace*. Roland's my great uncle. Natasha's his niece."

"Ah." If anything, this alarmed him further. His neck was reddening. "How nice. I didn't realize his family was involved."

"We're not much. He's a loner." More grinning. Made my face hurt. "Do you know him well?"

"Somewhat. I think you could say we're friends."

"My mother and I, we were closer with Uncle Rob."

Alan blinked. Purposefully to show his displeasure. "*Uncle* Rob? Who is Uncle Rob?"

"Roland's brother. He died a few years ago, poor guy."

"Oh! Robert Wallace, yes. I knew him too. I beg your

pardon, you've caught me off guard. You look a little like him."

I did not.

I said, "Our whole family, we're all giants."

"Mr. Wallace, I'm afraid I'm not an attorney. I have no ability to change his will. And even if I *did*—"

"Oh no. Whoa there. Settle down. We're not changing his will. I'm not a beneficiary, or at least I don't think I am, and I don't need to be. I do fine."

"Ah." He visible unclenched. A relieved smile. He spread his hands, palms up. "Then...?"

"He said he wanted a third party to look over his affairs. Not just his money but everything else too. Someone in the family. I think he trusts you, and I think he trusts his family, but he'd be happier if they verified one another."

"Quite understandable." Alan leaned back in his rocking swivel chair and adjusted his tie. "Do you have a background in personal finance, Mr. Wallace?"

"Estate planning, yessir, though I retired from it some years back."

"How nice."

"Yessir, only handle some personal accounts now," I said.

I was nailing the Texas accent. I wondered if Ronnie would like it.

He smiled with the minimal amount of courtesy. "Then you'll understand that I'm not legally authorized to hand over his personal—"

"Oh, yessir, I forgot." From my back pocket, I withdrew an envelope and dropped it onto his desk. "I brought a notarized letter granting power of attorney. I also have a letter of authorization, should you need it."

He picked the envelope up like it was covered in mud. Twitched it out and scanned the letters inside.

"A temporary authorization?"

I said, "Only need two weeks. Then I'll be gone. Like I said, I'm not here to alter things."

His eyebrows rose. He liked what he saw on the paper. I was becoming less of a threat. "This stipulates you can make no changes without his approval."

"I don't anticipate making a single one, Mr. Alan."

People in Texas use first names.

Another smile. Kinda. "You'll understand if I call Mr. Wallace on the phone, I assume, as a courtesy?"

"Of course. Tell him I said howdy."

"One moment."

He left for a conference room he shared with the others. Made a phone call on his cell. Roland was ready and waiting for it, at his house. My ruse was complete.

When Alan wasn't looking, I changed the order of his pens and pencils in the coffee mug, and moved his stapler to the other side of a decorative glass paperweight.

I didn't like the way his depreciated me with his smile.

He returned. Sat. "I apologize for that inconvenience. But Roland is a cautious man. So you'll understand that I am too."

"I get that impression, Mr. Alan."

He opened his mouth. Paused. Frowned at his desk. Something looked different. Said, "Roland explained the situation. He told me his brother didn't have his affairs in the proper order at the time of his death. And it worries him."

"What he told me too. But I can't speak to Uncle Rob's affairs."

"If you'll allow me twenty minutes, I'll print out a copy of Roland's entire portfolio," he said.

"And a digital copy too, please."

Polite smile. “Certainly.”

“Including his life insurance policy,” I said.

“Of course.”

“And his will. Just need eyeballs on it.”

A less polite smile. “I understand.”

“Who’s the executor?”

“I am.”

“Does he have an attorney-in-fact?” I said.

“Yes. Me. I am the designated fiduciary.”

I whistled. A Texas whistle. “I came to the right man. How’d you wrangle that?”

“There wasn’t *wrangling*, Mr. Wallace. I’ve been handling his finances for fifteen years. And, to be blunt, there’s no one else. He is a loner, as you earlier indicated.”

“That he is. Do you anticipate any issues with probate court?”

“Not until this meeting, no.”

“Hah. Good one, Mr. Alan. Maybe you can give me the general overview of the estate?”

“Of course.” He learned forward and rearranged his pens and pencils. I knew it. “Roland Wallace is a fairly straightforward man. He and I meet two or three times a week. He likes to talk money, as he says.”

“I know that kinda situation. He wants an update and doesn’t want to read it. I been there, partner.”

“I’m sure you have. He wants reassurance that his investments are locked in. Bonds, IRAs, his annuities—”

“Annuities? God almighty.”

For the first time, Alan looked at me like we might not be enemies. Like we might be on the same team. “Believe me, I understand.” He leaned forward like sharing a dirty secret. Look at us, best pals. “He insisted. Against my better judgment, I relented.”

"A damn shame."

"Indeed."

"Any real estate?" I said.

Leaned back, straightened his tie. "Only his land and home. As I said, straight forward. He likes to trade stocks as a hobby. That's the primary reason for our weekly visits."

"Like day trading?"

"Yes, but he prefers to pick ponies, as he calls them, and ride them for a week. Then pulls back and does it again," he said.

"Sounds like a good way to lose money."

A vexed nod. "He does. He's especially fond of shorting."

"Oh hell."

"It's frustrating, but it's his money. In general he's conservative. But for his *ponies*, he doesn't mind the losses."

"Anything gonna surprise me in the will?"

"The liquid assets, most will goto charity. His property is to be auctioned off and the residue distributed to the beneficiaries. His closer relatives, nine persons total, I think. A decent sum for each, enough to buy a new car and a vacation perhaps, depending on the value of his assets at the time of auction. His nephew—"

"Barry. Quirky kid."

"Yes, Barry. I will be appointed Barry's conservator upon Roland's death. Barry inherits a small family trust fund, enough to keep him comfortable the rest of his life," he said. He frowned at his desk more and rearranged the stapler and paperweight.

What a nerd.

I said, "Listen, Mr. Alan, let me drop a bomb on you. The only complication I'm expecting. Uncle Roland used to be married."

"Oh yes. That's not news to me."

"It's not? I'll be damned. Thought that secret was buried."

"He told me about her, the woman he met in Vietnam. The marriage didn't last long. But perhaps I could drop a bomb on you, to borrow your terminology. Roland has a son."

He was right. That was a bomb. No need to fake the surprise.

"He does *not,*" I said.

"He does, in fact."

"You shock the hell out of me."

"The boy wasn't born when she left him. Roland's only brought him up once, said he hoped the boy was doing well. I took the liberty of looking her up last year. Roland's ex-wife passed away two years ago. The son was married and living in Canada."

I said, "Canada? Why the hell's he living in Canada?"

"I wouldn't know."

"They never spoke?"

"Never, says Roland."

"He's not in the will?"

"He is not."

"Simplifies things, don't it. Forgive me, that was crass."

"It certainly *does* simplify things," said Alan.

"Well I won't keep you much longer. I'll come back in a few to get the financial records. You said he's giving away much of his estate to charity. Which one?"

"There are *quite* a few."

"You'll get me a list?" I said.

Another polite smile. And I thought, a forced one.

"Of course."

9

I arrived at Frankie Rowlands first. Manny and Beck came in soon after; he was a frequent patron for cocktails after work. He got the cocktails for free. I, merely Sherlock Holmes, did not.

Noelle Beck wasn't walking. She was being pushed in a wheelchair by Manny. A thin woman, a few years younger than me, who gave the impression her looks weren't worth spending more than thirty seconds on each morning. She had taken to wearing makeup and a nicer pantsuit, indications of Manny's influence.

On the other end of the spectrum, Ronnie spent an hour each day morphing from mere mortal to sun goddess. She arrived and created a gravity well of attention strolling the length of the restaurant. She was popular, perpetually en vogue, forced to chat with or wave to every table.

I got her chair.

Because I wanted people to know we were together.

Ronnie didn't sit yet. She'd been in JDR and circuit courts that morning, and she was still in no-nonsense, kick-ass attorney mode. She held up a finger to the server, a server who knew her proclivities, to order a pineapple martini.

Just one. After two she was forced to nap. I'd witnessed a third nearly kill her.

She dropped a heavy briefcase on our table. Remained standing.

"I'm furious with the marshal's insurance. Livid."

Manny didn't often tolerate marshal slander. He arched an eyebrow—I'd caught him plucking it once; no one's eyebrows are that perfect. "*Por que?*"

Ronnie had taken it upon herself to deal with Beck's medical claims when Beck received an exploratory call from the insurance adjustor. Ronnie said, "Those sonofabitches are hemming and hawing about covering Noelle's medical bills under the line of duty clauses. She's an NSA tech, not an 1811. They're saying she shouldn't have been assisting with an arrest, that's not why she's on loan to the marshals."

Beck did a demure shrug. "Technically, they're correct."

"You hush, babe. Focus on healing those sculpted abdominals. And next time, do not agree to a fucking recorded statement over the phone. Sorry for saying fuck."

She sat. Her drink came, an aureate nectar. So did my beer, Manny's beer, and Beck's ice water with lemon. We ordered. We all got New England lobster bisque and then diverged. I got salmon. Everyone else got a different type of salad.

Wimps.

"They told me insurance would still cover everything after the total out-of-pocket," said Beck. "And that's fine. I can manage that."

"No. *No.* Insurance is covering every cent." Ronnie was leaning forward, vivacious with judicial indignation. "Plus medical leave and incidentals and anything else I can think of. I'm sending them an armada of letters, threatening multiple lawsuits. I might set the letters on fire before personally delivering them."

Manny looked at me. "She like this in the bedroom?"

"Like sex," I said, "with Gloria Allred when she's furious."

We all drank more and Ronnie began to relax, sated with thoughts of future litigious violence.

Our soup came.

I didn't care much for lobster. But I cared a great deal about lobster bisque.

Ronnie and Manny and Beck sipped theirs, properly and without sound. Mine was more of a dog lapping water situation. But I finished first.

"How's your stomach?" I asked.

"Sore," said Beck. "A surgeon stitched up some inner muscles and those itch but they're under my skin. Not fun."

"She needs to eat more protein." Manny drained his beer. "I tell her. How's she going to regrow muscle without protein?"

Our salads and salmon came.

Near the end, as our bellies filled and complacency arose, Sheriff Stackhouse arrived. She was dressed for battle. Meaning, tight khakis and heels and a blouse half unbuttoned. Some sheriffs met with the mayor and city council and congress persons and local politicos, and they bullied their way though with brute strength and intimidation. Not Stackhouse. She played ruthless back alley politics, relying on guile and intelligence and raw appeal and deals cut behind the scenes. A formidable opponent.

She didn't wait for a server to bring her a pineapple martini. She went to the bar and got one—on the house—before sitting at our table.

She guzzled half her martini—unwise, I thought, but I didn't judge—set it down, and said, "Politicians should be forced to spend a weekend in jail. Earn the right to tell me how to do my damn job."

Manny and Beck both nodded.

She mumbled, "Calls to defund us while expecting us to do everything, including enforce social distancing. World would be better if legislators had to answer 911 calls."

"Calls to defund police," I said, "might drop if you guys quit running over suspects."

Manny made a scoffing noise. "Don't say 'you guys.' Not everyone does that, *amigo*. Only the best do that."

"Speaking of the marshal's insurance," said Ronnie, "that one ought to be fun. Nathan the Ninja will have his pick plaintiff attorneys. He was run over *twice*."

Stackhouse swirled her drink, watching it. "I'm not worried. He cut open a woman with a sword—a cute woman too—and then ran. Plus he was high on meth. No jury will side with him. Did you get photos? Of the injury?"

Beck shook her head. "Not yet."

"Yes," said Manny. "Gory ones."

"Good, that'll help."

Beck said, "You did? When?"

"In the car and at the hospital. With my phone," he said.

"Of my stomach?"

"*Sí*. Had a feeling we might need them."

"You pulled my shirt up?"

"I...no."

"Then how?" she said.

"You pulled it up. Maybe. Besides, I was keeping the wound closed, *señorita*. Only way to do it was go up your shirt."

Beck shook her head. "Good thing I wore my nice bra, then."

"Not at the hospital you didn't."

"Come again?"

"Let's say...maybe we need to blur out part of the photos before showing them around," said Manny.

"You took *topless* photos of me?"

"I documented the injury. The wound reaches your ribcage, Beck. They undressed you, not me."

"You've got nothing to be ashamed of, babe, with that perfect little body," said Stackhouse.

Manny nodded. "*Sí*. Photos look great."

"Manny." Beck was reddening. "Forward the evidence to...someone, I don't know who, someone *else*, and then delete them."

"Send them to me," said Ronnie. "I'm her attorney."

"Yes," I said. "Send them to Ronnie."

Beck pointed at me. "You don't get to look."

"In marriage, there are no secrets. And I'm a sucker for katana injuries."

"A lot of women would kill for Manny to have nudes of them," said Stackhouse.

"Not this woman."

Manny wondered, "Is the big sword in our evidence locker?"

"Yes. It's a big tourist attraction at the moment," said Stackhouse.

"I want it, afterward. Frame it on the wall."

Beck's face turned into...not disgust, more like distress. "Why?"

"Because you survived it, Beck. It's a trophy."

"Fine. Keep the sword, lose the nude photos. I don't want those circulating."

Stackhouse finished half of the remaining martini. Half of a half. “Speaking of circulating,” she said. “Rumors are swirling, Ronnie, that you’re dropping off a boy at preschool.”

Ronnie did a grimace and set down the pen she’d been using to scribble notes on a pad. I peeked—she was increasing her to-do list. She said, “Sometimes I wish Roanoke was bigger.”

“You start wearing longer skirts, you’d get blabbed about less,” said Stackhouse.

“But then how would everyone appreciate all my hard work with a barbell? I’m not doing front squats, back squats, and deadlifts in order to wear fucking pants.” She winced. “Sorry for cursing. But who cares if I drop off a boy at preschool.”

“It’s only the juiciest gossip in months. Mackenzie used to be your dirty secret everyone knew about. Is he no longer a secret?” said Stackhouse.

“He’s not a secret.”

I said, “Kinda.”

“You’re not. I swear you’re not. And anyway, I know you don’t care.”

“Not even a little,” I said.

“What do I need to do, take out an ad in the newspaper? Announcing that I got married?”

Beck smiled politely. “Most couples do.”

“Do they? You’re right, I’d forgotten that. But we’re only engaged.”

Manny waffled his hand. “*Más o menos*."

Ronnie picked up her pen and jabbed it, at herself. “But anyway, no. Hell no. I would be kowtowing to them.”

“Them who?” asked Beck.

“*Them*. The collective. The collective bitch who smirked

when I broke up with Darren Robbins and who disparages me behind my back."

"A pack of vipers." Stackhouse nodded, wise with experience. "I fit right in."

"No, you don't celebrate the misfortune of others. They're eager for gossip because each nugget might contain some kernel of a sordid disaster. And it's my fault, because I played that game for ten years." She was gripping my hand hard.

"So you don't want to tell them the truth about Mackenzie...why?" said Stackhouse.

"Because they don't deserve the truth. And they don't deserve Mackenzie. I don't want to fit in with them anymore. I don't want his name in their mouths."

"Good luck." Stackhouse finished her drink. Looked longingly at it. Looked longingly at the distant bar. "We're a covetous sorority, babe. Extraction is difficult."

"Maybe even harder than the mafioso," I said.

Beck shifted in her wheelchair, winced, and said, "I don't fit in with women either. The LDS women don't accept me because of...a lot of reasons. But I *am* Mormon so I don't have the active nightlife of most singles. I fit in with *no* women. My world is dominated by men and, it turns out, I like them better."

"Hear hear." Ronnie reached across the table to take her hand too and hold it.

"You're lucky as hell," Stackhouse said. "We, I should say, are lucky. We happen to be surrounded by the best of them."

"Aren't we, though?" said Ronnie. "They *are* the best. I spend most of my time trying to earn them."

"And for reasons that are beyond me, they try to earn us back."

Ronnie smiled, a marvelous, spectacular thing.

Pineapple martinis had given our table a microclimate of good cheer. “Unconditional love,” she said, “is too preposterous to be true. But getting close to it is good enough. And more than we deserve."

Manny, staring at the ceiling, shook his head. Just a little. But enough to indicate what he thought of white people and our complex emotions.

Good thing we loved him anyway.

10

The humidity was low that evening so I languished on the front porch, growing sleepy and listening to September crickets and Kix's baby monitor. The chessboard sat next to my rocking chair, untouched since Timothy August had stomped away in frustration, conceding his defeat. I might keep the pieces frozen a few days to remind him never leave his queen unguarded and trapped behind pawns on the back row.

Honestly, how old was he now, he should know better.

Liz Ferguson came down Windsor in a BMW. She'd given me a five minute warning, so I wasn't caught off guard. Not that I would be anyway.

Constant vigilance!

I didn't know a lot about BMWs. It was a two-door sedan and it was gray and it looked ten-years old.

She marched up my front walk. She did it wearing exercise gear—black leggings and a coral moisture-wicking long-sleeve workout shirt. Both were by Under Armour. Both were skintight, and the shirt was a crop top, exposing her abdomen.

Dammit. She was older yet she had better abs.

To be fair, she didn't have children and I'd never gotten my figure back after Kix.

I stood. Corrected my posture.

She also wore fancy-looking Reebok shoes, coral that matched her shirt. She marched onto my porch and slapped a pill bottle onto the chess board, knocking over both my king and queen.

"Walter called and interrupted my kickboxing class and said to get my sweet ass over to Roland's. So I did."

"He said sweet ass?"

She snapped a nod. "You know he did."

"I know he did."

"He checked Roland's medicine cabinet. Guess what he found." She nodded at the bottle.

I picked it up. Popped the top and spilled a few pills into my hand. Strychnine was beyond my ken, but these tiny pellets would only pass for aspirin if I wasn't paying attention. Or if I was seventy-five and had bad eyesight.

I said, "Strychnine?"

"Strychnine. Pretty sure."

I indicated the empty rocking chair. She paced instead.

I sat.

"How long has it been there?"

She said, "Walter thinks the bottle was bought yesterday. Angelina, the housekeeper, does most of the shopping."

I'd personally witnessed Walter helping Angelina carry groceries.

She said, "Someone's trying to kill that old man. It's a shock each time I find more evidence."

I felt the shock too. I was holding a murder weapon. Or an attempted-murder weapon. Doesn't happen often that one has the murder weapon but not the murderer. Usually the other way around.

"Good idea," I said, "planting Walter in the house. He might've saved Roland's life tonight."

"I know. So does he. Says he wants a bonus."

"Of course he does."

"Of course he does."

"So the bottle was in the house approximately thirty hours," I said.

"Right."

"Our six suspects had access."

"You know this from watching the place yesterday?" she said.

"That's assuming Zeus the groundskeeper and Yakira the nurse kept their schedules today. Alan Anderson, the finance guy, had the least amount of access. Or...wait." I stood. Went inside and plucked my notebook off the kitchen counter and came back. Flipped it open and scanned. "No. Alan Anderson the finance guy left before Angelina returned with groceries. He couldn't tamper with the aspirin."

"Not unless he returned today without telling us," she said.

"Or if there's more than one aspirin bottle floating around."

"Doubtful."

"Doubtful. Otherwise she wouldn't have purchased another," I said. "I'll verify with Walter."

"Should we strike Alan Anderson off our list of suspects?"

"Move him to the bottom." I set the bottle down. "We should've dusted for prints before I handled it."

"Walter said he groped it several minutes, trying to open

the childproof lid, and that other prints would probably be obliterated."

"I believe him. About his difficulty with the lid."

Although there was no residue on my hands, I used a water bottle to rinse them. Wiped them on my pants. Repeated the process. And I'd wash later with soap.

She sat now. "You know what I think? I think the killer is using strychnine because it'd be easy to assume suicide that way."

"I was thinking it too," I said.

"Liar."

"The killer has to know strychnine shows up on a toxicology report. It's a common means for suicide and that could preclude a homicide investigation quick."

She nodded and picked up the bottle again and glared at it.

I said, "I checked his life insurance today. He's had the policy long enough that it'll be paid out even if he kills himself. Or *kills* himself." I put the word in air quotes.

"So you think the killer is after money."

"Usually is. Only guess I got so far."

"I'll trust your instincts on this. My DEA experience was never about personal stuff like wills," she said.

"Be nice if we had a camera on Roland's bathroom."

"I ordered those nanny cams yesterday. They arrive tomorrow and I'll have Walter arrange them around the house."

"Did you tell Roland?" I said. "About the aspirin?"

"No. Should I?"

"Not sure. Roland might start walking around his house with that SIG .45 drawn, shooting shadows."

"Roland knows someone is trying to kill him." She

rattled the bottle. "This doesn't change anything. No need to tell him."

"Ask Walter if he can access Roland's computer. Take a look at purchases he made online."

"Looking for what? Strychnine?"

"I was the killer," I said, "I'd order the strychnine and other poisons through Roland's computer. Good chance Roland wouldn't notice it, not unless he's paying close attention and I don't think he is. Would make suicide look more plausible."

"That's a good idea, Mack."

"Obviously, Lizzy. How's Tom?"

A smile. A sad one, but affectionate. "He had a bad day. It happens now and then."

"Headaches?"

"Yes, but more like an increase in frustration with the headaches and seizures. I'm blessed as hell my job is flexible so I can be there. And I'm glad I hired you, Mackenzie, so I didn't have to worry today."

"Walter's the hero so far."

"Then we're screwed."

I grinned. "We totally are."

The screen door opened and Ronnie emerged. She wore activewear, similar to Liz, and she had a leather overnight bag slung on her shoulder. She was spending the evening at her place to get a handle on her fall wardrobe. Whatever the heck a fall wardrobe was.

"Liz!" she said.

But she didn't say it. It wasn't a shout either. More mellifluous than a shriek. Less than a scream. Not quite a hoot. Call it a happy and girly squeal.

These things matter.

Liz smiled and stood. "Hi baby. Sorry for the late night

intrusion."

Baby? I didn't know people called Ronnie baby.

They hugged. She'd hired Liz several times over the past few years. It'd gone well. Apparently. My clients never call me baby.

Ronnie said, "Mackenzie told me you were working together. Look how *fit* you are! I'm sick with envy. Your skin, it's like butter. I was happy with my appearance until this very second."

Laughter. Amusement. More feminine endearment followed that I didn't understand. Sixty seconds of it. They'd forgotten me.

I stood.

At least I was taller.

Liz said, "I gotta run, babies. Mackenzie, I'll call you tomorrow."

"Babies? We're almost the same age."

"Oh Mackenzie, it means she likes you," said Ronnie. "Don't leave, Liz. I'll get wine."

"I need to go, Tom's waiting. But thanks."

Lizzy left in her BMW. Took the pill bottle with her.

Ronnie leaned against me, smiling still. Watching Liz go.

"I just love her."

"She's solid," I said.

"She's been like my cool older sister ever since I first hired her."

"She called you baby."

"I know. Isn't it the best?" she said.

"The best."

"You have a crush on her."

"I do not."

She poked me. "You do too."

"It's the same way I feel about Tom Cruise."

"I imagine everyone who meets Liz Ferguson feels it, more or less. I sure do." She picked up her bag from where she dropped it. "Okay, I'm off to fetch two prostitutes."

"Sure. As one does."

She grinned and the stars hummed. "Fetching them from the emergency department at Carilion Hospital. Someone beat the shit out of them. They're staying at my place tonight and as long as they need."

When Ronnie said her place, she meant an old building she'd purchased downtown. She'd renovated one hallway thus far and arranged for police cruisers to drive by the door regularly, keeping away prurient malcontents. Her quest to help prostitutes save themselves.

She kissed me. Although my hands were no longer contaminated, I wasn't touching her with them. She said, "Then I'm going to my apartment to work on clothes until I fall asleep. If you get lonely, come join."

"I hate working on clothes."

"Some of them are skimpy."

"Some?" I said.

"Most of them are skimpy. I'll try on anything you like."

My eyebrows perked. That sounded more fun than the book I was reading.

She said, "Mackenzie. I take it back. You can come join, but I can't fool around tonight. It's already late and I have thousands of dollars worth of stuff to sort."

I nodded. Thoughtfully.

"Wait," she said. "No, I take it back. You can't come. Because I will be seduced by the sight of you in bed, and then we'll lose an entire hour and I'll fall asleep without getting anything done, and I still won't have anything to wear."

"You're a tease."

"Well, whose fault is that! This house has zero closet space."

"It was built a hundred years ago. They didn't know women would need to house a wardrobe befitting Buckingham Palace."

"Aw, that's sweet. I wish. Poor Manny has to rent a climate-controlled storage unit," she said.

"Manny's issue is not closet space."

She kissed me again. Then once more. "I'm gone. Call me if you get lonely."

"I will be. Manny is sleeping at Beck's."

"Isn't that the most darling thing. On the floor of her bedroom, do you think?"

"Told me he was," I said. "With a James Bond novel."

"I bet she doesn't sleep a wink, knowing Manny is in the same room. Goodnight Mackenzie."

She left.

On the monitor Kix made a noise in his sleep.

I went inside to wash the murder weapon off my hands. Dried them. Stared at my fists, blissfully free of poison. Unlike Roland's house, where he expected to die any minute.

An awful way to live. If it could even be called living.

I went upstairs to check-in with Timothy August, grabbed my keys, and got in my car.

Unfortunately I wasn't headed to Ronnie and her skimpy outfits.

11

I motored up the drive of Roland Wallace. His house loomed large on the brow of the hill and increased in size as I traveled toward it. Which I did without headlights, moving through thickets of black and cones of soft landscape glow. Didn't want to wake Roland or Barry.

I stopped a short distance away and a dark silhouette detached from the porch. I got out and gently closed my car door. Insects were abuzz in the fields and flowerbeds surrounding Roland's house, crickets and cicadas. My Honda Accord's engine clicked and sighed, and I guessed the air temperature was about five degrees cooler up here than on Windsor Avenue. The stars were brighter too.

The dark figure from the porch joined me behind the car. Walter Lowe, huffing some.

He said, "Think we get overtime for this?"

"We're paid by the day."

"How much we gotta work, that's what I want to know. Should be eight hours a day max."

Being somewhat of a comedic savant, several biting retorts sprang into my mind, centered around his laziness.

The retorts would've been hilarious. He would be amused but also stung. Hurt but appropriately chastised. He'd see the error of his ways and thank me for my jokes being the impetus of his evolution.

But I detected tension. Lowe was on edge—he'd found a murder weapon. That held some gravity. He was rubbing elbows with a would-be executioner. I was spooked by the strychnine dust on my hands; I bet Lowe was too scared to sleep. Every creak a killer.

I said, "You want an avuncular pat on the shoulder?"

"The hell's that mean?"

"Means, don't give up. We'll catch him. Or her."

"Christ, we better. I'm exhausted. Sitting around all day somehow's work. This is your thing, not mine. I just take pictures most times. I'm freaked out, Mack, honest to God I am."

"Tell me everything, since that aspirin bottle came into the house," I said.

"That's why you're here? It's late and you woke me up for this? What if it's Barry, you thought about that? Maybe the killer is in the house with me. This is bullshit, August."

"That's why I'm here."

You absolute asshat.

He sniffed and rubbed his eyes with the heels of his hands.

I said, "Angelina bought the aspirin bottle, right? I saw you helping her with the groceries."

"You did?"

"I did. Posted up with binoculars."

"You're a weird guy, Mack. But I don't blame you peeping on Angelina. Hard not to."

"You saw the aspirin then?"

"Yeah. Angelina popped it open and took a few," he said.

"*Heyo..*"

"Think it's a clue, her opening the bottle?"

"Probably not. But I love to jump at inferences."

"You got a good look at her? Because, I'm telling you, Mack, she could be a model. She's built like you wouldn't believe and she's thrilled about it."

"Super news, Lowe. Just super. What happened to the bottle then?"

"I'm not sure. I decided to check the medicine cabinet and there it was."

"When did you check?"

"Right before I called Liz," he said.

"What compelled you?"

He did a shrug. "Got bored."

"Nothing occasioned it?"

"Nah."

"Does Angelina ever go upstairs?"

"No idea. How do I know that?" he said.

"It was a trick question. Of course she does."

"Then why'd you ask? And how do you know she does?"

"She's the housekeeper. She tidies up," I said.

"Oh. Look at you, Mack, deducing shit. This is why you get paid more than me, huh. So yeah she had access to his medicine cabinet, sure, but I don't think she's the killer."

"Why not? Don't say her breasts."

"For starters, her breasts. They're huge, Mack." He cupped his hands and held them out, demonstrating size. Through a heroic act of willpower and restraint, I didn't punch him in the navel. "No, but being serious, she seems to like Rolly."

"Rolly."

Good detectives always repeat stuff.

He said, "That's what she calls him. Rolly. They get

along. She teases him and it goes back and forth. They're friends. And, Mack, think about it. If she wanted to poison him, she'd could easily dump it in his food."

"She's the cook. We'd know it was her."

"Oh. Well yeah."

"Who else goes upstairs?" I said.

"The nurse. The Yaka girl."

"Yakira."

"That's it. Yakira's upstairs every day."

"Was she the day of the aspirin purchase?"

"Yep, and today. I bet it's her."

"Give me your impression of her," I said.

"She's kinda cold. Her boobs are smaller. Hey, what, they are, maybe that matters. She's a nurse, you know, she's all business. Doesn't call him Rolly. She orders him around and helps him build muscles or whatever and gives him some shots and she leaves."

"Does she talk to anyone else?"

"Mmmm. Not really."

"She's quiet," I said.

"Sure."

"Alan Anderson ever go upstairs?"

"The finance guy?" He scratched at the scruff on his neck. He was two days overdue for a shave. "No. And he wasn't here today."

"He had no access to the aspirin then."

"Guess not. Hey, a clue. Alan's innocent."

I said, "How often does Barry go upstairs?"

"Dunno. I'm sure he does. He lives here full-time, after all. Haven't seen him do it though. But he could. Nice kid. He's writing a book about superheroes. Won't shut up about it. Wants me to read it."

"Confess to him you can't read."

"*Can't* and *don't* are different things," he said.

"Debatable. Zeus the landscaper, he doesn't go upstairs, but he was here. Right?"

"Yeah, he was. But I don't think it's Zeus."

"Because?"

"Intuition," he said.

"You don't have a simulacrum of that."

"I don't know, Mack, I just don't. Guy's too quiet, too hard-working."

"You think we should strike off everyone who's hard-working and quiet? That leaves you," I said.

"I'm not a suspect and you don't gotta be mean."

Somewhere nearby, an owl hooted. Walter did a little jump and turned around.

I said, "Zeus could've tampered with the bottle in the kitchen, depending on when it got moved upstairs. He could come into the kitchen for water or food. His job is landscaping. He has access to strychnine."

"Yeah I guess. Hey, that's true, maybe it's Zeus. Crazy, Mack, how you think of this stuff."

"Could there be another bottle of aspirin?"

"Haven't seen one."

"Look around, Let me know."

"Sure. Jeez, I do all the work, huh." He said it through a yawn.

"Was Johnny here today?"

He nodded. "Yeah. Guy's here most days, I think. They're best friends. Roland doesn't talk much except to Johnny."

"Did Johnny go upstairs?"

"Not that I saw. But maybe, I don't know. It's been a long couple days, Mack, and you're asking too many questions."

"Think. Does Johnny go upstairs?"

"No. I doubt it. He gets a beer and the chess board, that's all. Sometimes he goes to the bathroom."

"Tell me about the bathroom," I said.

"What, it's a bathroom. It's near the stairs. There's a hallway back there. Close to Barry's room, on the main level."

"So it's close to the kitchen."

"Kinda."

I said, "He could've grabbed the open bottle, taken it to the bathroom, poisoned it and then returned it."

Walter snapped his fingers. His stupid fat fingers. "Mack, you know what I just remembered? Johnny said his back was hurting and he asked Roland if he could take some aspirin."

"Did he."

"He did!"

"How the hell," I said, "are you just remembering this now."

"I don't know, it didn't seem important, stop being mean. He said it this afternoon."

"Johnny went inside then?"

"Yeah. Roland told him there should be some in the kitchen."

"Is there?" I said.

"No. There's none in the kitchen. But I was outside. I didn't see if he went upstairs. But why would Johnny kill his best friend?"

"Why would anyone kill him? He's their primary source of support. That's what we're being paid to figure out," I said.

"What happens if I get poisoned?" He said it through another yawn. I was running out of time, because Lowe was running out of lucidity. His eyes were bleary.

“Call 911 or drive yourself to the hospital. And call me.”

“I can’t afford the hospital. You think Liz would pay me worker’s compensation? You got health insurance?”

“I do. You have health insurance,” I said. “Right?”

“Course I don’t. I don’t have a rich attorney girlfriend.”

“She doesn’t pay for my health insurance, Lowe.”

“Where do you get yours?” he said.

"I buy it.”

“Must be nice. Some guys have all the luck, huh.”

“Walter, what do you think we’re doing out here? Right now?”

“Working too hard and not getting overtime, that’s for damn sure.”

“We’re doing our best. Usually takes more than eight hours a day.”

“Oh jeez, gonna give me another speech?”

“If we do a good job, Roland stays alive. Maybe he hires us again, maybe he tells people we did well, and we get referral business. And the referrals lead to more business, which leads to more referrals. These things compile into a successful career. You want health insurance? Work your ass off, Lowe. It’s not luck.”

“Hurtful. I don’t want insurance that bad.”

"Easier to go to sleep, you work hard. The sleep’s better. You earned it,” I said.

“What’s that got to do with anything?”

“It’s an example of why hard work is good for you. I used sleep to illustrate my point.”

“I’d sleep better if I wasn’t in this damn house.”

“But if you...never mind. We got a pearls before swine situation here.”

“Mack, I’m too tired to understand the weird crap you say. I’m going back to bed. We didn’t figure out much.”

"Tomorrow I want you to use his computer to see if anyone bought—"

"No. Maybe. Text me. I'm not listening to anything else tonight. Because you want me to get shot and I don't have insurance."

"Somebody's gonna shoot you, Lowe, chances are it'll be me."

"That's not funny. By the way, you have a retirement fund?" he said.

"You don't have an IRA either, do you."

"Nope. Don't even know what IRA means."

"I'll help you set one up."

"Can you just give me some money? Ask your rich girlfriend if she wants to upgrade to me."

"You don't need an IRA. When it's time, it'd be an honor to put you down."

He turned to go. A shuffle up the drive. "That's also not funny. You think you're funny but you're not."

Of the many things Walter Lowe got wrong in life, that might have been the biggest.

12

The following day.

Roland and I sat on his front porch.

A safe bet, you need to find me, I'll be on a porch somewhere.

I didn't mention I'd been there only twelve hours previous. We watched Zeus ride a green and yellow John Deere and cut grass on a distant lawn. Walter was inside watching television with Barry, Roland's nephew. Yakira the nurse had left. Angelina the cook and housekeeper wasn't coming in today.

"You found something," said Roland. He said it without looking at me.

I wished we were playing chess. But he didn't offer. I was good at it and eager for ways to demonstrate my superiority.

He went on. "You found something, I know. The fat guy, Walter, he's sweating like a whore in church. And my medicine cabinet was open."

"He found more strychnine."

Roland cursed. He did a thing like chewing on his lip,

his jaw jutting forward. Eased to the side, getting quicker access to the pistol on his belt.

"Dammit," he said. "Got'dammit. I want to kill someone. I want to kill the sonofabitch in my house, in *my* house, trying to poison me. Hear me, Mack? I want to punch holes in them. I want to knock chunks out of them."

"You never shot someone," I said.

"No I haven't."

"You won't like it."

"The hell I won't. You had someone try to kill you?"

"Sure."

That stopped him. Turned his attention to me, the delusional lunatic in the adjacent chair.

"I mean," he said, "*really* try. Like with poison."

"Yep."

He waited and indicated I should elaborate. But I didn't want to. Naples, Italy and the bloodsport tournament would blow his mind.

"Been a weird few years, Roland. But I'm alive and I'm grateful," I said.

"This keeps up, I'll be neither."

"You kill someone and you'll go to jail."

"You won't snitch me out, Mack."

"I won't need to. They'll pull bullets out of the person you killed, or tried to kill, and match them with your gun and you'll spend the rest of your life locked up."

He made a mmphf noise.

"And," I said, "you'll wake up queasy. Often. Because your brain is replaying the tape of you sending pieces of metal into the flesh of another person. A horrible thing. If it was self-defense, you can cope. You can go back to sleep. Otherwise, maybe not."

He did the grunt again. "You let me worry about that part, August."

"We'll see."

"Tell me what the hell you're doing to fix this thing."

"I'm looking through your finances. There's a lot of paperwork."

"Good." He turned his gaze back on the lawn. Squinted. "Good. Follow the money. That's usually it, right?"

"Quite often. Tell me who benefits when you die."

"Barry." He said it quickly.

"From what I read, and I'm still only dipping my toe in, Barry benefits no more than he does now. Less so, probably, because his quality of life is so high at the moment. With you alive, he gets to live here."

"The boy doesn't think clearly. Maybe he's stewing, maybe he's wishing the old man would die, because he'll get that trust."

"He likes living here?" I said.

"Assume so. He was alone in a dumpy apartment before. We don't talk a lot. Or...he yammers some. I don't always listen. Some days I regret taking the boy in."

"No one gets more than Barry?"

He shrugged and shifted, the pistol clunking against the wooden chair. "Barry's trust will pay far more than anyone else gets. I forget exactly how it works, August. I don't have immediately family. A handful of my distant relatives get a chunk. Thirty or forty grand, but I forget, you'll have to tell me."

"I'll chase them down. See if anyone's in dire financial need."

"Good," he said.

"Would your brother Robert have inherited anything?"

"My brother, the man you shot."

"I didn't shoot him," I said. "But yes."

"A marshal shot him."

"That's right."

"You know the marshal?"

"We're friends."

"Does the marshal wake up at night, like you said? Queasy?"

"He does," I said. "I know it for a fact."

"Because he shot my brother."

"Because of a lot. He *should* have shot your brother. He had to. But it still caused damage on both side of the barrel."

Roland took a deep breath, like all this talking wore him out. "What was Robert shot with?"

"A .357."

"Good God."

"He is, I think."

"Marshals carry .357s?" asked Roland.

"This one does."

"A .357 gets the job done. Killed...killed Robert quick, I bet."

I nodded. It had.

"Where was Robert hit?" Roland's fingers were gripping the arm rests.

"Twice in the back."

"Shot in the back? The marshal's a coward?"

I said, "How do you think these things should go down? You watch a lot of wild west movies?"

"A real man doesn't shoot another in the back. That's for damn sure."

"A real man does what he can. He does it as best he can and then lives with the consequences," I said. Irked at his fictional nobility. "Your brother was shooting at me. He'd already fired twice. He wouldn't miss again. The marshal had no choice."

Roland's pale eyes latched onto me again. "Shooting you?"

"Shooting *at* me."

"Papers said Robert shot the priest."

"He did that too," I said.

"Why the devil was he shooting at you?"

"A lot of reasons."

"You wake up at night queasy?" said Roland.

I nodded. "I married someone who hugs me when I do. And I reciprocate."

"Good for you." Said it with a sniff, like he didn't really think it was good for me. Which, I thought, was rude. "Good for you. But it's too late for me for that."

"Will be if you go to jail. All the more reason you shouldn't shoot someone. Would Rob have inherited anything from you?"

He growled the growl of a man unaccustomed to his personal life being invaded. "Does it matter?"

"It might."

"No, Robert wouldn't get a damn thing," he said.

"Because you had a falling out."

"That's right. Robert turned into a religious zealot. An absolute bastard."

He wasn't wrong about that. Only bastards shoot at me.

I said, "What happened to Robert's belongings?"

"Got no idea. He left me nothing."

I made a note to find out.

"What're you writing?" he said.

"I want to know Robert's beneficiaries."

"That matter?"

"Probably not."

"But you're thorough," said Roland.

"All I know how to be."

"Good. Good, keep it up and you'll do well."

I already am doing well, old man. Maybe tell Walter instead of me.

"You were married," I said.

He coughed and wiped his mouth. "I suppose that matters too?"

"Might."

"How'd you find out?"

"Wasn't hard. She doesn't benefit?"

"Course not. She's dead, besides."

I made a note. A mental one. How'd Roland know his ex-wife was dead? He was checking up on her? Alan Anderson told him?

"Any children?" I said.

"She had two."

"Either yours?"

"You know the answer, don't you," he said.

"I know the answer. One of her sons is yours."

"The bitch took off before she knew she was pregnant. Marriage was a disaster from the go."

"She was a bitch?" I said.

A silence. He didn't answer right off. Pale eyes on the horizon turning watery.

Zeus finished the field, now a uniform verdant carpet. He disengaged the blades, raised the deck, and rumbled into Jettie Frizzell's lot. Took his straw cowboy hat off and wiped his forehead.

A minute passed. Then another. Roland held a deep resonating silence within.

"No." A whisper finally. "No she wasn't. It was mostly me."

~

Two in the afternoon.

Quitting time for Zeus.

I waited for him near the bottom of the mountain. At two-thirty, he passed in his Ford pickup. I followed at a distance.

Strychnine was commonly used as a rodent poison. Zeus, as a groundskeeper, would have access to oodles. Could that be a clue? I loved those.

He drove into Roanoke City and stopped on Williamson at Carniceria Lily's food truck. He ordered food and ate it out of the wrapper, chatting with other guys doing the same. Roanoke had a thriving Hispanic culture if you knew where to go.

I texted Manny.

You ever eat at Carniceria Lily food truck?

He replied.

>> No. Too authentic. They laugh at me.

Aren't you their king?

>> Sí. Means I don't eat with my subjects.

Soon Zeus left and went to Reyna's Produce. A Mexican grocery. Fifteen minutes in and he emerged with straining white plastic bags. Put them into the passenger seat.

He motored onto 10th Street. Crossed over 581 and into Washington Park. A less affluent part of town and houses could be rented for cheap. As I followed him a block back—Mackenzie August, master of camouflage—I tracked our progress using a map on my phone. When he turned onto Rockland, I didn't follow. Because that was a dead end. I went to the next street over. At the cul-de-sac I found a spot on the curb with a view overlooking Rockland. *Eureka!* I saw Zeus's truck parked at the end. A dilapidated little house with two cars plus his truck. The concrete foundation looked exhausted and the driveway needed to be paved and the patchy yard needed over-seeding. Three kids running around the back yard, calling in Spanish.

I stayed there for an hour and a half, watching. Enough to learn that two families lived inside that little house. Based on activity and furniture I spotted through windows, it had two bedrooms and one bath, a living room and a little kitchen. Plus a basement. The main level had maybe a thousand square feet, unfinished.

Best guess was Zeus's family and the other family were immigrants living here illegally or on work visas, waiting in the green card line. Doing their best.

A full house. And as happy as their circumstances would allow, seemed to me. Better than where they came from. I assumed. Else why do it.

Zeus changed shirts and sat out back on a lawn chair in the shade. A woman came out. She brought him a beer and they talked and she kissed him. Zeus had a faint scar, mostly healed, that ran from the corner of his mouth down his neck. It was visible as a tug when he spoke.

Getting close to five, he lit charcoal and sautéed chicken and peppers on an iron wok, or something like a wok. When the children called, he flicked pieces of chicken in the air for them to catch in their mouths.

He watched the kids and cooked without smiling. But he wasn't frowning either. He did it like he was tired and the kids brought him peace.

I liked Zeus. We had a few things in common.

Including the likelihood that we both had people sleeping on our bedroom floor.

13

At the beginning of the investigation, I fretted the would-be killer was someone outside our list of six suspects, though unlikely. That fear was allayed with the second batch of poison, the one Walter found. It had to be someone inside that house.

So what did I know?

I knew Angelina was the housekeeper and cook and that Walter thought her breasts were great, and I knew that she purchased the aspirin and she opened it. She had access to the upstairs bathroom. Suspicious as heck. However, she seemed to have a good relationship with Roland. Rolly.

I knew Yakira was quiet and hard-working and that she had access to the upstairs bathroom. She tinkered with his medicine every few days. However, she'd lose her income if Roland died. I checked; she wasn't a beneficiary.

I knew Barry the nephew had access to the aspirin bottle and the upstairs bathroom. However Walter had never seen him go up the stairs, and he had financial reasons to *not* want Roland dead.

I knew Johnny was the talkative best friend and that he'd

asked about the aspirin. Walter had seen him go inside. But Johnny wouldn't kill Roland, they were old friends.

I knew Zeus better than the others. He had access to strychnine. He had access to the kitchen, but not the upstairs bathroom. Be nice to know when the aspirin bottle was spiked. Be nice to know a lot of things. I liked Zeus, though. Intuition might not be worth a hill of beans, but my intuition didn't even blink at the guy.

Alan Anderson hadn't been anywhere near the aspirin between its purchase and its discovery. Plus, if Roland died he'd lose his client. So he wasn't guilty. *Probably* wasn't guilty. Of anything other than being a snit in a tie.

In summation, the culprit could be anyone except Alan Anderson, but none of them had reason to kill Roland.

My job would be easier if killers wore signs.

~

THAT EVENING Manny didn't come home. Texted that he was out. Presumably doing the stuff Manny did and doing it with machismo and conviction.

I put Kix to bed. It'd been a day at the Montessori school, and those wiped him out. He smiled from his crib like a drunk, happy with everything.

I went into my bedroom to discover Ronnie on the bed, wearing the red nightie. I loved the red nightie. A flag flown by the locus of pleasure.

She once told me women never felt sexier than when wearing lingerie, so I should let her wear it awhile. Easier said than done, but I heroically did my best.

Tonight she found my restraint charming but tedious so she tugged it off herself and there was marital bliss.

Sex wasn't as simple as I thought it'd be, being married.

The timing had to match up and sometimes there were hidden hurt feelings and conflicting desires and expectations. Like anything good in this world, sex took work, especially beforehand. Who knew. But when we got it right, the whole world changed, a pure catholicon. The thing had a way of correcting the earth's axis, of erasing pain, aligning broken pieces, smoothing over rough spots. The air turned sweeter.

Plus. Hot damn was it fun.

Afterward I lay in the darkness, a bright beautiful darkness, and she sat beside me brushing her hair. My hand on her spine.

Eventually she stopped brushing. Laid down with her head on my stomach. Released a deep sigh.

"Thank you."

"For sex?" I said.

"For being in love with me. And showing it."

"Anytime, anywhere. Were you feeling unloved?"

"I was feeling...things. I was *feeling*, essentially. Which is something I didn't allow myself for years and years. I lived in a state of showmanship. Not authenticity. And now I feel new and I have authentic emotions." There was silence as I scratched her back. Outside, on Windsor, a couple cars went by. When she spoke, I felt the vibrations of her chest transfer into mine. "I think that's what's bothering me. People are gossiping about me, about us, and it makes me angry. Because I *have* changed. I'm new. Or I'm being renewed, I guess. And those bitches....no, those gossiping women represent the old me. And they don't respect that I'm not the old me anymore."

"Makes sense," I said.

"Did you know that's what was bothering me? This divide in my life?"

"No."

"But you had guesses."

"I had guesses."

"I feel like I'm stumbling around in the dark with this. Why don't you tell me your guesses when I'm upset?" she said.

"Because you're a human being, far too complex to be simplified. And you, more so than most, are fascinating beyond reason."

"Your opinion matters to me. I want to hear your theories."

"My theories about your current unease?"

"Yes. Tell me, please."

"Sure." I stared at the ceiling fan, far more perfect and grand after sex. Collected my thoughts. "You don't want their opinion to matter. And the opinion of any one woman probably doesn't. I think the collective opinion, however, does. You spent your whole life adjusting your actions and appearance to appease the collective opinion. How could you suddenly stop? You can't. You wish you didn't and that's a sign of growth. Actualized change. But change is slow. And, to top it off, you're a little embarrassed."

"Embarrassed? By?"

"Me. Us."

She sat up quick and twisted to face me. Pinned me with a glare. "Bullshit. That is not true."

It was, I thought, difficult to focus when Ronnie was nude. I did my best.

"Sure it is. You married a private detective. His roommate's a cop. He shares a house with his father, an elementary school principal. Your socialite group of friends work their way *up*, not down," I said.

"That doesn't mean I'm embarrassed."

"I didn't say unhappy. Think of it this way. For a while, I was a guilty pleasure. A toy you showed off. Look how naughty I am, because he's a side piece and I'm really engaged to a big time federal prosecutor destined for a presidential appointment someday. But marriage to me is different. You're making a declaration of who you are. What you're attaching yourself to. You love me and you wouldn't change a thing, but it's a radical departure from your old life. You're not ashamed. Shame is different. But it causes some embarrassment because marrying me is a public proclamation that you were wrong. That everything you believed and worked for previously was in error."

Her shoulders slumped some. She picked at the quilt. The thousand-dollar Vera Wang quilt with hand-stitched diamond hourglass pattern, God help us.

I said, "You like who you are. You like who I am. But you don't want to face the former friends and defend it."

A whisper in the dark. "I don't."

"I don't blame you."

"I'm not embarrassed to be married to you. I'm so *so* proud to be your wife, Mackenzie. Or fiancée, or whatever the hell I am."

"But your friends don't know I have the strength of ten men."

I felt her smile. A slight shifting of the atmosphere.

"At least ten."

"At minimum," I said.

"I didn't like that version of me. I'm changing, as quickly as I can. But...I'm still spending a thousand dollars a month on my appearance. I don't plan to stop. So I'm also embarrassed by my hypocrisy."

"Good," I said, "heavens."

"In most ways, I still am one of them," she said. "One of

the vain gossipers. So...when I face the mob, they'll have ammunition against me. I'm still this pathetic superficial fake, they'll say, who gets botox."

"You get botox?"

"Of course I get botox, look at my wrinkles," she said.

"You don't have...ah. I get it."

She laid down again. Using my stomach again as a pillow.

"I'm two people, Mackenzie, the old and the new."

"I really like them both."

When she spoke, her lips moved against my skin.

"That," she said, "is the only reason the new Ronnie exists."

14

Kix spent the day with Roxanne, his sitter when he wasn't being inculcated at the Montessori school.

Georgina Princess came with me to my office, downtown Roanoke. The building's central air was pumping and I opened my windows open to let in some noise.

I passed the morning researching beneficiaries of Roland's will. It wasn't a long list and none of our six suspects were on it, other than Barry and his trust. Barry's mother, Roland's niece, lived nearby in Lynchburg. I called Roland and he said she rarely came by, but they were friendly. Might need to visit the niece, though her background was as clean as everyone else's. And her credit score was the highest. Higher than mine.

As I poked around the internet, I watched electronic feeds from four cameras positioned in Roland's house. One in his bedroom, aimed at the bathroom. One in the kitchen, aimed at the refrigerator. And one in the television room, with a view of the front door. Walter had done his best...or probably he hadn't, but it was tricky because Roland didn't want anyone knowing he was onto their schemes and the cameras had to be plugged into a power source. I could hear what happened in the house and I could see it too, because Walter had connected the cameras to the house's wifi. Liz had the camera feed running at her house, too, and she recorded it.

Yakira the nurse helped Roland up and down the stairs several times and led him through stretches. She hadn't gone into the master bath.

Angelina was there now, in the kitchen, humming and cooking.

Walter was playing on his phone, keeping an eye on her. With the shorts she wore that day, it was hard to blame him. But I did my best.

Ronnie called.

"I'm leaving Beck's apartment now," she said. "I took her flowers and gift cards."

"How is she?"

"In a fair amount of pain. And overwhelmed by Manny."

I grinned. "He can do that."

"I'm only now realizing the guilt he's under. He took her injury personally. She was riding along to document it as part of a continuing education thing, as a favor to them. He thinks it's his fault, the poor guy."

"Beck's his partner in that black ops group. She's tough. She's not a federal marshal, but I get the impression she's been through a lot," I said.

"That doesn't change the fact that a sword sliced her open. He's cleaned her apartment. He threw out her bar stools because they were from IKEA, and ordered her handmade, solid wood stools from Amish country." She snickered, a lovely breathy sound in my ear. "He's cooking her steaks and chicken and fish and she doesn't know what to do with it all. If I didn't know better, I'd say it was romantic."

"It's not. But it's more than friendship," I said.

"It's breathtaking, that's for sure. Then again, the relationship you and he have could be confused for romance to a casual observer."

"I wouldn't correct them."

"She refuses to let him bathe her but he's still trying."

"He's never offered to bathe me. So she's got that going for her," I said.

"What are you doing?"

"Boring research. I hate doing the work that I hate to do."

"But you look so good doing it."

"Come do it with me," I said.

"I can't. I'm in court soon. But Mackenzie?"

"Yes Ronnie."

"I am so in love with you."

She hung up.

THE AFTERNOON I spent with Roland's charities. Not with Ronnie.

Only nine people would receive any inheritance from him, but there were dozens of charities that benefitted. I hadn't pegged him for altruism, but the guy was giving away millions. Close to twelve, if my numbers were right.

I knew some of the list. I knew St. Jude's Children's Hospital. I knew the Make A Wish foundation. I'd heard of the Libertarian Party. I knew World Vision and Red Cross. I'd heard of the Roanoke Foundation, a college grant.

Some I didn't know. The Responsible Trust for Virginia Veterans. The Financial Literacy Initiative of Roanoke City.

The Southwest Federation for Parents of Children with Special Needs.

I read and I researched and I clicked, looking into the charities I didn't know. Soul crushing, mind numbing labor. I rewarded myself with a dram of nectar, Johnny Walker Blue, each hour. Even that wasn't enough. I'd rather be pulling weeds with Zeus. Charities were charities it seemed to me after learning about the seventh, but these rocks had to be overturned. And I Sisyphus.

Or something like that. I was tired and might be botching the allusion.

Eventually Georgina Princess whined and suggested we call it a day. My back ached after long hours at the computer and my butt agreed with the dog.

I stood and stretched. A lesser man would feel frustration at learning so little.

On the way out, I glanced at the camera feed again.

Not a single person in sight.

Except Walter, asleep in the television room.

Us private detectives, worth every penny.

15

Lo and behold and wonders never cease.

Walter did something helpful and he sent it to me that evening. He engaged Barry the nephew in a conversation and he recorded the encounter with his phone. He sent me the file and I pressed play.

Barry was in his room, on his bed. Walter was holding his phone in a way that I could see the room. Looked like maybe he had the phone dangling from his hand, and he knocked on Barry's door.

"Hey Barry."

"Hi Walter. What are you, what are you up to?"

"I saw you playing Clash of Clans earlier."

"Oh yeah." The camera caught a big grin on Barry's face. His legs were straight on the bed and he wore black running shoes and white calf-length socks pulled up, and his shirt was buttoned up to his chin. His smile struck me as innocent and genuine. The world could use more of those. "Oh yeah, I like...I like it quite a bit and I've, I've been playing for quite some time."

Walter said, "You got room in your clan for one more?

Mine's not active much anymore."

"You want to, you want to be in my clan?"

"If you got room, sure."

"Would you like to, would, would you like to come in?"

"Yeah thanks." Walter walked into the room, the camera bouncing. He set his phone on Barry's desk or maybe his nightstand, the camera facing up. "I play the game on my iPad. Helps with my fat fingers. I can sit in this chair?"

"Sure, that would be, sure, that's fine. I'll send you a clan invite right now," Barry said.

"What's your town hall?"

"I am an, I am an eleven. See, I've had quite a bit of trouble getting to twelve. I don't like to press and I don't like to spend money on it."

Walter tried adjusting his phone's camera but it was awkward without Barry noticing. I got a brief glimpse of Barry on the bed, rubbing his palms nervously on his pants, before the phone fell and Walter let it be.

"You're better than me. I'm a nine," said Walter.

"Oh I don't, I don't know." Barry was smiling, evident in his syllables. If it's possible to express enthusiasm in a monotone voice, he did. Happy to have a friend. "Maybe I have been, maybe I have been playing longer than you. Is your, was your clan quite active?"

I talked myself out of fast-forwarding for the next ten minutes, enduring the longest and most tedious video game jargon imaginable.

Finally Walter asked, "How long have you lived here, Barry?"

"In this, in this house with Uncle Roland? Quite a long time. A few years, I'd say. It's been, it's been quite a while."

"Do you two get along?"

"I guess, I guess so. Uncle Roland doesn't talk very much," said Barry.

"How old is he now? Any idea?"

"I don't know. He's not that old yet. You know, you know I'm surprised I haven't heard of you before. We're related, I guess. Do you, do you think so?"

"Not by blood, I don't think. I'm on the other side?"

"How are you related to Uncle Roland?" said Barry.

"I don't know. Who knows how that stuff works. His third cousin, maybe."

Sometimes on tombstones, a quote is attributed to the deceased. On Walter's tombstone it should read *I don't know*. He said it. A lot.

"Who is your, who are your parents?"

"My parents?"

"Yes, I wondering, I'm wondering if I have heard of them."

"Bob and Carol," said Walter. Their voices sounded thin and hard, picked up by the mic on the table. I still couldn't see them.

"Bob and Carol. I think, maybe, I think I have heard of them. Bob and Carol."

"We're on the other side. Who knows."

"Yeah, that's, that's quite a good point. Who knows."

"What'll you think happens to all Roland's stuff when he dies?" said Walter.

"I think, I would think his relatives will inherit it. But to be quite honest, I am not sure."

"I don't think I'm getting any. I'm too distant. How about you?"

"I don't, I don't know. My mother might," said Barry.

"Your mother?"

"Yes. She and Uncle Roland have always been good friends. That's what, that's what she tells me."

"How'd you end up here?" said Walter.

"Well that's a, that's a, that's quite a funny story. Uncle Roland, he took, a few years ago he took me in, and, well, I was, I wasn't working, and I wasn't, I wasn't doing quite well, and I was working on my novel."

"Oh yeah?"

"Oh yes, I am writing a superhero novel. I would, I would be happy to show it to you."

"You told me about the novel. How's it coming along?"

"Oh it's, oh it's coming along quite well. I really have the villain as a nasty guy and he's, he's creating quite a few problems for the heroes. I would love you to read it. It's quite, it's quite good."

"Sure, I guess, you can email it. I'll take a look," said Walter.

"I have it here on my laptop. Would you like to read it right now?"

"To be honest, Barry, I'm getting kinda tired. Thinking of going to bed."

"Yes I understand. I will be happy, quite happy to email it to you."

"Has Roland read it?" said Walter.

"No. He doesn't, he doesn't seem to want to have anything to do with, he is not a reader. And he says, he says he is not into superheroes."

The phone jumped and the video shifted position; Walter had picked it up and aimed it. I could see Barry standing near his bed, holding a black laptop and smiling.

"Do you want to know something I think, that I think is quite funny?"

"Yeah sure," said Walter.

"I named, I named the villain Roland." He grinned bigger and snickered. "I think that is quite funny."

"That's a good one, Barry. And I won't tell Roland. He doesn't need to know."

"Good. That's, that's good," said Barry.

"You're secret's safe with me. You can share stuff and I won't tell anybody."

"I think, I am glad you glad you moved in, Walter."

"Me too."

"I'll send you the story and you can read it tonight. I think you'll find the characters are quite good."

Walter said sure and walked out of the room.

It was late but I knew he wouldn't be asleep. I texted him.

Nice work.

>> i know

Are you reading the story?

>> i tried

>> i don't read a lot

>> but i know his book sucks

Read the parts about Roland the villain

>> how

Use the search feature

>> how

>> that sounds hard

I set my phone down. It was late and I was tired. Maybe Barry would name a clown after Walter.

16

Day seven of our investigation. Everyone who knows anything knows that on day seven you stalk the nurse.

Yakira Chen.

She lived in a modish apartment building near the Carillion/Virginia Tech medical school. I got up early with the dew and found her little red Nissan Sentra in the parking lot and waiting for her, parked illegally on the street. I lowered my window so I could listen to birds as I drank coffee and read the Bible.

I was trying to read it in a year. The Israelites had incurred the wrath of God—again—and he was pleading with them to change their ways before destruction arrived. His primary complaints were they'd forgotten him, they took their blessings for granted, and they were unkind to the poor and the immigrants.

Good thing America didn't have those problems.

Yakira emerged, ending my confused stroll through the minor prophets. Often you could tell a nurse by the way she moved. Or he moved, but Yakira was a girl. She walked quick, posture alert, moving with purpose like she had somewhere to be and she wouldn't suffer nonsense when she arrived. The nursing scrubs and comfortable running shoes were also indicative.

She drove to At Home Nursing first, a nondescript office on Jefferson. According to the website, they employed eighty nurses providing in-home care of various levels depending on your needs and budget. Yakira came out ten minutes later holding two bags. A guy came with her hauling two cardboard boxes, which he loaded into the trunk. He said something I couldn't hear but she didn't seem to care for the guy. She slid into the car and headed north on Jefferson while he watched from the curb.

I eased into traffic and followed her to a house in South Roanoke. She marched inside, carrying one of the plastic bags.

I sat a block away and called At Home Nursing.

A guy answered, "At Home Nursing, this is Jeff, how can I help you?"

"Hi Jeff. I'm a nurse working in northern Virginia. The Woodbridge area, and I need a change of pace. Are you hiring?" I said.

"We're always hiring, bud. Application is online."

"A friend of mine recommended you. Yakira Chen. Do you know her?"

"Yeah, I know Yakira," said Jeff. "She was just here."

"Cute girl. We went to nursing school together."

"Oh yeah?"

"Just don't get on her bad side, am I right?"

Jeff made a snickering noise of agreement. "Bud, you ain't playing. Gotta watch what you say around her."

Me and Jeff, the best of friends

"She doing a good job for you guys?" I said.

"Sure, she does fine. No complaints. What'd you say your name was?"

"Hang on, getting a call, one sec," I said and I hung up.

Brief and sweet.

What did I learn?

At Home Nursing wasn't a front. Jeff likely hit on Yakira. And you had to watch what you say around her. Deep stuff.

And I hated being called bud.

An hour later she drove a tenth of a mile and parked at the curb and went inside the brick ranch house, carrying a cardboard box.

While I waited I brought up Roland's charity beneficiaries to research but Walter Lowe called me first.

I answered. "Let me guess. You got stuck inside the microwave."

"That's not funny. How's that funny?"

"I'm hilarious, Walter, wake up."

"Are you doing anything? Honestly. I've been here forever. I'm bored shitless. Why haven't you caught the guy yet?"

"Or girl," I said.

"What are you doing?"

"I'm tailing Yakira the nurse and learning about her."

"It's her. It's Yakira, she did it, she's the killer," he said. He was chewing something, directly into my ear. "Trust me, she's mean."

"Did you hit on her?"

"What? No. Did she say I did? I was polite."

"Did you hit on Yakira, Walter?"

"I was friendly, Mack," he said. "What kinda girl doesn't like compliments."

"Gotta watch what you say around her."

"Yeah, otherwise she'll poison me to death."

"Please stop eating," I said.

"I did. I'm going outside. Why're you tailing her? She doesn't come to Roland's today."

"That's precisely why I am. Elementary, my dear Walter."

"I passed elementary school. Took everything I had."

"Did you check Roland's online purchases for strychnine?" I said.

"No. I don't know how."

"Look on his computer or phone."

"I don't know where they are."

"You didn't ask him," I said.

"No. Think he'd let me?" There came a rushing sound on his end, like he was blowing into the receiver.

"Tell him it might save his life if he grants you access to his computer. But you're busy outside, lighting a cigarette."

"Of course I'm outside smoking a cigarette. Liz is coming soon. She'll be here most of the day so I can go do stuff."

"You have no stuff to do," I said.

"I have stuff. Perverted stuff, I bet you think."

"Crossed my mind."

"You're wrong. I need to see my mom. Check my mail. Feed my cat," he said.

"You don't have a cat."

"No but I could. I just gotta get out of this got'damn house a few hours, Mack."

"I get it. And I don't blame you."

"Thank you. Do me a favor and catch the killer. It's Yakira."

We hung up.

Yakira herself emerged from the house soon after, walking the quick nurse walk.

She didn't look like a killer.

SHE STOPPED at Chick-fil-A for lunch. Praise the Lord for his mercies are new every morning. I utilized the drive-thru and purchased two—*two*—spicy chicken sandwiches. No fries because I'm not a caveman. I listened to Colin Cowherd on the radio and watched Yakira. She sat alone near a window and ate a salad and played on her phone.

The whole time, every single second, I wished I'd gotten fries.

Her next client was in Botetourt, a thirty-minute drive. I listened to Colin en route and wished he'd talk baseball more, and I also wished the Nationals would buy another big bat before the trading deadline.

Yakira turned off 220 in Botetourt and onto Country Club Road, then a left on Shawnee Trail. On my phone's map, I noticed Shawnee had no outlets so I parked; I'd be busted for sure if I followed now. I waited five minutes and then entered. The neighborhood was one of rolling green hills, meadows, Civil War split rail fences, and great trees. I found her red Sentra on Stonelea Drive, parked at a modern farmhouse. I wrote down the address and retreated back to 220 to wait for her. Did this have anything to do with Roland's predicament? Almost certainly not. But who knew.

While I waited, I opened up his will and scanned down to the odd list of charities benefiting upon the event of his death. I'd researched several already. For example, the Give Back Yoga Foundation was real. Roland was bequeathing them a hundred grand, specifically to provide yoga access to veterans and active members of Alcoholics Anonymous.

Another odd name, Patriot PAWS. Also real, also getting a hundred grand.

That left The Responsible Trust for Virginia Veterans.

The Financial Literacy Initiative of Roanoke City. The Southwest Federation for Parents of Children with Special Needs.

I called The Responsible Trust for Virginia Veterans. Left a message. Couldn't find much about them online.

Next up, the Financial Literacy Initiative of Roanoke City. They had a post office box downtown and a decent website, displaying happy children with calculators in a school classroom. Also I found a mission statement about the growing challenge of boys and girls growing up with no sense of the power of a dollar. Wasn't that the truth. They would be bequeathed...I checked the paper...four million dollars.

Jiminy Christmas.

I checked the paper again. A cool four million bucks.

I called the number.

It rang a lot. I was prepared to leave a message but a woman answered on the seventh ring. "Hello there! This is the...Financial Literacy Initiative of Roanoke City. How can I help you?"

I gave her my Texas.

"Afternoon. How the heck are ya?"

"Well I'm doing fine, and how about yourself?" she said. With some perk.

"Couldn't be finer. Where are you located? I'd like to drop by and speak to one of your officers, if possible."

"Well. Um," she said. And she paused. "The initiative doesn't have a...a physical location. We're a...voluntary workforce."

"Is that so," I said.

"Yes sir, it surely is."

"How kindhearted."

"Isn't it? Our instructors teach classes at elementary

schools and also at the Rescue Mission. We do the classes on site, so we don't need a dedicated facility."

The lady was speaking in a peculiar fashion. Like reading the lines but she wasn't good at reading.

"How often?" I said.

"Depends on how often they ask."

"Pro bono?"

"Pro bono!"

Then why, I thought, do you need four million dollars? Four *million*.

"You're not one of the officers, ma'am?"

"Oh no sir, you could say I'm the...administrator. To be honest, it doesn't take much time."

"Could you pass a message for me?"

"Oh *absolutely*."

"My name's Clayton and I'd like to speak with an officer at their earliest convenience," I said and I gave her my phone number.

"Got it! I'll see he receives the note."

"Who?" I said.

"Who?"

"You'll see *who* receives it? From whom should I expect a call?"

"Oh!" A pause. I thought I heard papers shuffling. "Erik Foreman."

"Perfect. I look forward to hearing from Erik Foreman. And what's your name?" I said.

"My name?"

"Why yes ma'am, your name. I apologize for not asking earlier. My momma raised me better than that."

"My name's...Sally." She stuttered it.

"Thank you, Ms. Sally, and I look forward to hearing from Mr. Foreman."

"You're welcome, Mr. Wallace! Have a nice day," she said and she disconnected the call.

"Something," I said to the cosmos, "was weird about that."

The cosmos said, *Yeah we noticed.*

I said, "Why is Roland giving them four million bucks?"

The cosmos replied, *Because people are strange.*

Yakira finished her appointment and came zipping off of Country Club Road and drove toward Roanoke.

I followed.

As I followed, I called the Rescue Mission. I was connected to the Recovery Program, and a very nice woman answered my questions.

Yes, she knew the Financial Literacy Initiative.

Yes, they taught a two-night class about personal finances, approximately twice a year. Very nice people, usually the same man.

Yes, it was pro bono.

No, she couldn't remember the man's name, but yes it might be Erik Foreman. Should she look it up?

"No, that's fine, thank you," I said and we hung up.

Humph. Maybe the financial literary charity wasn't as weird as it seemed. Maybe Sally the administrator was just super duper odd. Maybe they'd be gobsmacked to learn they'd inherited four million. Four! Million!

Yakira Chen made one more stop, bringing the day's total to four. As usual, she took in supplies and came out an hour later, succor delivered. She drove to Kroger and then home to her apartment.

I left her there and did the same—Kroger and home.

I did so with the nagging feeling that Yakira had had a much more productive day than me.

THAT NIGHT. An epiphany.

I sat up straight in bed at 10:30, startling Ronnie next to me, and Manny and Georgina Princess on the floor. Nobody was asleep; we were all reading, except the dog.

Are you okay because I am right here and I love you, said Georgina Princess.

From his air mattress, Manny asked, "I need to put in earplugs?"

"No. Something's been nagging at me and I just got it."

Ronnie placed her hand on my spine. "What?"

"I made a phone call earlier. The woman took a message and she asked for my name. I told her Clayton. That's it, just Clayton. But when we hung up, she said, Goodbye, Mr. Wallace. She knew my last name, even though I never told her."

"Wallace," said Manny with a yawn, "is not your last name. You are dumb, señor."

"It was today. And she knew it."

Ronnie copied Manny's yawn. Asked, "How'd she know?"

"Alan Anderson. He's the only person who knows the name. He warned the charity that I might be calling," I said.

"Why'd he do that?"

"That, Ronnie, is an excellent question."

17

The next morning Liz came to the office wearing tight jeans and a light leather jacket, the kind with no collar or buckles. She brought two coffees and a box of Duck Donuts. My warm platonic feelings for her became more ardent.

"I figured you for a donut guy," she said. "And Roland's paying, so why not."

"My blood pressure, that's why."

"You're already on your second and no one's forcing you."

"Don't be ridiculous, Lizzy."

She opened a laptop to check the video feed from our nanny cams in Roland's house.

We chatted and drank coffee and I called Walter Lowe on speaker. He answered and Liz said, "Get somewhere you can talk."

"I'm in my bedroom with the door closed."

I said, "You should be near Roland."

"It's not even ten yet. Don't be a bully. Besides, he's still in bed."

Liz's eyes were on her computer screen. "No he's getting coffee in the kitchen."

"I'd rather get paid for doing nothing, if you don't mind. Am I on speaker? Are you two together?" said Walter.

Liz nodded, even though Walter couldn't see her. "Yes and yes."

"You doing anything kinky? Can I get a video?"

"We're eating donuts," I said. "And it's very kinky."

Liz grinned at me.

Walter said, "So selfish. Why'd you call?"

"I want to touch base, make sure we're all operating from the same pool of knowledge," she said.

"I don't know anything."

"Agreed," I said. "Walter doesn't know anything."

"Focus, boys. I'll go first. Walter, one of the cameras keeps glitching. Did you know?"

"No. Which one?" he said.

"The kitchen. I think it's wifi interference because it seems to happen when someone walks by."

"How long does it cut off?" I said.

"A few minutes. Once for three hours. Happens once or twice a day."

"Both video and audio?"

"Yes," she said.

"Alright, I'll take a look. Maybe I'll put it somewhere else." Walter made noises like he was moving. The rustling of sheets.

"Look later," I said. "Roland's in there now."

"And if you're going to the bathroom, put the phone down," said Liz.

"You don't want to hear me piss?"

"I do not."

Walter's phone thumped—he'd set it down. He was going to piss.

Liz told me, "In the DEA, I never had to tell anyone that, to put the phone down first."

"Bet they had to tell you that. Because you're uncouth."

"Is that supposed to be flirting, Mackenzie?"

"It is not," I said. "Even though Ronnie said I could."

"Why'd she say that?"

"She thinks highly of you. But I think highly of her so I don't flirt with other women. When I said you were uncouth, it was a genuine insult."

She laughed.

Nailed it.

"I am not uncouth," she said.

"You know the saying, beauty is on the inside? Well. Inside you're just awful."

She laughed some more. I was elite at not flirting.

Walter came back a minute later.

"That's better. Please continue."

Liz wiped the smile off her face. Down to business. She said, "I've been researching Barry, Roland's nephew. Get this. He spent a week in a juvenile correction center during high school after he stabbed someone with a pencil. It was Barry's *second* stabbing. HIPPA prevented me from getting his psych evals but I got a talkative school administrator on the phone. She worked there eight years ago, when Barry was a senior. She told me Barry can't handle teasing from his peers. He just snaps. When I suggested Barry was autistic, she didn't push back."

"He's twenty-six now. What'd he do after high school?" I said.

"It's a gray area, and I can't find much. Roland said Barry's father is long gone and his mother has a weak mind and kicked him out. Barry moved in with his aunt for a while, and last year Roland plucked him from a cheap apartment. I didn't find a criminal record."

On the speaker, Walter cleared his throat. "Seems like a nice kid. But I never tease him so what do I know. It's probably him, trying to kill his uncle. Let's wrap this up."

Lis said, "Walter, do you get the impression anyone suspects that you're not Roland's distant relative? That you have an ulterior motive?"

"Nah. Maybe. Johnny asked me if I knew who you were. Call you the hot black girl."

Liz made a light sucking sound at her front teeth. "I take issue with all three of those descriptions."

"Johnny's old, like sixty or seventy. It's okay. It's probably him, wants to kill Roland. Let's wrap this up."

I said, "What's he call Angelina?"

"Dunno."

Liz shrugged. "I was there most of the day yesterday and Johnny came, but Angelina took the day off. I saw nothing of consequence. Mackenzie, what'd you do?"

I said, "Tailed Yakira. I learned she's industrious and doesn't like it when guys hit on her."

Walter said, "It's Yakira. Wants to kill Roland because he hit on her."

"I'm going through Roland's will and calling charities. One of the local charities, a pro bono financial literacy initiative, is getting four million dollars when Roland dies. And I deduced that Alan Anderson called them to warn I might be in touch."

"It's a clue! It's probably him," said Walter.

"Warned him?" Liz frowned. "Why does a financial literacy initiative need to be warned?"

"Precisely."

"Could be nothing," said Liz. "Alan Anderson might have a close relationship with the charity and was paying them a professional courtesy."

I said, "Could be. Maybe they're a disorganized crew and he didn't want them to be embarrassed."

"It's possible. But you don't like it."

"I don't. The lady on the phone was out of sorts. The charity is legitimate, I verified that, but the whole thing rubbed me the wrong way. I'll circle back after I investigate the others."

"It's Alan. He's a killer. Let's wrap this up," said Walter.

"Alan never had access to the aspirin. Never had a chance to spike it," said Liz.

"I was joking. Alan's no killer. He's a wimp." Walter made a disgusting throat-clearing noise. Waking up for him was hard. "This sucks, what are we doing? We're getting nowhere. Alan's suspicious but he had no access. Yakira *isn't* suspicious but she has the best access to his medicine. Angelina and Roland get on great so it's not her. Barry's violent but it's not him because Roland rescued him. Everyone's guilty and no one is. What the hell are we *doing?*"

Liz filled her chest with oxygen and let it out slow. Like a parent reminding herself to remain calm. "We're compiling evidence, Walter. It's not easy, especially since our client stipulated the suspects be kept unaware. This is part of the work."

"Work's good for you, Walter. Work is a duty that echoes from deep below. Makes you realize you exist."

"Okay, Mom and Dad, thanks. How about this, though—Zeus is the killer. He has the strychnine, right? Let's wrap this thing up."

I said, "I don't like him for it. I followed him home. He

needs money and he doesn't benefit if Roland dies. Plus he reminds me of me."

A quick smile from Liz.

Walter said, "Fine, whatever. By the way Mack you need to come here tomorrow. Keep watch while I go do stuff."

Liz and I shared a glance. I shrugged. She shrugged.

"Sure," I said.

"Good. Roland asked for you. Wants to play bridge."

"I don't play bridge."

"Well, you lazy asshole, learn. He wants to play. And he said to bring the marshal," said Walter.

"Manny?"

"I don't know who Manny is. He said bring the marshal. He wants to play cards with the two guys who killed his brother, he says."

"Yep," I said. "That's us."

Liz closed her eyes and pushed at a spot between her eyes. "Good grief. That's quite a conflict of interest."

I grinned. "Anyone know how to play bridge?"

18

Ronnie and I jointly deposited Kix at the Montessori school. He screamed and shouted for his dad, expecting to be murdered any second. Drop-off shook Ronnie every time, filling her with doubt about the school and the wisdom of Kix's attendance. She was subdued after, quietly kissing me goodbye and walking to her car. At the door she took a deep breath and closed her eyes and shook her head. Did it again. Stood still. Kept doing it. Nodded to herself, practicing a technique taught to her by her therapist. A final dispositive nod. Opened her eyes, some inner order restored. Smiled at me and winked and got in her Mercedes.

I watched her go.

I liked a lot of things about Ronnie. I liked her laugh and her sigh. I liked that she frequently said my first name. She didn't know what she believed about her creator and the afterlife but she loved and respected me enough to investigate it. She'd risked her life and her financial stability to rescue me from Italy. She was intelligent and cunning in legal affairs. She was a fighter, overcoming absurd odds to remain alive and mentally stable. She adored Kix. She adored my father. She adored our house. She watched baseball with me and refrained from disparaging remarks about its monotony. She loved what I loved, and I liked that.

Also I liked her ankles and her feet. They were elegant and trim, but strong with muscle. Not the feet of a woman praying her high heels wouldn't betray her. Not the feet of a woman moving listlessly through the universe. Not the ankles of a couch potato. She'd taken dance lessons her whole life and she'd kept the balance, the poise. Her lower half was predatory and active. She grabbed the earth with her toes and moved with vitality, vigor. She moved like a tigress.

It was worth watching and contemplating after she'd gone. Which I did at the window, simmering in my cathexis until Stackhouse came downstairs.

I thought she'd left already.

Perhaps I'd been too lost in my thoughts about Ronnie's ankles.

Stackhouse came to the window where I was standing. She was tucking in her shirt. She smelled healthy, like soap and hair that'd been shampooed and dried.

"Ronnie left?"

"Yep," I said.

"That poor girl. How I love her."

"Poor girl," I said.

"Yeah."

"Why's she a poor girl?"

She finished with the shirt—all her shirts looked tight across the chest, a fact I did *not* notice—and she buckled her belt. Turned to inspect me. Although I stood nearly a foot taller, it often felt reversed.

"You know, babe, for a detective you can be obtuse."

"My detective powers were focused on her ankles," I said.

She grinned and went for a travel mug of coffee. "Think about life from her point of view."

"No. It's too early. Tell me what I should know."

"She started a new life. For you. She left her friends. She left the restaurant where she worked. She left her fiancé. She left her apartment. She's changing the way she talks, the way she does business. Hell, she killed her own father." She raised her hand to indicate I should shut up. "I know, you know, we both know, most of those changes were good. They needed to happen. She was a wreck. But let's not kid ourselves that her life is easy now."

"I believe you."

"Good." She poured a dollop of cream into the steaming travel mug and sealed it.

"But, because I am obtuse, give me an example. And use small words, as if you're speaking to an idiot."

She said, "Driving Kix to school. Think about it, babe. She shows up with a kid who calls her Robbie, who screams for his dad. She feels the eyeballs. The world thinks you and her are a temporary thing, and she knows it, and she feels like an intruder in the world of legitimate parents. She's right about the gossip, you know. The irony is, she feels more like a prostitute now more than ever before."

My knees almost gave out. Good grief.

"She told you this?"

"No. I see it." Stackhouse walked to the front door, where I stood. Grabbed me by the collar and pulled me down. Kissed me on the cheek. Rubbed it off with her thumb. "Did I make you feel bad?"

"Exceptionally so."

"None of it's your fault, babe. You're worth the work. You

earned her and she earned you. And there's not much you can do except support her and understand it. It'll get easier soon."

A noise outside got our attention. Manny's supercharged Camaro growled up Windsor. Turned into our drive and slid to a stop in the gravel. We watched him get out of the car.

"Is he just coming home from Noelle Beck's?" she said.

"Spent the night there."

"You think they're fooling around?"

"I think they are not," I said.

Her sigh clouded the glass. "What the hell are they waiting for."

"They have scruples."

"They won't be young forever. Scruples are for the elderly, like me."

"You're only fifty," I said.

"Fifty-one. Old enough to have scruples."

"Did living without scruples make you happy in your thirties?" I said.

"I was miserable in my thirties. I'm happy now."

"Your logic isn't holding weight."

"I don't need logic. I have scruples and happiness and plastic surgery," she said.

"You don't require logic after turning fifty-one?"

"Age does weird things, babe. Thus the plastic surgery."

"I think," I said, "age is messing with my client. Suddenly Roland wants to prove how strong and important he is. By shooting another man."

"How old is he?"

"I forgot exactly. Mid to late seventies."

"I can't imagine. I'll never be that old." She left, crossing paths with Manny as he came in.

I got more coffee and sat. Manny poured some too and

also sat. Mine had cream. His, he said, didn't need it because he had testosterone.

"*Amigo*, what's this favor you need?" he said.

"Remember Robert Wallace?"

"No."

"Religious nutcase, owned a big house on the border of Franklin County."

"No," he said.

"You shot him to death in a bunker in his backyard in the driving rain."

"Ah, *sí*, Robert Wallace."

"His brother is Roland, my current client. Wants to meet the man who shot his brother. Wants both of us to play bridge at his house this afternoon."

Manny stood. Washed his empty Yeti tumbler in the sink. Dried it with our drying towel.

"I don't know how to play bridge. But I'll go beat his ass, you want."

"I found a YouTube video on how to play. Wanna watch?" I said.

"Watch a YouTube video about bridge?"

"Yep."

"You want me to throw a chair through our front windows?" he said.

"I do not."

"Then you watch the video." He snatched the dog's leash off the wall and whistled. Upstairs we heard GPA scramble to her feet. "I'll take the dog for a walk and you tell me about bridge later and we'll play with what's-his name."

"Seems less destructive that way."

He and the dog left. Perhaps, I thought, to walk off some guilt about Noelle. Because life was fragile.

19

Roland Wallace stood and waited on the expansive porch as I parked near his garage. He wore the SIG on his right hip.

Still in the car, Manny said, "He gonna shoot me?"

"Maybe."

"I don't like being shot, *amigo*. Maybe I shoot him first."

"You trying to exterminate his entire genetic line?"

He smiled—although I was heterosexual, I admired the smile—and he said, "He got any other siblings I need to kill?"

"Don't think so. And you better hurry, you want to be the one to kill him."

"Your job is to keep him alive, I thought," he said.

"I'm not good at it."

We got out and closed the car doors and went up the steps. Johnny was already there, sitting in a rocking chair near a card table. I hadn't met Johnny. If we'd done our jobs well, Johnny had no idea he was under investigation. Walter Lowe was already gone for the day, leaving before lunch. He'd texted that he'd come back after dinner.

"Roland, meet my good friend, Manny Martinez," I said.

Manny threw him a nod. "Señor."

Roland didn't return the nod. "You killed my brother." Half statement, half question, and a little passion thrown in.

Manny nodded. "I did. Just in time, too."

"Was there a warrant for his arrest?" said Roland.

"No."

"Why was a federal marshal at Robert's house, then?"

I said, "He was looking for me."

"I knew you were there...Clayton," said Roland, using my undercover pseudonym, which impressed me. Maybe I should be using my Texas drawl. "But why was a federal marshal looking for you?"

I said, "I'd disappeared. My friend came looking."

Manny did a shrug. "I didn't shoot Robert in my role as marshal. I shot him in my role as Mack's *amigo*. I mean, Clayton's *amigo*."

Roland was glaring and his eyes were red. He was jazzed up for this encounter. The red didn't look like malice, though. The emotions looked like those we deal with when discussing tragedy. There was a lot of the emotion in him, more than he knew what to do with, and I thought it surprised him.

He said, "It was personal?"

"Someone shooting at *mi amigo?* It's personal." Manny nodded at Roland's holster. "Gonna draw on me?"

Roland chuckled and wiped at his eyes, angry at the tears there. "Probably not, Marshal. You look quicker than me. I'd have to catch you by surprise and that's not what men do."

"It ain't?" Manny looked to me for verification. "Men don't catch bad guys by surprise?"

"Roland thinks real men face off at high noon to settle their differences."

"I don't do that," said Manny.

"Yet you own several quick draw and accuracy records at Glynco. Why go through all that training if not to settle disputes in pistol duels?" I said.

"First lesson at Glynco. Don't stand in the open and let guys shoot at you," said Manny.

Roland made a dismissive growl and walked to the card table. Wiped his eyes again. He indicated his friend Johnny.

"This is Johnny Barnes. My friend since Vietnam. He'll be my partner."

Johnny stood up and shook our hands. He wore a Vietnam Veteran's hat and his hands were tough and gnarled with old injuries and arthritis. He was a short guy but stronger than most men his age. He didn't look at me like he suspected I was investigating him on the sly.

He introduced me to Johnny as his nephew, Clayton.

Johnny said, "You're a big guy, Clayton. Football player?"

"Once upon a time. Now I do finances."

"Clayton," said Johnny. "Clayton Wallace?"

"Yep," I said.

"Alan mentioned you."

"Alan?"

"Alan Anderson. Roland's tax man," said Johnny.

My heart, the coward, did a little jump. I could be on the very cusp of a clue.

"Oh yeah, I met Alan Anderson. Uptight guy."

Johnny enjoyed that. He laughed, kind of a smoker's cackle. "He is! Nice guy, though, I like him fine."

I said, "What'd he say about me? That I'm trying to weasel into Roland's will?"

Johnny, still grinning. "Something like that."

"Well you tell that tight-ass that Clayton Wallace isn't a

snake-belly." I jerked a thumb at myself. "I'm not in the will and I don't plan to be. Right, Uncle Roland?"

Roland thought the charade childish so he produced a noncommittal grunt. We sat.

I said, "What'd you do in Vietnam, Johnny?"

"I was a tunnel rat." He spoke with a smoker's rasp.

"Oh shit," said Manny and Johnny laughed. He enjoyed our surprise. "Those the guys go face first into the mud holes?"

"That's us." Johnny nodded at his forearm. An old faded blue tattoo of a rat holding an hour glass. "Wasn't alway mud, though. Mostly hard dirt."

"You're the only guy here qualified to talk about what a real man is," I said.

Roland coughed. He picked up the cards to shuffle. "He got picked to be a tunnel rat because he's little. Bastards didn't give him a choice."

"Didn't have a choice? Shit, that isn't true, we had a choice. They asked the smaller soldiers and we'd volunteer. You volunteer and the guys leave you alone because they knew you're crazy as shit," said Johnny and he laughed again. Kind of a cackle. "You get harassed when you're little, but not after you join the rats. Had to be short, yeah, but you had to be thin. That was the thing, how thin were you. The Viet Cong, they were tiny and their holes were too."

Manny asked, "Meet any guerrillas down there?"

He nodded. Lost some of his enthusiasm. "Three times I did. Tell you what, though, I'd rather meet a guerrilla in a tunnel than deal with the bamboo snake falling from the ceiling. Got bit by a scorpion down there once. Fucking awful. I'd rather fight a VC than snakes and centipedes in the dark."

I wanted to ask him more about his three encounters

with an armed enemy fifteen feet underground in a tiny black tunnel but he'd glossed over the fact, a good indication he'd prefer not to discuss it. Couldn't blame him.

Manny said, "You two are Vietnam amigos?"

"Who, Roland?" Johnny laughed, a rattling sound in his chest. "Old Rolly wouldn't last a day in the shit. He was there but he was a civilian. An engineer working on roads."

Roland stared fixedly at the cards in his hands. Not looking at me. He'd given me the impression he was a combatant in Vietnam. An intentional falsehood.

That nerd.

A little red in the face. He said, "Appears I'm the only man at the table who hasn't had the chance to test his mettle and kill his opponent. But that'll be addressed soon. Meantime, let's play cards."

Johnny, enjoying the moment of attention, said, "I went down twenty-four holes. Craziest thing I found down there? An armory. A cave of American shells. Big ones dropped from our bombers, the ones that hadn't gone off, the duds. Those little Uncle Ho bastards took the shells underground to repair. You imagine that, taking a bomb that didn't go off underground to tinker with it? How insane is that shit?"

"Enough of Vietnam. Bad memories for Johnny. And for me." Roland made a grunting noise and started flicking cards to us. "You know how to play."

"A little," I said.

"Very little," said Manny.

Roland and Johnny walked us through the first few hands. Without grace. They mocked our deficiencies. Told us we played the cards poorly but it was our bidding that was truly deplorable. We had no idea how to properly evaluate our starting hand, they said. Manny, not enjoying the mockery, became furious when told he was the dummy after the third contract. Although there was a dummy every round, he demanded we change the name.

After an hour of slow progress, Johnny announced the score, 960 to 80. We assumed that was correct. If he'd said the score was four rainbows to eight unicorns, we'd assume that was also correct.

Flying a plane would be easier than learning bridge.

I was dealing cards when Roland said, "Why the .357?"

The question was for Manny. "*Qué?*"

"You shot my brother with a .357, Marshal. Why?"

Without much interest, Manny replied, "That's what I had on me."

"Your Glock would've done the trick, too?" He indicated Manny with his finger. He'd seen the holster Manny wore at the small of his back.

"*Sí.* Not as quickly."

"Aim's a little easier with the smaller gun, and that's good because with the smaller caliber you need to hit your opponent in more critical spots," said Roland.

Johnny chuckled. More like one of his cackles. "Old Rolly's an expert on guns he ain't ever fired."

Manny said, "You fired the SIG?"

"I have not." A gruff reply.

"You're wearing a gun you haven't fired, *amigo?*"

"I know how."

I said, "Go to a range, Uncle Roland. Shoot that thing. A lot. Get some accuracy. Or even better, get a bottle of mace."

"Mace? Absolutely not, mace, just because I've never killed a man," said Roland.

Manny shot me a glance and grinned. "Roland watching too many westerns."

"I don't watch westerns, Marshal."

"Mace works, *hombre.* I use it."

"You didn't use any damn mace when you killed my brother."

"Didn't have time," said Manny. "Mace's great. You don't miss with mace. Besides, watching a guy suffer from it, that's entertainment."

Roland hit his fist on the arm rest of his chair. "When the time comes, I won't have time to fetch a damn can of aerosol! Neither did you."

"When what time comes, Rolly?" said Johnny. "Why're you carrying around that piece anyway? God awful things, guns."

"Only two percent of crimes are solved." The way Roland was talking, he produced spittle from his plosive syllables. "Did you know that? Two percent of major crimes! Look it up, that's a fact. I trust the police for nothing. Hear me? Nothing! Look around. Look at what I built." He flung his hands at the porch. The yard. The house, the sky. "You think I'll let some bastard come and...and *steal* it? While I hunt for *mace?* Or wait for the damn police to come and botch the job? No." He tapped the holster. "No, I'll handle it myself."

"You're gonna miss, buddy. Hitting's harder than you think it is," said Johnny. "Wanna get the job done? Use a grenade."

"Mace," I said.

Manny jerked his chin at Johnny. "You don't carry."

Johnny held up his tough gnarled hands. "Nope. No sir, not me anymore."

"Because of suicide?" said Manny.

"Damn right because of suicide."

"Suicide?" Roland made a scoffing sound. "Don't be absurd. Johnny's not suicidal."

Johnny looked down at the table and gave it a dark glower. He pressed his lips closed, so I answered for him.

"Johnny crawled into dark holes on the other side of the world, Uncle Roland. He knew going in that the mud would be boobytrapped. He knew he'd die of poisoning down there. He knew it'd be an awful, claustrophobic death and his friends wouldn't even know what happened in the black, but he went anyway."

"*No puedo imaginar*," said Manny. "You don't come out of the holes the same guy you went in, I bet."

"So yeah, Johnny's thought about suicide. Who wouldn't," I said.

Johnny made jerking motions to wipe his eyes, like he had some control over his hands but not all. "And then...you come home and your country tells you...don't talk about the tunnels," he said. When Manny and I arrived, we hadn't planned on making old guys cry. But that's what we were doing. He continued, "And your countrymen think you're a...a crazy asshole. A villain. I know a lot of boys who did. Killed themself. If I had a gun in the house? I'd'a shot myself a dozen times by now."

"Hard to blame you," I said.

Roland did one of his grumpy noises. Did a lot of those. "Well. He's fine now. I don't see the use upsetting him."

"He's not fine now. Never fine after stuff like that, señor Roland," said Manny.

"Johnny hasn't had a steady job since! I worked my ass off while he takes it easy. He flew to Mexico after the war. *Mexico.* Just to drink. He goes back every couple years, and I've never been."

Johnny grinned. "I had war money to burn and I did. Even though money's cheap down there, it didn't last two months. I bought a house. Still own it! More like a shack in a bad neighborhood, but it's mine. Short walk from the beach."

"You see? His life can't be that difficult, Marshal. You know what I did after the war? Came home and got to work. Worked my whole damn life!" Roland was shouting now. Might as well be pleading, *Take me seriously. Please tell me I'm a real man. I feel incompetent.*

Johnny grinned and patted Roland on the arm. "Relax, old Rolly. Getting worked up for nothing."

I thought about hitting Roland. Johnny wanted to baby him, but I wanted to kick his ass. We're talking about tunnel rats dying underground and Roland's complaining he doesn't get enough credit.

He was saved by Angelina, the Costa Rican cook and housekeeper, racing up the driveway. She drove a rattling Chevy Malibu, twenty years old. She got out and fixed her hair and called, "Sorry I'm late, Rolly!"

He waved her off, still fuming. "It's fine."

She came to the stairs. Up close, her full-figured architecture was even more impressive. "Did you eat lunch?"

"Did I eat lunch? It's late afternoon. Of course I ate lunch."

"I'm sorry, Rolly. I'll start dinner."

"It's fine." Under his breath, "She's late a lot."

She smiled at us. Saw Manny and she tripped. A big trip, catching herself with her hands on the steps.

Manny stood. "Vaya, ten cuidado."

Be careful.

He went to help her but she hurried the rest of the way, blushing. "Gracias. Estoy bien."

Thank you, I'm okay.

"De dónde es tu acento?" said Manny.

Where's your accent from?

"Costa Rica," she said. Fixing her hair again.

"Es muy bonito."

"Gracias," she said, and she fled inside, Manny's attention and his perfect face was too much to bear after a fall.

Manny sat again.

"*Ay caramba.*"

I nodded. "*Ay caramba.*"

"Your wife, Roland?" said Manny.

He grinned, with a hint of lecher in him. "My helper. I admire, that's all. Usually."

"She looks like trouble," said Manny.

"She's a lot of damn trouble."

Johnny said, "That's Angelina. She's got a boyfriend. What do you mean, Rolly, you look *usually?*"

"A couple years ago, something happened, you might say." He winked. "But I felt bad after and I told her I felt bad, and since then I keep my hands to myself."

Manny wrinkled his nose. "Don't tell the story."

Johnny looked disgusted. "Gee-zus, Rolly, you're an old man."

"I wasn't an old man that afternoon. Best ten minutes I had in years," said Roland, and the rest of us thought about throwing up. "But like I said. I told her then, we shouldn't do it again. She's a sweet girl." We didn't know the proper way to express our abhorrence and sordid curiosity about those ten minutes, so we said nothing. He stood with grunt. Stretched his stiff back. "I need to piss, then we'll play a couple more rounds of cards. I'm getting tired and the game's ruined with talk of war. Anyone want a beer?"

"Hell yeah I want a beer," said Johnny.

Manny and I also accepted and Roland went inside. When he opened the door, Angelina's humming drifted out.

"Good Lord, I wish I didn't know that. About Angelina,"

said Johnny. He removed a pack of cigarettes from his jacket pocket and fished one from the pack.

Manny said, "You got a lot of patience with your old buddy Roland."

Johnny gave us chagrinned. "You gotta know him. He's not an asshole. Not usually. Just talks like it."

"You two met in Vietnam?" I said.

"No. Met here afterward. The dummy was telling everyone he'd been in Vietnam. And he had, I guess, but not in combat. I knew he was lying but I liked him. Been friends for forty years."

"Lying about Vietnam and feeling up the help. Not a good look," I said. Fueling his fire.

"Never said the guy was perfect." He flicked the lighter.

"That Vietnam thing would drive me nuts," I said.

"It does. It does. But Rolly, he's taken care of me too. Been a real good friend for a long time."

"He'd have the—"

We were interrupted by a scream. Angelina. A real scream, terrified.

Manny and I jumped up.

Someone else shouted inside, a man's voice. I reached the front door as a big sound rocked the house. A gun shot. I yanked the glass door open and peeked around the heavy wooden inner door. Made sure no one was aiming the barrel of a pistol at me. A second blast, impossibly loud, deeper within the house, then another. Three gun shots total.

In the kitchen Angelina had her hands in her hair, clenched. Breathing heavy, eyes wide, staring at a hallway.

"Where?" I shouted

"It's...he's...*ay dios*..."

This was the first I'd been inside Roland's house. Overstuffed furniture, high ceilings.

I reached the hallway she stared at. Slipped my pistol free. Manny behind, looking everywhere, his gun already out.

A wide hallway, hardwood floors. Bright light spilled from the bathroom. Roland stood in the light, swaying. I heard him groan, though I saw no injury. His pistol was in his hand, the barrel smoking. The gun slipped from his fingers. Landed with a hard thump beside a splintered hole in the hardwood.

At the far end of the hallway was a bedroom, and someone was squirming on the bedroom carpet. Scooting backwards, away from Roland, and gasping. Next to the bed, a revolver on the floor.

The person scooting backward was Barry. Staring at his Uncle Roland, eyes wide like a struck dog, his mouth working but producing no sound.

As he writhed, he left a deep crimson stain on the carpet.

Roland had shot him.

20

Everyone started moving again.

Angelina got on the phone quick, called 911. She was screaming—there'd been a shooting, help, someone had been shot.

Not the wording I'd use. Now we had a bigger mess on our hands.

Barry was hit in the shoulder. There wasn't much left of his trapezius muscle—a .45 round destroys more than just the tissue it touches. Manny and I pinched the wound closed and wrapped it tight with bedsheets. Manny kept pressure on it.

Blood pumped into the sheet but not a fatal amount. Barry would survive this and I told him so.

He wasn't talking, which spooked me. I removed the pillowcase from his pillow and picked up his revolver with it. Manny was cracking jokes, trying to get Barry to smile.

Angelina, still crying, called from the kitchen.

I met her there and accepted the phone. I talked with the 911 operator and outlined the situation, explained it was an accidental shooting, which was kinda true and kinda not, and asked how far the ambulance was because I could transport the kid myself. It was close, less than five minutes, she said, don't move him. I gave the phone back and washed blood off in the sink.

Roland was in a big chair, sucking oxygen and trying not to cry.

What do you know, I thought; he got his wild west moment. Shot his opponent face to face.

Roland's hands were shaking. Mine were too. In my left hand, I had the pillowcase with the revolver inside.

The revolver that hadn't been loaded.

THIRTY MINUTES later there were three police cruisers out front. Lights still flashing, effectiveness reduced in the daylight. There was an ambulance too, the medics inside with Barry.

I had experience with forensics. Based on the hole in the floor and the two holes in the wall, Roland's first shot had been accidental, nearly clipping his foot. The second shot missed Barry by two feet. The third got his shoulder.

Barry was in shock, but not circulatory shock. He hadn't lost that much blood, not enough to deprive his organs. Something in his nervous system had tripped and he wasn't talking. Shocked speechless.

Johnny was shocked too. He paced the front lawn, smoking. Gunshots brought nothing but bad memories.

I sat on the front porch with Manny and Angelina. Nearby, ashen faced and sitting in an Adirondack chair, Roland listened to Detective Green and mumbled answers.

I knew Green. He worked homicide for Roanoke County. I liked him well enough. He had on khakis and a blue police polo. A trim guy, he wore fancy sunglasses and gel in his hair like he was big time. Somehow his shoulders looked bunched up too high. He had good cheekbones so that was nice for him.

Another cop stood inside doing nothing. But if something happened, he was ready. The third and fourth cops were near us, vigilant, watchful. Crime scenes are weird, even for police officers. A lot of times they didn't have anything to do, but they felt like they should, and everything was awkward.

This was a case where there wasn't much to do.

They all knew of Manny and watched him, wondering if the legends were true.

Detective Green left Roland alone and came to talk with us. Leaned against the porch rail. "Where's Liz Ferguson?"

"On her way," I said.

Green took his sunglasses off and cleaned them on his shirt. The corner of the glasses read Armani. "She's who I talked with, last time. You'd think, with two reputable private eyes and a federal marshal, this would be a safe house."

"Any house with me in it is a dangerous house, detective," said Manny.

"Yeah I heard. Anyway, you mind walking me through it one more time? I know, I know, but I'm getting everyone's story straight."

"Once more should do the trick. First two, we were lying about it all," I said.

He was writing on a notepad and recording everything with his phone. "Uh huh. Okay. Roland, Johnny, and you two are all outside talking on the porch. Roland's wearing the SIG. Angel, you're cooking in the kitchen."

"Angelina," she said.

"Right. Angelina. Tell me about it. *Again*."

She nodded and pushed her hair back. Her breathing was still shaky. "I went to the bathroom. When I come out, Roland is in the hallway. We pass each other and he makes a gasping sound." Her Hispanic accent was minor but it was there. "Because he looked into Barry's room, *sí*? I turn around when he gasps. I see Barry and he is pointing a gun at us. I scream. I did not mean to, but I did, and I think it scared Rolly."

"And you guys," said Detective Green, pointing at us, "you hear the scream."

"We heard it so good. That's where we get our reputable reputations, our hearing," I said.

Green did a little eye roll. "Yeah sure. Keep going, Angel. Angelina."

"I scream. I run out of the hall. Then I hear the gun."

"We did too. We're great at hearing," I said.

"You told me. Two gun shots, right? Just the two, Angelina?"

He was doing that stupid thing where he gets facts wrong to see if people correct him, see if people are listening, see if stories change. Also he'd called her Angel on purpose and he was flirting with her.

She said, "Three, I think."

"Then what, Angelina?"

"I'm in the kitchen. I am afraid to move. I did not know, I hadn't seen...I thought Barry shot Rolly. I did not know."

Green said, "Then you two guys run in."

"We did it so good," said Manny.

"Sure you did. Great at running and listening, you two." He swallowed, looking at his notepad. He was nervous around me and Manny. We were known. "You find Roland in the hallway. He drops the gun. You secure Barry. He didn't talk, and he still hasn't. Right? What else?"

I said, "Manny keeps pressure on the wound. I talk to the 911 operator. I pick up Barry's gun with the clean pillowcase. A minute later I get Roland's. You and the cavalry ride to the rescue five or ten minutes later."

Down the hill, Liz's gray BMW sedan motored into view and turned into the driveway. Detective Green slid his Armani aviators back on and watched.

I said, "Did you tell Roland that Barry's gun was empty?"

"Just did. He's shook. Says he doesn't believe me. It's hard to learn you shot your nephew for no reason. I showed him a photo of Barry's gun and Roland says it belongs to him. Said it'd been stolen weeks ago, before the poison, before Liz got involved."

Angelina was looking at me a little funny.

She said, "A minute ago, he called you...what, a private police officer with a good reputation? Something like that? I thought you were in finance, here to look over Rolly's bank records, yes? You are his nephew?"

I spread my hands, palms up. "Cat's out of the bag. I lied. It's a weird story, Angelina, and I'll tell you the whole thing soon."

"What about poison?"

"We'll talk about that too," I said.

Manny mumbled, "You're not good at being under cover, *amigo*."

On the lawn, Johnny lit another cigarette.

Liz parked behind the cruisers. Slammed the door and walked our way. Detective Green took off his glasses and pointed at her with them. "I told you, didn't I. What'd I tell you?"

"Hello, Detective."

"I told you attempted murder isn't something you should handle without me. Without the police."

She ignored him. Looked at Roland, still alone and shaken in his chair at the far end of the porch. She asked me, "Tell me what you know?"

I said, "Barry had Roland's stolen revolver. It was empty. There was an unopened box of ammo in his nightstand. He was playing with the gun in his room and Roland saw him and got scared and shot him."

Liz pushed at the spot on her forehead like she did when frustrated.

"What do you mean, playing with the revolver?" said Detective Green. "Roland said he was taking aim, not playing."

"It's an educated guess. Barry's an adult who writes bad superhero stories and lives with his uncle because he has a hard time functioning. Chances are, the reason he had the empty pistol in his hand in the bedroom is he was playing make-believe. There are inferences to be drawn."

Angelina, eyes red, watched Liz, one more surprise from a heart attack. "Are you a private police officer?"

"Yes, sweetie. We'll talk it all through, soon as we can."

Detective Green said, "Barry has a hard time functioning? Tell me about that."

Angelina answered him. "He is autistic or something. He is a big sweet kid. He cannot grow up or hold down a job, not really."

"You clean the house? Did you know Barry had the missing pistol?"

"No. *No*, I swear I didn't."

"Roland's convinced the boy was going to kill him," said Green.

"Not without bullets, he wasn't," I said.

Manny shrugged. “Could throw the pistol real hard. I’ve done it.”

Green slid the glasses back on. He liked doing that. “You killed someone by throwing a gun?”

Manny’s eyes went far off, looking through us, remembering. “No. No that guy didn’t die. But he bled a lot. It was a good day.”

“Are you faking too?” Angelina asked Manny. “Or are you a real police officer?”

“Sí, soy policía y soy el mejor,” said Manny.

Yes I am police and I’m the best.

“Will Rolly be arrested?” she asked.

Liz said, “*No*.”

Detective Green said, “Maybe, maybe not, but not today. I need to talk to Barry first and to the Commonwealth.”

Liz whacked Green in the chest with the back of her hand. Not many people get away with that. Liz Ferguson, however, could. “C’mon, Detective. Roland's gun was stolen and he was scared and he walked into someone aiming it at him. Roland stood his ground in his own house.”

Detective Green held up three fingers and ticked them off, one by one. “Negligent discharge in a residential area. Malicious wounding. Attempted murder. From what I hear, Barry might be mentally incompetent and he was *playing* with an *unloaded* weapon, so there’s no justification for using deadly force. So yeah, Liz, we might charge him.”

Roland had been listening. He made a groaning noise and stood up. Came to the card table, still with bridge hands laid out. He picked up the cigarette Johnny’d discarded earlier at the sound of gunfire. And the lighter. Returned to the far chair and tried without success to light the cigarette with quaking fingers.

Detective Green told Liz, “On the bright side, you found

your culprit, right? Roland hired you to find the guy who stole his gun. Case closed?"

Liz didn't respond, her arms crossed, watching Roland with a frown on her face. I didn't respond either, because I was thinking the same thing she was—we didn't believe Barry had stolen Roland's revolver. No way.

So who'd given it to him?

21

Ronnie told me, "The gun was missing and Barry had it. That's compelling evidence. Convincing a jury otherwise would be tricky."

Saturday night, the day after the shooting. We were sitting on our front porch, listening to insects buzz and chirp in the dusk. She held a glass of wine. I held her bare feet in my lap, a beer beside me, next to the humming baby monitor. She'd put to Kix to bed thirty minutes ago. I would spend as many fall evenings on the porch as decency allowed.

"From what I gather," I said, "Barry doesn't do dishonesty. He thinks straightforward. When he got teased in high school, he stabbed the guy with a pencil immediately. Good and bad, no gray. He thinks in binary. Barry kept his bedroom door open at the house because he has nothing to hide. Doesn't even occur to him to hide. And he never goes upstairs."

"Can you prove he never went upstairs? Or that he had nothing to hide?" she said.

"I don't have to prove it to anyone. Just what I believe."

"Roland terminated your services. You could prove it to him?"

"He's not thinking clearly at the moment," I said.

"Are you upset about it? Being terminated?"

"I think it's a mistake. Someone wants Roland dead and it's not Barry."

"What's Liz think?" said Ronnie.

"She's forlorn. She feels like a failure on a few levels. She agrees, that Roland's still in danger."

Ronnie made a slight moan as I pressed a thumb into the sensitive fleshy spot on the bottom of her foot. I could spend the rest of my life manufacturing that noise.

Yesterday, after the police left Roland's house and after the ambulance had whisked Barry off to the hospital, Roland had retreated to his bedroom, a broken man. Liz and I told Angelina and Johnny the whole story—Roland had evidence someone wanted to kill him and he'd hired us to find out who. Angelina cried more. Johnny lit another cigarette and left in his truck. Liz went upstairs to talk but Roland told her to leave.

Eyes closed, Ronnie murmured, "You're going to keep investigating, aren't you."

"Probably."

"Even without a paying client."

"Even so," I said.

"Mackenzie."

"Yes Ronnie."

"I like that about you," she said. "But I like everything about you."

"You like it when I flush billable hours down the drain?"

"I'm a successful attorney who lusts after you and will pay all your bills." She smiled, eyes still closed in a dream-like state. "It turns me on a little, the idea of financially providing for you."

"Prurient and oofy. Those are a few of my favorite things. Or adjectives."

"I don't know what oofy means."

"You don't have to. You're pretty."

"Tell me," she said.

"Means wealthy."

"Oofy does not mean wealthy."

"It does."

"I'll look it up later. If you're lying, I'm going to pinch you," she said.

"And if I'm not lying?"

"I'll scold you for using archaic words. Either way, I'll still lust."

"Win win." On the monitor, Kix made a noise. I thought he said something about Robbie. Called her Robbie in his sleep, which was adorable. I drank beer. "Do you think the Commonwealth Attorney will charge Roland?"

She said, "I doubt it. Those guys are pretty backed up. I'll ask. If the CA knows I'll get involved, he'll likely let it slide."

"Are you not overworked?"

She shrugged, something she did that looked supernal. "A little. But Roland's rich and I like rich clients."

"Me too."

"Our jobs aren't so dissimilar, Mackenzie. Do you know what the biggest difference is? You discover the truth, while I tell everyone what I want the truth to be."

"Do you not find it destroys your soul a little?" I said.

"It does. But then you make it better." She yawned and after it she sipped her white wine. "Speaking of my destroying soul, I'm skipping church tomorrow."

"Marcus will worry. Our pew population matters."

"Marcus pedals cocaine. He doesn't get to judge."

"Marcus...keeps a clean workplace environment for other guys who pedal cocaine. Distinction is important."

"You don't have to tell me. I make a living on distinction," she said. "I'm skipping because I have a lunch date with friends."

"Uh oh."

"Indeed."

"Bitches who start rumors?" I said.

"They aren't bitches. They're...industrious with the tools they have. Distinction is important. And I will tell them I'm married to the man of my dreams, and they'll think that's childish and then they'll move on to discuss their new lake homes at Water's Edge."

"I love Water's Edge."

She smiled, eyes still closed. "I know."

"I should charge more."

"No, I make plenty and I have enough in the bank to buy a lake house with cash," she said.

"But."

"But I'm happy. We're happy. So so happy. No reason to rock the boat. Maybe some day."

"Will they believe you're happy?" I said.

"No. Or they won't know what to do with it. Do you know what I wish for them?" She sat up straight. Pulled her feet out from my lap to place them on the wooden porch slats. "I wish I could bring them here, the friends from my former life. I wish they could eat with us. Cook with us. Sit at the table and wash dishes afterward. Then watch television and talk. I wish they had the opportunity to put Kix to bed and sit on this front porch. It has to be *this* porch and that kitchen inside with these people, with you and the rest. And afterward, I would say, see? *Look*. Look at this. Look at

Kix and look at these men. Listen to them talk. Can you blame me for getting out of the bullshit game of ascendency? It's heaven. I found heaven. And I'd tell them it was a gift. This guy, this perfect man, he fell in love with me and none of this is based on my merits, not really, and it's all a gift. And they'd understand, Mackenzie. And they would be so jealous and resentful and dubious, but they'd understand."

"Dubious," I said, enjoying her passion.

"Yes, dubious. They'd fall in love with you and this house too. This Kingdom of God here on earth. But they'd doubt it'll last because they know the old me and they know I don't deserve it. But even so, I wouldn't have to fumble my way through a defense of my new life. They'd understand, because they felt it. They felt the joy."

On the monitor, Kix made noises. He was either awake or was trying. I said, "Perhaps your former friends already found their joy."

"You don't believe they have, though."

"I try not to judge. From what I've seen, joy is difficult to reach when climbing the wrong ladder."

Ronnie said, "As a girl who climbed that ladder hard, who went to bed alternating between smug satisfaction and cold despair at the world's cruel comparisons, I affirm that life without ceaseless striving is better."

"A tough position for you to defend, counselor, to your friends. That's a lesson learned through experience, not lecture," I said.

She sighed and sunk back into the rocking chair. "I know. That's why I wish they could live here for a day. Except I kinda hate them."

Kix uttered a cry. A mournful wail we heard through the monitor. Despair at finding himself alone in the dark.

Father! I'm alone in a dark room and usually I'm fine with it but I had a bad dream. This is embarrassing and I'd rather not keep shouting! Daaaaad!

Inside, Georgina Princess whined in solidarity.

"Speaking of ceaseless." I finished my beer and stood.

Ronnie remained seated. Smiled peacefully upward. "You're a good father."

"I'm a sucker, is what I am. It's a tough world we live in. Other kids his age are already working in the coal pits. I should let him cry himself back to sleep. Self-soothing."

"But you won't let him cry it out. Because you understand, now and then, we all need a Mackenzie August to hold our hand," she said.

"I do okay at it."

"You're the best at it."

"Well," I said. "Hard to argue with logic."

And I went in.

22

After church I picked Liz Ferguson up from her house in Wasena, a mile from my home in Grandin. Timothy and Stackhouse kept Kix, and Ronnie was at her dreaded lunch date.

Gray September clouds blocked out the blue and kept Roanoke warm and damp. I tried not to judge. But I thought it was a poor showing from September, one of my favorite months.

Liz didn't speak a few miles and when she did, "I should have checked Barry's room."

"You weren't hired to find a stolen revolver. That wasn't what he asked you to do."

"I should have checked. However, if anything, the idea of Barry playing with the gun like a little kid solidifies his innocence, in my mind. The bedroom door was open, damn it. He was hiding nothing. He didn't steal it from Roland's closet," she said.

"Be nice if he could tell us where he got it."

"His mother, Roland's...niece, I think, she signed him out of the hospital yesterday evening. She's not exactly a highly functional adult either. I called her this morning and Barry isn't talking. His insurance will pay for counseling and he starts Wednesday. She hasn't decided if she'll press charges, but a blood-sucking attorney will talk her into it sooner or later."

"If Roland's smart, he'll offer a big settlement, pre-blood-suckers," I said.

"You know what I think?"

"You think someone took the gun and planted it in Barry's room without telling Barry." I drove us into the eastern hills of Roanoke County, via the Blue Ridge Parkway.

"That's exactly what I think. I think one day he opened a drawer and there it was."

"The thief thought, if Roland dies one way or another, the police will look for the murderer, and wouldn't it be nice if Roland's stolen gun was in Barry's room? If Barry stole the gun, maybe he's capable of poison, the police will say. Or, maybe the would-be killer would get lucky and Barry would do the job for them with the pistol," I said.

"Exactly. I told Roland this theory. Over the phone."

"And?"

She wore her leather jacket and it crinkled when she crossed her arms and shrugged. "And he thinks private detectives are worthless. I'm not sure he's wrong."

"We're not the one drilling holes in his nephew."

"You should tell him that, Mackenzie. It'll go over well." She sighed at the window, her breath fogging it for an instant. "What a mess."

"It is."

"Did the shooting scare you?" she said.

"Of course."

"If half the stories about you are true then you've had a

far more adventurous career than me. And I should have anticipated a shooting when I hired you."

"Rumors of my magnificence," I said, "are potentially exaggerated."

"I heard you had something to do with the shooting of Sergeant Sanders a couple years ago. How about that? It was whispered in our circles that you personally avenged the death of your girlfriend, Kristin Payne, but I imagine that's off limits. And it was widely reported in the news when you shot your colleague, a fellow teacher, in South Hill. Of course, the North murders in Los Angeles. Plus the—"

"Okay, Lizzy. I'm a big deal. I forgot."

She sniffed, a little laughter. "Do you see? That's enough danger for three career lifetimes in law enforcement. Do you know, my time in the Army and the DEA, and now working privately, I have never shot someone? Not even shot *at* and missed?"

"Maybe you hang out with the wrong people."

"Nice decent people?" she said.

"Or you're not trying hard enough to see the worst in them."

"I'm just...sad, I guess. I've never had a case end this badly."

"Keep working with Walter Lowe and you'll have lots."

A little more laughter. "He wasn't even there when it happened. But you're probably right."

~

ROLAND DIDN'T ANSWER the doorbell but we spotted him through the window, sitting at his kitchen table. I opened the front door and we went in.

He was smoking. Tendrils of haze drifted lazily around

him, giving the kitchen a fug. The television was off. The radio was off. The lights were off.

"I don't smoke," he said. "Or I hadn't in twenty years. What do I do when shit hits the fan? The first thing I do, I reach for a damn cigarette."

Liz wrinkled her noise at the haze. "Your house is too nice to smoke inside, Roland."

"Too nice for a lot of things." He wore a long-sleeved blue pajama outfit with a terry-cloth robe over it, and socks and leather slippers. I thought he looked shrunk, diminished. Roland never struck me as elderly until this moment. He coughed, producing puffs of blue from his nostrils. "Feels empty, doesn't it. This big damn house. No Walter. No Johnny. No Yakira. No...no Barry. It's a Sunday, so it'd usually just be Barry and me. Sometimes Johnny. I can't remember the last time the house was empty."

"Walter moved out?" I said.

"I made him. That fat bastard didn't do a damn thing."

"I want him back in here."

He stubbed out his cigarette and glared at me with bleary red eyes. "Why?"

"This house needs someone else in it. And your life's still in danger," I said.

"It's not, but even if it was, what would Walter do about it? Life's not a game that can be played from a phone." Talking seemed hard for Roland. He reached feebly for a mug of coffee. Picked it up but found it empty and set it down. "Walter. Fat Walter doesn't even carry a gun."

His words connected with his ears and he grimaced. The inner conflict was plain to see. The cognitive dissonance, the belief that real men carry guns and duel each other versus the reality that he'd shot his nephew.

"Roland, Barry didn't steal your gun," said Liz.

"Barry stole it. He intended to...use it. And I dealt with him."

"Your nephew had no intention of shooting you."

"You already told me! And I gave you my response. Yes he damn well did. Boy's not right in the head."

"Did you ever see him upstairs?"

"He did it when I wasn't looking." Roland's hand flexed and released and flexed again, like he needed something in his fingers.

Roland's insistence on Barry's guilt was understandable. If Barry hadn't stolen the gun, then Roland had truly gunned down an innocent kid. And that was a heavy thing to live with.

"I think the more plausible answer is that someone who is upstairs frequently found the revolver and took it."

"Why would they do that?" said Roland.

"Maybe they didn't like the idea of you being armed. Maybe they wanted to frame someone. Maybe they were stealing it, panicked, and hid it in Barry's room. Maybe a lot of things, each of which makes more sense than Barry sneaking upstairs to steal it and then not caring if he got caught."

"Seems farfetched, inspector." The way Roland said inspector, it wasn't a respectful title.

"I know. But Barry never went upstairs and he isn't... sharp enough to poison you. You are his benefactor and the only family who cares about him. You're in danger, Roland, because someone wants to kill you and it isn't Barry."

"Maybe you damn bloodsuckers just need a client to drain," he said.

"Your bloodsucking theory manifests from pain and emotion and it's wrong," I said. "I'll work free."

"You..." He stopped to cough into his fist. Blinked at the tears the coughing produced. "You'll work free."

"I will."

"Why?"

"You're going to die soon," I said.

"I'm going to die soon." He said it again, a second time, under his breath. "Well. Maybe I deserve it."

"I'm doing it for me, not for you."

"Say again? Why?" he said.

Liz turned to watch me. Like I was a lunatic. And she had good judgment. So...

I said, "You're still my client, old man, whether you pay me or not. You hired me to catch the culprit and keep you alive. Job's not done. I am undeterred by obstacles. If you die, I'll have failed."

He thought about this. Liz did too. I could tell she thought my decision a poor financial one. Hard to argue with her math. But Roland nodded at me and said, "I forgot that about you. You're thorough. You do life right."

"And, on less somber days, I'm hilarious."

"How long?" His itchy fingers picked up his lighter. Toyed with it. The motion made him want another cigarette. He reached for a new pack but couldn't get it. Liz did a sigh and got out of her chair and retrieved the little box. "You can't keep me alive until I'm ninety-nine."

"I'll catch the guy within a week."

"A week?" said Roland.

"Or girl. The killer could be a girl," said Liz.

"You're right. Equal opportunity. My apologies."

"How do you know, a week?" said Roland. Liz still had the pack. It was fresh and full but already open. She held it up for him and he plucked one out.

"Just a guess, a week," I said.

Liz gave me inquisitive. "Based on?"

"Based on variables bouncing around. There's math and educated guesses happening between my ears that I'm not privy to, but somehow the answer is delivered. Years of experience tells me this'll be wrapped up inside of seven days. Pressure is building and pressure makes people do dumb things and the dumb things will happen soon. Plus, more importantly, I'm having a good hair day and it's made me optimistic."

Liz rolled her eyes. But she smiled.

"Fine. Fine." Roland lit the cigarette and sucked in the ash. Exhaled and spoke a cloud into existence. "Fine. I'll retain your services, you and Elizabeth and Walter, for one more week."

Liz was frowning at Roland.

I said, "Walter moves back in."

He said, "Walter can move back in."

"Has any of your help quit?"

"No, and I don't think they'll—"

Liz snatched the cigarette out from the corner of Roland's mouth, like it might explode the next second. She set it on the marble kitchen counter and smashed it, scattering tobacco.

She glared at the tobacco and she said, "Roland, who was here today? Anybody?"

"What in God's name is wrong with you people?"

"Earlier today? Anybody here?"

"No," he said. "Was something wrong with the...?"

"What about yesterday?"

"What *about* yesterday?"

"Who came over yesterday?"

"First tell me what's wrong. I demand you tell me what's wrong," he said.

She held up the box of cigarettes. "Where'd you get this?"

"I bought it."

"*You* bought it?"

"I had Angelina buy it! Tell me what's wrong!" He shouted it and his voice wavered with powerful emotions, like fear and anger.

"Maybe nothing." Liz was eyeing the pack.

I saw it then. I said, "It's a fresh pack that's already open, Roland. Open but no cigarettes were missing. That's weird. Liz spotted it. Why was it already open?"

"I must've opened it earlier."

"Did you?" she said.

"I don't know!"

"Someone is trying to poison you," I said, "and an open pack of cigarettes represents an oddity. Caution is good."

"You got the pack yesterday? Or, I mean, Angelina did?"

"Yes!" he said.

She carefully shuffled the pack at an angle. The cigarettes slid onto the table. "Angelina was here yesterday. Anybody else?"

"Alan Anderson came." Roland watched the cigarettes with fear and loathing.

"The finance guy," I said.

"He heard about the…he heard about Barry. He came to check. He's a good friend."

Liz said, "Anyone else?"

"My nurse."

"Yakira."

"Yes Yakira. I called her because I needed…I needed something to help me relax."

I said, "What about Zeus?"

"He was here. Or, he was outside. It rained so he...well, I forget what he did."

"Anybody else?"

"No," said Roland.

"What about Johnny?"

"Johnny didn't come over yesterday. He should have. He's my closest friend and I had a damn bad day."

"So Angelina, Alan, Zeus, and Yakira. That's who was here since that pack of cigarettes came into the house. Right?" I said.

"Yes." He poked at them. "What are you looking for?"

"That." I picked one up and held it for Liz. She took it. "It's been tampered with."

"You're right." The cigarettes were uniformly perfect. Crisp and cylindrical. Except the one she held. It looked a little ragged and it bulged in the middle. Not a lot. If the other cigarettes were in mint condition, this one could be classified as used but good. Roland would've lit it without noticing a difference, most likely. She plucked a knife from the wooden knife block.

"It looks funny," said Roland. He spoke in a whisper.

She laid the cigarette on the marble. Sliced the paper open like a surgeon with a scalpel. Peeled the paper back.

Inside the evidence was clear to see.

The tobacco had been carefully extracted. Then a foreign substance stuffed inside, filling half of the cigarette length. And then tobacco reinserted, filling the remainder of the cylinder, so it looked normal. Or almost normal.

Liz poked at the foreign substance with her finger. "Those are poison pellets."

I felt a chill. "Same as the bottle of aspirin."

"Strychnine. Again."

"Our killer isn't deviating from the plan."

She said, “Is strychnine lethal if smoked?”

“I don’t know. Couldn’t be good.”

Roland started to cry. He got up, stiff and jerky, and walked into the living room, the room with the big television where Walter liked to sleep.

A hell of a thing, seeing evidence *again* that someone wanted you dead. And realizing that you’d shot your nephew, an innocent kid, for no reason.

He tried not to make a sound but it came out anyway, a low wail. We gave him space.

I said, “Our would-be killer isn’t very sophisticated. He or she keeps trying strychnine, even when other poisons would be better. Amateurish.”

“Fortunately for Roland.” Liz held up four fingers. “Alan. Yakira. Angelina. Zeus. It has to be one of them.”

“Probably,” I said.

“Probably?”

“Remember the aspirin bottle last week. Alan never had access to it. We moved him to the bottom of our list. Maybe we were right, maybe we weren’t. It’s not as easy as striking people off the list, like a game of Clue. So probably the killer is on that list of four. But I like to be certain.”

“Let’s pretend, for a moment, that the killer *is* on that list of four. Zeus never goes upstairs. He couldn’t have stolen the gun, and he had the least amount of access to the aspirin bottle. So if we move him and Alan to the bottom, we’re short-listing Yakira and Angelina. But you like to be certain,” she said.

“As often as possible.”

“But that list of two, Angelina and Yakira, gives us a place to concentrate.”

I nodded. “We don’t rule the others out...”

“But we focus.”

We were talking quietly, heads together, while Roland mourned and paced in the adjacent room. He could see and hear us, because there were no walls, but he didn't want to.

I said, "By now, all six suspects *know* they're a suspect and they know we're investigators."

"Maybe not Yakira or Zeus. But the others know. Wait, Mack, you said six. Is Barry still on your list? It's impossible for him to have poisoned the cigarette. He was in the hospital."

"Good point. Five suspects."

"But they know about us now, or will soon. Our game's up."

"In fact," I said, "the game's afoot."

"You're quoting Sherlock Holmes." She was smiling. Although she'd discovered another attempt at murder and that was a rough thing to find, we were using clues to narrow down suspects. We'd gone from six to five possibilities, with two looking exceptionally probable. After a week of no progress, this felt like running down hill. And that felt good. "Aren't you."

"You'd think. But, like most things worth quoting, it originated with Shakespeare."

"Really."

"King Henry's famous Unto the Breach monologue. Impressed with my useless knowledge?"

"We should probably focus on the murder weapon on the table," she said.

But I could tell. She was.

Who wouldn't be.

"Now that the game's afoot," I said, "we can conduct a proper investigation. We rattle them, with verve and élan."

"Whatever that means." She looked over my shoulder

and make a face of disappointment. "The cameras are gone."

I twisted to follow her gaze. There should be one in the corner on a wooden shelf. But there wasn't.

"Walter took them."

"He was in a big hurry to wrap this up. Probably wants to sell the cameras on eBay," I said.

She spoke through clenched teeth. "It would have been helpful to watch that video footage."

"Nothing about Walter is helpful, except the minimal chance that he dissuades the murderer from open violence."

Roland came back into the kitchen. His fists were shaking.

"Don't tell the cops," he said. "Don't tell them a damn thing. We handle this ourselves."

"You handle nothing, Roland. Liz and I are professionals," I said.

"Get me a name. That's your job. I'm going to kill them." He turned to shuffle toward the stairs. "What'd I do with my pistol?"

Liz rubbed her forehead and sighed. "The police took it."

"Get me another one."

"No," I said. "Hell no."

"We'll see. We'll just see about this. I'm going to kill them. Hear me? I'm going to kill them."

23

I dropped Liz at her home and I went to the office. On a Sunday. My life's hard.

I pulled up the recorded footage from the nanny cams and realized Roland had been wrong. We'd been wrong. Someone else had been at Roland's house yesterday. Walter. He'd been there until lunch.

Even though that didn't alter our list of suspects, and Roland's omission of Walter was not critical, it was a good reminder that there were things we didn't know. We forgot about Walter; what else were we forgetting?

I watched him help Angelina unpack groceries. There, there was the carton of cigarettes. Walter pulled them from a plastic grocery bag and frowned, and he said, "Since when does Walter smoke?"

On screen, Angelina replied, "Since today. He asked for a carton. Gross habit, *sí*?"

Their voices sounded hollow and tiny. After that they didn't speak, but I could hear their movement.

Roland kicked Walter out around 1pm, because that's when Walter went to each camera and the screen went dark.

As he approached the camera in the kitchen, the cigarette carton was visible on the counter, still wrapped.

Why, oh why, did you unplug them, you nincompoop.

I called him. He answered on the third ring.

"Why, oh why, did you unplug the cameras, you nincompoop," I said.

"Nice to hear from you too, Mack. How you been?"

"Go back."

"Go back?"

"Go back to the house and live there and surreptitiously plug the cameras in."

"You said syrupy?"

"No. Shut up. Someone tampered with the cigarettes. We'd know who it was, maybe, if you'd left the cameras," I said.

"What cigarettes?"

"The cigarettes Angelina bought. Our killer opened a pack and poisoned one of them."

"What? No they didn't. When?"

"Since you unpacked them."

"Check the carton for fingerprints. Boom, there's your killer," he said. "I'm so good at this."

"I gave the pack to Stackhouse for that reason. My hopes aren't high. Did you see anyone tampering with them?"

"No."

"Did you leave right after unplugging the cameras?"

"No, probably an hour later. Maybe two. I packed my suitcase and cleaned up my room. Watched some television. He gets the golf channel and I don't."

"Did you see anyone other than Angelina?" I said.

"Angelina wasn't there."

"Yes. Yes, Walter. Yes she was. She brought the groceries."

"Oh yeah. She was there. No, no one else. Wait. Zeus was outside. No one else inside," he said.

"What about Alan the finance guy?"

"He wasn't there while I was. Or if he was I didn't notice him."

"Of course you didn't. You don't notice things."

"Hurtful."

"Go back," I said.

"I don't want to. People get shot and poisoned in that house."

"You haven't unpacked your suitcase. I know you haven't. You're not an unpacker."

"You're right, that thing will sit there for two weeks, if I'm being honest," he said.

"Go back. Live there another week. Deter more attempts."

"Okay. Fine. I'm being paid? I'll go back in a few minutes."

"Go back now."

"I'm in the bathroom. Gonna be a while. Ate a big lunch. Guess what I'm—"

I hung up.

"This is why private detectives work alone," I said. Loudly. To no one. "Mackenzie August, man of steel and intelligence, sitting alone in his office, thinking about his bottle of scotch, had realized why guys like Sam Spade and Philip Marlowe didn't collaborate with other private dicks in town. Because the other private dicks in town were asshats who took calls from the can. Why'd they take calls from the can? Because they were without class, that's why. Because they didn't treat their body like a temple, that's why. Because life's hard and they tried to fill the void with hamburgers and Jim Beam, that's why. Mackenzie would be better off working with a gerbil, that's why. Another reason he didn't work with them, they'd look at him funny when he employed the occasional illeism, that's what Mackenzie thought."

I pulled out the bottle of scotch and watched the rain fall and smear on my window.

It was one of those days.

I WENT HOME AROUND DINNER.

Ronnie had Kix and they were out, shopping for new shoes at Target. Who shops for shoes on a Sunday evening? A rainy Sunday evening, for heaven's sake, and the Cowboys were about to play.

Timothy was in the kitchen and he expressed the appropriate amount of pleasure at seeing me. So did Georgina Princess. He asked how poor Roland was holding up. Timothy asked, not the dog. I told Timothy that within the past twenty-four hours someone had poisoned Roland's cigarettes, another attempt to kill him.

Timothy set down his iPad. "You're kidding."

"I never kid."

"Yes you do."

"Yes I do," I said. "But not about this."

"Poisoned his cigarettes."

"Yes. And he refuses to involve the police. He wants to kill his would-be killer."

Timothy, watching me as though I was responsible, shook his head. "What the *hell* is going on inside that house?"

"An excellent question. Someone should find out."

24

Angelina called Roland Sunday night. She left a sixty-second voice mail. I know because Roland called Liz after and played it for her. Liz recorded it as an mp3 and sent me the file.

And now, Monday morning, sitting outside her house in my car, I listened to it again.

"*Hola*, Rolly, it's me, Angelina." She said it like Angeleeena. "Listen, Rolly, I am scared. I am freaked out. Okay? Someone is trying to kill you and you shot Barry and I am scared. That was a awful day, yes? It was probably Barry, I guess, poisoning you? It was him? He had the gun... Right?" A deep sigh here and then a long shaky breath. "*Ay, no lo sé.* You are my *Rollitico*. And I love you and I am not trying to poison you. I promise, okay? I am scared that you think I am, but I did *nothing.* And, Rolly, if I can be honest with you? Um, I need the money. I don't have a lot. So I am coming to your house to cook and clean like I always do. This is a bad time and we'll take care of each other, yes? If you do not want me, please call me back, but I promise Rolly...I'm not trying to hurt anybody. So, um, please don't shoot me? Hah hah. I know it is not funny. But...okay? Okay. *Hasta mañana,* Rolly."

I'd brought Georgina Princess with me. She sat in the passenger seat. She looked at me and I looked at her. We both shrugged.

I played the message again.

And learned nothing. Again.

If I was guilty, I would make a similar phone call.

If I was innocent, I would do the same.

"Who knows, GPA. Not me, Mackenzie August, master of evidence assessment."

I am bored, said my dog. *This is boring and I am bored but I love you and I am comfortable.*

Angelina lived in a little brick ranch in Vinton. A *pequeña* brick ranch, probably a rental. Smaller than Zeus's house because it didn't have a basement, only a storage space reached from a hatch outside. If she remained a person of interest, I'd search the house soon.

Her Facebook page said she was married. And her Instagram had photos of her wrapping her arms around a thin white guy.

However. I hadn't seen a ring yesterday. Nor a ring tan line. And she hadn't mentioned a husband to me or Walter or Roland or anyone else.

She emerged from the front door at 8:45. She carried a purse, a brownish Louis Vuitton or a Louis Vuitton knockoff, and a big stainless steel rambler with a cap, issuing steam. She was dressed in black leggings and a pink t-shirt that was probably too big but she tied a knot in it. The knot pulled the shirt to the side, making it tighter, stretching it over and under her breasts, making her figure even more eye catching. Which, I thought, was probably her goal. She locked her deadbolt using a key and she yawned. Her hair was up in a ponytail.

For a car that looked twenty years old, she could make it zip. She drove her rattling Chevy Malibu into South County, just off 220 into a neighborhood called King's Chase. I didn't follow; my cover would've been ruined and no way around it. But I parked on Buck Mountain and saw her on Kings Court Drive through the pine trees. I zeroed in using my binoculars. She was yawning still, retrieving two carrying trays of cleaning bottles and rags from her trunk.

I drummed my fingers on the steering wheel. Now, in fact, might be a great time to search her house. I could find strychnine. Or a big signed confession. But as I considered, Liz rang.

Over speaker, "Mack. It's Liz, one sec, I'm calling Walter too. For a phone conference." The phone went quiet and thirty seconds later she came back and said, "Okay we're all here. How's everyone?"

"I expect to be shot accidentally any moment," said Walter.

"It'll be on purpose. Trust me," I said.

"Hurtful."

"Boys," said Liz. "I just heard from the police lab downtown. The cigarette box had only my fingerprints on it. Whoever opened the pack, he or she wiped it afterward."

"It's Yakira. The nurse girl," said Walter.

"Good to know. How's Roland?"

"Hasn't come down yet. He shot his nephew, remember. He's sad."

Liz's sigh was audible over the phone. "Thanks, I'd forgotten, Walter. Go check on him, make sure he's alive?"

"He's alive. Yakira's already been here, that's how I know it's her."

"Elaborate," I said.

"Yakira always gets here at 8:30. Today Roland started shouting in his bedroom. Woke me up. So I go listen at the stairs. He was demanding she open her purse to see if she had poison or a gun. He called her a gook."

"A gook? What's a gook?"

"A slang for Asians. Used a lot during the Vietnam War," I said. "Which is where Roland spent part of his early adulthood."

Liz issued a sigh that was part exasperation and part mirth and part disgust. I thought she nailed it. "Well. Shit," she said.

Walter carried forth. "So then Yakira starts shouting back. Did you call me a gook, she says. Poison? Why would I have poison? And she says she doesn't own a gun. What was wrong with him, she says. Roland keeps shouting, tells her someone's trying to kill him and he knows it's her. She says, what? What do you mean? He says, I'm being poisoned. Those people who started hanging around, they're detectives trying to catch the killer and now I know it's you. Now she really starts screaming. You think it's *me?* So then he says, now I do! And he says, open your purse! She wouldn't. I hear them wrestling, and she's screaming *let go, let go of my purse*. I start going upstairs but she passes me coming down. She's holding her purse tight. I hold up my hands and smile and say, can I look in your purse? She says no. If you're innocent, you have nothing to hide, I tell her. She shouts at me, if I had a gun I'd shoot you both, and she runs out."

"What a disaster. Why didn't you call me?" said Liz.

"I would've. But I went back to bed. I'm tired. But you see? She was hiding something in her bag."

"Or she values her privacy," said Liz.

Or, I thought, she was hiding something in her bag. Why

would a nurse bring her purse in? Had she done that at the other houses? I couldn't remember.

"So it's her, right? Let's arrest her," said Walter.

"She's a significant person of interest."

I drank some coffee from my stainless steel mug. Similar to Angelina's but smaller. Said, "Do you know how to arrest someone, Walter?"

"Sure. Shout at them until they lay down and then call 911."

"If Yakira's guilty, she'll come back," I said. "If she's innocent, Roland will be shopping for a new at-home nursing agency."

"That's true. Good one, Mack. If she comes back, bingo," said Walter. "Hey I'm curious about something, Lizzy."

"Liz."

"I'm curious, Lizzy. Did you tell the police why you wanted the cigarette box dusted for prints?" he said.

"I told them we're looking for evidence."

"So we don't have to report the poison? I mean, is it illegal to *not* tell them?"

"It's a gray area," she said.

"How?"

"We're not aiding or abetting a crime. The victim isn't a child and we're not classified as mandatory reporters. Plus we're actively trying to prevent the assault. However, attempted murder is a felony, so if we're questioned we have to answer honestly. If Detective Green returns, we can't lie. But we're not compelled to report it and our license provides us with some leeway in the gray area."

I kinda knew all that, but I kinda didn't. Usually it was my sparkling wit that got me out of jams with police procedure.

Liz said, "Mackenzie, you're following Angelina?"

"I am. She's cleaning a house in South County now."

"I bet you're staring at her with binoculars. Pervert," said Walter.

"Gives me something to do while I keep researching Roland's beneficiaries."

"It's not Angelina. It's Yakira. She's mean. Trust me, she had poison in her purse. Besides, what can you even learn by following people around?"

"If they make a mistake," I said, "I'll see it. For example they might go by the strychnine store. Also, it kills two birds with one stone."

"What do you mean?"

"I mean, the charity research I mentioned previously. I can do both."

"You work too hard, Mack," he said.

"You want to hear a speech about hard work?"

"God no. But I think researching the will is a waste of time. You're just sitting in your car reading boring documents and calling boring people? What kind of life is that?"

"At the moment, it's banal."

"You're not going to point out that it's hypocritical for me to tell you that you're wasting your time but I'm still in bed?" he said.

"I knew you'd get there on your own."

"I'm researching beneficiaries too. His niece in Lynchburg, his closest relative," said Liz. "She's probably not involved but we're meeting later today. Mackenzie's made me want to be certain of things."

"It's probably her. The niece. And Yakira. This is boring now. Hurry up. Good bye," said Walter. There was a clicking noise and the texture of noise coming from my speaker phone shifted and he was gone. Just me and Liz now.

"Good," I said, "grief."

"You're less patient with him than with most people."

I scratched my jaw. Needed a shave. "I know."

"It irks you that he sullies the good name of our profession," said Liz.

"Our profession doesn't have a good name and it's because of him."

"Hey Mackenzie." Liz paused. "While I have you. I want to say…thanks."

"For my sparkling wit?"

"For…for being complete. For not feeling like you have to compete with me, or wrest control away, or be an alpha male. For not being an ass or hitting on me or letting me know you're better at this. And you are, and I know you are. But you seem very grounded and secure in who you are and you don't need anyone else's approval and you don't need validation through me or from me. And it's refreshing. So thank you."

"I'm not doing it for you," I said.

"I know. And that makes it even better. Because it's not a Camelot act. You do it for you, not an audience."

"Want me to say something nice about you?"

"Nope," she said.

"Good. I can't think of a single thing."

She laughed.

I'm hilarious. I wish I could be friends with myself.

I LED GPA for a short walk around my car. She peed in the grass and got back in. Then I peed in the grass and got back in.

Angelina left the house in Kings Court and drove to

Kroger. Thirty minutes later she loaded six plastic bags of groceries into her car and motored east, to Roland's.

I trailed off and parked at a convenience store en route. She would come back this way in a couple hours.

I consulted my notepad, where I kept track of my correspondence with Roland's charities. I'd chased most of them down and they checked out, even the goofy financial literacy initiative with the goofy receptionist named Ms. Sally who'd been warned by Alan Anderson that I might call. That was a real charity that did real work in the community—I knew because the Rescue Mission told me so— even if they were goofy as hell and even if I hadn't spoken to Erik Foreman, the director.

The two charities who hadn't returned my calls were...I consulted the notepad...The Responsible Trust for Virginia Veterans and also The Southwest Federation for Parents of Children with Special Needs.

Three calls each, no response.

Based on their names, I understood why these charities drew Roland's altruism. Johnny was his buddy, a veteran from Virginia. So the Responsible Trust for veterans made sense. And Roland was the caretaker for a guy with special needs. So the Southwest Federation made sense too. No judgment; give your money to whomever you like.

But.

But they were each getting two million dollars.

No, I looked again. Virginia Veterans was getting *four* million dollars.

And they couldn't be bothered to pick up the phone? Or return a call?

GPA whined and I fed her a treat from my pocket. One of those bones requiring an hour of work to fully enjoy.

How hard was it to commit charity fraud? Were the

Responsible Trust and the Southwest Federation both a 501(c)? Was Roland trying to beat the tax game? Was it complicated to set up one of those nonprofits? Could Roland do it himself? I knew nothing of the world.

I poked around online until finding the National Association of State Charity Officials. I surfed there and clicked on Virginia's charity registration.

If Roland's odd charity beneficiaries were truly recognized nonprofits, I'd find them here...

...and I did. There they were, before my eyes. Official as heck.

The Financial Literacy Initiative of Roanoke City.

The Responsible Trust for Virginia Veterans.

The Southwest Federation for Parents of Children with Special Needs.

How about that. Maybe Walter was right and I was wasting my time with this.

Of the three, only the Financial Literacy Initiative had bothered to take my call. So I clicked on them.

I found the articles of incorporation. The bylaws. The employer identification number. Their tax exemption status. Their board of directors...

I sat up straighter in my car.

"*Heyo*," I said. Georgina Princess looked happy for me. Then back to her bone treat.

The Financial Literacy Initiative had two officers listed. A president and a secretary.

Erik Foreman was not listed. Even though Sally, the goof on the phone, had told me that the director was Erik Foreman.

You know who *was* listed?

Alan Anderson. He was the president.

And Sally Barker was the secretary.

Barker. I knew that name. Barker was the last name of Alan's receptionist. It'd said so on the stationary outside his office.

Sally had answered the phone when I called the Financial Literacy Initiative. She'd answered it from Alan Anderson's reception area.

My mind spun. What did this mean?

It meant...

...Alan Anderson was the director of a charity that would receive four million dollars when Roland died. It meant he'd instructed his receptionist to take my call and lie to me. And that meant he didn't want me to know he was the director.

"*Heyo*," I said again, pleased and expressing it organically.

25

I delved into the other two charities, the ones for veterans and parents of children with special needs. I didn't recognize the officers, but I found them online and they appeared to be real people. Or at least they had real Facebook pages. I was researching further when Angelina drove by, away from Roland's.

I didn't follow her. I drove to Roland's instead. Walter's car was parked there, under the loom of the imposing mansion, and all looked quiet.

I went inside. Walter slept on the couch. He was barefoot and snoring and his shorts were unbuttoned.

Upstairs I found Roland in bed, reading a novel, *The Guns of Navarone* by Alistair Maclean. Couldn't fault his taste in literature. He looked at me over his reading glasses.

"August. Come to kill me yourself?"

"Wouldn't that be something." His bed was a large solid wood, four-poster thing. Cost more than my car, maybe. His dresser and mirror matched, oversized, dark and beautiful walnut. His bed sat on a camel rug, looked like silk and wool, a high pile. Paintings of wildlife on the walls. No television. No pictures of family. His venetian blinds were closed. The place felt like a sarcophagus. "Let's talk money."

"You want more," he said.

"No, I want the truth."

"The truth?"

"Like Lt. Daniel Kaffee," I said.

He closed his novel. "Like who?"

"Nothing. I'm being glib." I laid a sheet of paper on his lap and sat on his accent chair near the dressing mirror. "I'm looking over your will."

He picked up the paper. "Okay."

"I need to know about that charity at the top."

"The Financial Literacy Initiative of Roanoke City," he said.

"Yes. What do you know about it?"

"Nothing."

"It's in your will," I said.

"I'm giving money to a lot of charities, August. I don't keep track of them."

"That charity is directed by Alan Anderson."

"Oh." His eyebrows rose. "Oh. Oh yes. I remember. Alan's charity, yes, I know it."

"You're aware you're leaving four million dollars to Alan's charity?" I said.

"It has to go somewhere."

"Four million of it."

"He's a good man and he does good work and the money will stay in Roanoke."

Roland Wallace, taking some wind out of my sails.

"It was your idea?"

"Yes."

"To leave Alan four million," I said.

"Not him. His charity. And yes it was."

"How did you know he ran a nonprofit?"

"He mentioned it a few times," he said.

"Did he."

"It came up, yes."

"What's the purpose of the charity?"

"I'm not sure. Helps children learn math, I believe. Finances. Underprivileged children."

"Look at the other two," I said. "At the bottom of the paper. Nonprofits for veterans and for parents of children with special needs. Recognize them?"

"I...remember choosing charities that would benefit veterans and also kids with special needs, yes."

"You left them a *lot*."

"I can leave money to whomever I damn well please."

"Did Alan help you choose these charities?" I said.

"He was involved, I'm sure."

"Did he make suggestions?"

"I don't remember," he said.

"Look at the names of the officers. Do you recognize them?"

"I don't."

"I don't either," I said.

"Does that mean anything?"

"I don't know. Did it not occur to you," I said, "how financially beneficial your death will be to Alan?"

"Beneficial to a damn *charity* he works with."

"He's the president, the only officer other than a secretary. He can pay himself an exorbitant salary. The funds can be used at his discretion."

"I...didn't know that." He seemed to sink a little into the pillows. "But. It was me who offered. He didn't ask. I named the charities and the amounts, not him."

"That doesn't change the fact that Alan is the only

suspect who is also a beneficiary. That puts him in rarified air. It's a clue. We love clues, Roland."

"It's not Alan, Mr. August."

"How about you leave the deductions to me," I said.

"Liz Ferguson told me that Alan never had access to that damn pill bottle. And Alan visited me *before* Angelina bought the cigarettes. He couldn't be my killer. Isn't that correct?"

"Alan came before the cigarettes?"

"I'm almost positive," said Roland.

Rats.

I'd watch the camera footage to verify. But I assumed he was correct.

I stood. Snatched the paper from his fingers. "Darn it. Darn it and rats."

He gave me a hard smile from his cocoon of pillows. "Sorry to burst your bubble. But I'm relieved I won't be forced to kill Alan. He's been good to me."

"You're not going to kill anyone, Roland."

"The hell I'm not."

"Who are you comparing yourself to?"

"Beg your pardon?" he said.

"You've got it in your head that you're inferior until you kill someone, until you prove your worth. Who are you inferior to?"

"I...I don't know. I don't feel inferior."

"Sure you do," I said.

"August, I do not enjoy being spoken to by a man I hired."

"Oh dear."

"Excuse me—"

"Who are you comparing yourself to? Your brother?"

"I'm *not* comparing myself to anyone, especially not my damned brother," he said. Getting close to a shout.

"Me? Manny, the guy shot your brother? Johnny? Other guys in Vietnam who didn't take you seriously?"

"Get out. Get *out.*"

"Stop comparing yourself. It's stealing your joy. Don't let temporary insecurities ruin the rest of your life."

"You've made me angry, August," he said.

"Good. I wanted to. Now we're both angry." I crumpled the paper with the nonprofits in my fist.

"What are you angry about?"

"Everything. Including you," I said.

"You're angry because you're supposed to be good at this. Everyone said you were. But you can't crack this one."

"Not yet. I'm getting warmed up, though."

26

It annoyed me that Alan would inherit a windfall. But the annoyance came from personal reasons—I thought Alan was false and cloying and affected.

That didn't make him a killer. And it didn't disqualify his nonprofit from a bequeathment, no matter how hard I wished it, though I hoped my revelations today might prompt Roland to amend his will.

My annoyance remained throughout dinner that evening, at the table with people I loved. And it remained during our evening stroll while Ronnie pushed Kix in his stroller and he babbled about the dog and Robbie. Ruining a September evening was no small feat. The humidity had surrendered, and most leaves held onto verdancy but the poplars were gold, and the sky deepened into a shade of pink and orange only found in the fall. Many evenings in Elysium would look like it.

"This is unusual," said Ronnie. She wore form-fitting activewear, black and yellow. Nothing could ruin that for me, not even attempted murder. "Of all the people in the world, you're the least prone to moodiness."

"Watching you walk helped."

"We're almost home and you haven't spoken."

"It's that house. Something's going on inside," I said, "but I don't know what it is."

"And unless you figure it out, your client will die."

"Or end up very sick. That's part of it. Chances of him injecting enough strychnine to die are slim. If he'd smoked the cigarette, he would be hospitalized but it wouldn't be fatal. I should be able to catch an amateur."

"Fish," said Kix. "Fish dog. Robbie, fish dog."

Fetch. Georgina Princess, fetch the stick. Robbie, please make the canine fetch a stick. I require entertainment.

"Your killer isn't good at killing," said Ronnie.

"No. But he or she is quite good at covering his or her tracks. After poisoned water, two poisoned aspirin bottles, and one poisoned cigarette...how could I not solve it?"

"Could it be two people coordinating? The financial investor and the nurse? The groundskeeper and the cook, who are both Hispanic?"

"It could," I said. "That's why Liz and I have been following them. And one reason why we have nanny cams in the house, to spot alliances. But so far, there's nothing."

"If Roland allowed the police to be more involved, would the culprit already be caught?"

"Possibly but I doubt it. There isn't a lot to go on, and their only real weapon would be threatening the suspects. And Roland's still espousing real men don't involve the police."

"The problem with the world is that fools and fanatics are so certain of themselves," she said.

I finished the quote. "And wise men are too full of doubts."

"Who are we quoting? I forgot," she said.

"Bertrand Russell. A man certain of himself."

We stopped at our house's front walk. Ronnie bounced the stroller, rocking it backward on the rear wheels. Kix laughed about it.

This will work. Well done, Robbie. Again please.

"Are you enjoying working with Liz Ferguson?"

"Meh."

"Meh?" said Ronnie. "You're kidding, meh?"

"Liz is great but I don't see her. We chase different leads. We follow different people. What I do is largely solitary."

"And what's-his-name? Does he remain worthless?"

"Walter Lowe isn't worthless. But he's not not worthless either. I'd rather have a good watch dog," I said.

She took one hand off the stroller. Slipped it around my waist and stood on her tiptoes to kiss my chin.

"Mackenzie. You survived Italy. You beat Darren. You beat all of Darren's thugs. You'll beat this."

"Darren knocked on my door. This time, the killer is hiding," I said.

"You'll still win."

I nodded. "Almost certainly."

Our street lights flickered on. Dusk had fallen, bringing the evening breeze.

Ronnie said, "You can't lose while Liz is watching. I'd be so embarrassed."

My phone rang. I looked at the screen.

"Speaking of Liz," I said.

"Oooh, tell her to come over. I'll make drinks."

I answered and Liz said, "Mack, I'm being followed." An urgent whisper.

I stilled. *Being followed.*

I had a lot of questions. But I started with, "Where are you?"

Still talking soft. "I'm walking my dog through the Grandin cemetery. Someone's behind me. I'm playing ignorant."

I twisted to look her direction, a mile distant, through two big neighborhoods in the dark.

"What kind of dog?"

"A cockapoo. She won't be much help," said Liz.

"That's not even a dog. And who walks alone in the cemetery at night? I'll be right there."

"Don't call the police. Let's do it, you and me. But get here quick because I'm not packing."

"Which way at you traveling?"

"I'm closer to the east gate."

I put my hand over the phone and told Ronnie, "Going to help Liz."

"I heard and I'm scared. Please go fast."

I did. Got my keys from inside the front door and slid into the Honda. Drove up Windsor. As I crossed Lee Highway near Too Many Books, Liz's dog started barking through the phone. Liz's breathing became harsh and she shouted. I pressed the accelerator farther, doing fifty-five in the twenty-five, around corners. I didn't waste breath trying to ask questions. I listened. Listened and sweated. I was gonna do the mile trip in two minutes.

"Shit...Mack, he's chasing me...." Liz shouted again. Unintelligible. A grunt. Lots of noise and movement.

Sounded like she was running.

A cry.

The phone popped and cracked and the call disconnected.

Rats. Rats rats rats.

Houses flying by. Evergreen Cemetery to my left, dark, lit infrequently with street lamps. I laid down a slick of rubber breaking at the entrance. The thick gates were closed for the night. I left the lights on and I ran through the little opening for walkers.

"Liz!" I shouted. The cemetery swallowed up the noise.

"Mackenzie! *Mack!*"

I saw her. I saw *them*. She was under a tree. Dark figures, outlined against the dotted distant neighborhood. Figures wrestling. Beyond the range of my car's headlights.

A dog was barking, thin yaps, furious.

I sprinted. Gun gripped in my right hand.

My blood was warm. In the mood to pull a trigger. You can't jump women in a cemetery.

She screamed. Anger and pain.

I cut through the grass, aiming at the tree, and I lost sight of the figures. Some headstones were taller than me, others were flat. Like a minefield in the dark. I caught one in the shin and landed in the grass. I cursed and my eyes watered. Held onto the gun. Climbed up and kept moving.

"He's gone! He's running," cried Liz. She was still under the tree. To my right. "That way!"

"*Which* way?"

I was moving fast but with a limp. That marble headstone come close to breaking my tibia.

"To the...west, away from your car," she called. "The exit closer to Grandin!"

I veered from her tree. I hit another tombstone, taller. Caught it with my hip and I staggered. Idiot, not bringing a flashlight.

"Where?" I shouted.

Then Liz's cockapoo leaped at me from the dark. It was a tiny tiny dog, so I survived. Snarling, yapping, biting my pants. I kicked her off. Kept running but she came back, tripping me. I hit the ground again and she mauled my ear. Tried to tear it off.

I hit the dog with a backhand. It yowled and came back as I stood.

I turned in a circle, lost. Got my bearings based on the tree and my distant car. Searched the dark and let the cockapoo tug my jeans.

I didn't know which way to run. I knew the far gate was *that* way...or was it? The cemetery was vast and I'd gotten disoriented.

"Liz!" I shouted.

"You okay?"

"I think he's gone. I don't see him. He could go for the gate or climb the fence, and I'm lost."

Her voice came from my right. "It's fine. You saved my ass, that's enough." She was talking in a groan.

"I hate your dog. It nearly killed me. I kicked it a few times, though, so that's good." I limped her direction, dragging the cockapoo.

"Don't kick Jackie."

"Like, Jackie Brown?"

"You know it."

I called her phone. It rang near the paved road that wound through the grass. I envisioned what happened—she'd been walking the path when her stalker accelerated, they'd fought here and then among the tombstones, closer to the tree. I altered direction and retrieved her device. Clicked on my phone's flashlight—should have done that earlier—and found Liz under a big maple tree, sitting with her back against the trunk.

"You're hurt," I said.

"He hit me with a big Maglite." Her face near the cheek and eye was cut and already swelling. Tomorrow that eye would be closed. Her shirt was torn and her neck was red and scratched.

"It was a guy?"

"Yeah. Male," she said. "Jackie! Let go, baby."

Jackie released her death grip on my Levis and went to Liz.

I handed Liz the phone and she said, "Dammit. The screen cracked."

I sat beside her. I was jumpy and lightheaded with adrenaline. And my leg hurt, a sharp pain along my right shin.

She clicked on her phone's flashlight. Gave a half grin.

"Damn, Mackenzie, look at yourself."

The dog had ripped my cuff, and the right leg was bloody from the tombstone impact.

"Not my best pursuit," I said. My hands shook.

"And your ear! Mackenzie, you're all busted up."

"Your dog tried to take it off."

Nervous laughing. "Your ear? Does it hurt?"

"Yes, Lizzy, it hurts."

"There's blood all over your face and neck." More laughter. Not hysterical, because she had control, but close to it. Drunk on life and safety after the fight. "Jackie's so little, Mackenzie, how'd you let her do that?"

"She looks at me funny, Imma shoot her," I said.

"Christ, Mack, I'm glad you got here when you did." Smiling, talking through it, voice quavering. "That was some scary-ass shit. I just wasn't ready, you know? It was the fear that got me. I should've been ready."

I shined the light on my hand, which trembled. "I know about the fear. Look at me."

"Which way'd he go?"

"I never saw the guy, not really," I said.

"If I hadn't been so spooked, I could've handled him. I lost the mental battle, you know?" She scratched the dog and hugged her knees. "He grabbed my shirt and spun me around. I just wasn't ready."

"No idea who it was?"

"He never said anything. I hit him in the head twice, pretty good, and he grunted. That's it, the only noise he made."

"Big guy? Little guy? Did you see his face?"

Hugging her knees and rocking. "I'm not sure, Mackenzie. I…jeez, I handled that poorly." She put a hand to her head and winced. "He caught me by surprise. That's why… He had a hood and something over his face."

"How do you know it was a man?" I said. My heartbeat, loud in my ears, was slowing.

"His size."

"Could it be random? A stranger robbing you?"

"I don't think so," she said. "I didn't have my purse, he could see that. And he didn't say anything, didn't ask for money."

"Could it be Angelina? She's not small."

"I…I don't know. Don't think so, but maybe?" she said.

"Zeus? Alan Anderson?"

"I don't know, Mack, I'm sorry."

"Don't apologize. You got jumped in the dark and you survived. You did good."

Hand to her face, she lowered her head to her knees. Groaned. "You're patronizing me because I blew it."

"Nah. That was scary. Want me to drive you home?"

"Yes. But I need a minute."

"Your dog can't come," I said.

She snickered against her knees. "Yes she can. She tried to save my life."

"By taking mine."

My phone chimed. A text from Ronnie.

>> Manny's headed your way, following your phone's location!

>> Are you hurt??

>> How's Lizzy? I NEED an update!!!!!

>> I'm even praying!!!!

I smiled. It's good to be loved.

I said, "I got a better idea."

"What's that?" said Liz.

"Let's go to my place first. Ronnie mentioned making drinks. And you can fix yourself up before your husband sees you."

"I accept. Gladly."

27

We stood in the kitchen, debriefing. Debriefing with ice bags and margaritas on the rocks, poured by Ronnie.

Sheriff Stackhouse paced the front porch, talking on the phone with three patrol cars cruising up and down streets near the cemetery. I doubted they'd find anything.

Liz was angry. The fear and adrenaline had burned away, leaving fury and embarrassment. She sipped her margarita and Ronnie rubbed her back.

"I shouldn't have called Mackenzie. You know? That changed my whole mindset. I turned into a victim, waiting for help to arrive, and I stopped thinking about my training. Does that make sense? It's all mental and I wasn't ready," said Liz.

Manny, arms crossed and leaning against the counter, nodded. "The coward used surprise and darkness to attack someone littler than him. Not your fault, *señorita*."

Liz smiled her thanks. Hearing it from Manny helped.

She said, "I don't believe it was Johnny. But...maybe?"

"He was a tunnel rat. Those guys are crazy," said Manny. "I respect them, but...*esos hombres están locos.*"

"Johnny is tough and strong and maybe crazy," I said. "But I don't know if he moves well enough to escape like he did. Guys pushing seventy-five don't scamper through cemeteries. I think he's innocent."

Liz shrugged. "Then...it was Zeus?"

"Maybe."

"None of this makes sense."

"We're missing something and I hate it," I said.

She took the ice bag off her face. The skin was already purple. She'd caught the Maglite in her shoulder too, resulting in a gash.

"Who's your cleaner?" said Lizzy, indicating our house with her chin. "I need one."

"We don't have a cleaner."

Ronnie smiled, still rubbing Liz's back. "I asked the same thing when I first came around. I assumed they had weekly professional cleanings or they were showing off for me. But, I learned, fastidiousness is their natural state."

Liz shot us a look, a piercing inspection to see if we were collectively in on a joke.

She said, "There's no dishes in the drying rack."

Manny shrugged. "They were dry."

"The floors gleam."

I said, "Rubbing alcohol, vinegar, and dish detergent."

"You make your own?"

I snorted. "Obviously."

"But," said Liz. She held out her hands toward indicate the main level, indicating all the things she didn't have time to name. "But."

"I'm the messiest," said Ronnie. "And I'm told so."

"Why does it smell so nice?"

"That's testosterone," said Manny.

"Is the upstairs neat?"

Ronnie said, "Even the bathrooms."

"I don't give tours of my bedroom," said Manny. "But for you, señorita, I'll bend my rules."

"It has something to do with their careers. They couldn't be the violent, dangerous men they are if they... No, I should say, that *considering* their violent and dangerous professions they wouldn't still be alive if they didn't have strict order in their personal lives."

We heard Kix, then. He hadn't fully gone to sleep and he was furious about it. His little voice came down the stairs.

Liz smiled. "Aw. He's calling for daddy."

"Demanding, more like it, the terrorist."

"Does he ever call for mommy?"

"No," said Ronnie. "I'm Robbie. He asks for Mackenzie when he's scared or hurt, and he asks for Robbie when he wants to be spoiled."

"That's cute."Liz's phone rang. "Probably my husband." But the caller ID on her cracked screen displayed surprised her. "No," she said. "It's Walter. That can't be good, this time of night."

Manny said, "Who?"

"Local pain in the ass private detective," I said.

"Be nice. He's trying." Liz answered the phone. "Hello Walter."

She listened. As she did, her eyebrows inched upward.

She said, "Where are you now? ...one sec, let me talk to Mackenzie." She lowered the phone. "You'll never guess."

"He shot himself," I said.

"He was just attacked. He and Roland and Johnny were playing cards on the front porch, and they heard noises. Walter investigated. Someone attacked him."

"Well," I said. "This night's not all bad."

Ronnie's mouth fell open. "*Mackenzie.*"

"I know. I *know*. But I can't stop."

"They didn't see who it was but Walter was hit with a shovel. A minor head injury." Liz returned to the phone and talked another minute and hung up. "Walter's not going to the hospital. Yakira is working on him. She says he might need stitches."

Manny grabbed his keys. "I'm police. I'll walk around his house, make sure all bad guys are gone." He went out the front and we heard him leave in his growling Camaro.

I said, "Yakira and Johnny were there. Kinda late."

"I thought so too. Is it a clue?"

"No idea. And I thought Yakira quit."

"Roland called me earlier this evening and said he apologized to Yakira and she forgave him. She was there administering his evening medication."

"Roland screamed at her, insulted her, called her a gook, and she went back," I said.

"So I was told."

"And someone went to Roland's house, hid in the bushes, and hit Walter with a shovel when he investigated."

"Yes."

"What," I said, "in the world is going on."

Ronnie said, "Is that detective jargon for you're about to solve the case? I hope so."

"Any minute. And it'll surprise us all, even me."

I WATCHED the nanny cam video early the next morning.

It showed Walter and Roland stepping outside to greet Johnny at 7:34 p.m. They played cards on the porch, though I couldn't see it.

I fast-forwarded the cameras approximately an hour.

Yakira arrived at 8:30 to administer Roland's evening medicine, the stuff he took through a needle. (I'd looked it up; she gave him a cocktail of a muscle relaxer, a statin to lower cholesterol, an anticoagulant, and a gentle sedative for sleeping, adjusted based on vitals. He could get the job done himself if he had to, but he preferred a nurse. Concierge medical care, what a life.) Yakira and Roland went upstairs at 8:45. At 9:06 the camera picked up shouting. Then a minute of silence. Walter staggered in, holding his head, aided by Johnny. Yakira hurried downstairs and ordered Walter to sit on the chair so she could see his head.

I paused it and called Walter. He told me his attacker was male and the guy was talking in Spanish.

"Spanish," I said.

"Yup. Pretty sure."

"What'd he say?"

"Nothing, more like mumbling. Grunting."

"What words were used?"

"I don't know."

"How do you know they were Spanish?" I said.

"They sounded Spanish. Duh."

Thanks, Walter. I told him I was glad he survived. Which was almost entirely true.

I returned to the video of last night's drama and Yakira cleaning a gash along the crown of Walter's skull.

I made a note that Roland should get one of those Ring door cams. That would be handy.

Other than that, I learned nothing. A distressing trend.

Facts and guesses ricocheted between my ears, finding no purchase. Approximately fifty-five minutes had passed between Liz's attacker vanishing in the cemetery and Walter being hit with a shovel. Fifty-five minutes was more than enough time for the same person to do both. The attacker would have to hustle but it could be done and it would confound an investigation, just like it was confounding me. Because it could be one person, but more likely it was two.

Why had Liz's attacker been silent but Walter's had been grunting in Spanish? What was the attacker hoping to accomplish at Roland's?

Something else odd, Yakira had gone back. She didn't strike me as charitable or forgiving. Had she returned because that was the easiest way to murder Roland?

I crossed my feet on my desk and stared up at the ceiling. I made a list of things I knew for sure.

My ear hurt and my shin throbbed.

And I hated Liz's dog.

That's it, that was the list of what I knew.

Oh, one more thing.

I sure hoped Zeus had an alibi for last night.

28

Day thirteen of my investigation. This had gone on long enough. I had a reputation to uphold.

Zeus was checking a lot of boxes. He had easy access to strychnine. He was big enough to attack Liz and escape. He knew Roland's yard well enough to sneak to the front porch, and he knew to get a shovel from the tool shed. And he was one of the few suspects who'd been in a position to spike both the pill bottles and the cigarettes.

I saw no motive, however. He didn't benefit financially from Roland's death. In fact it would be financially problematic for his family struggling to make ends meet.

He and I were going to chat. Later that morning. I knew exactly where he'd be—on a mower in Roland's yard.

It was, however, Angelina's day with her other clients, and I wanted to chat with her too. I didn't know where she'd be later so I had to catch her early. Look around her house. Apply some pressure and see if anything popped.

When she emerged from her house that morning, wearing the black spandex pants and a button-down plaid shirt, tied in a knot at her hip, I was waiting at her car. She saw me and nearly dropped her steaming coffee.

"Señor August! You scared me."

"Sorry. I didn't want to knock this early," I said.

"You are here to arrest me? But I didn't! I did nothing!"

"I don't want to arrest you. I want to talk."

"Now."

"Yes," I said.

"Okay but it is early and I have houses."

"Call them. Say you'll be twenty minutes late."

She was frozen at the door, ready to lock the deadbolt. And she morphed. Her expression changed from fear to something else. Something predatory? Instead of a threat, I felt like a target. Someone she could manipulate. Her chin tilted it up and she gave me a come-hither smile. Like a prostitute getting into character.

"Twenty minutes," she said. "You want twenty minutes with me."

"To talk."

"To talk. Yes okay. Come in." She opened the door and I followed her. A small house. One living room adjacent to a kitchen and laundry. The kitchen had no dishwasher. No table, but a stool at the kitchen counter. The ceiling was cracked and the couch was threadbare. A basket of laundry near the television. Wires running along the floorboards. No paintings, no framed pictures. A Costa Rican flag was fastened to the plaster wall with pushpins. "I am sorry it is a mess."

"I don't mind a mess."

"You want to talk on the couch."

"I'll stand and talk."

"I'm glad you are here, Señor August. I feel safe with you around." She smiled and squeezed my arm. I did not flex, for her sake. Her perfume was strong and she generated heat, a constant sexuality.

"No one's trying to kill you, Angelina. You're safe anywhere."

"I will get you coffee."

"No thanks. I have coffee."

She went anyway. She brushed me as she passed.

I took the moment to turn in a full circle. I spotted no signed confessions or bags of poison.

She poured a cup from the pot and returned and the top three buttons of her shirt had come undone somehow. Hints of a hot pink bra under the shirt.

I took the cup. She remained close, steady eye contact, smiling, shoulders back, like an offering waiting to be consumed. "I hope you enjoy it."

"The coffee."

"The coffee, yes."

A strange and heady sensation, alone with a buxom woman giving herself to me. Her clothes already half off. The couch, the bed. No one would know. And me, a man who liked women. And there was a lot of this woman to like.

I said, "Let's get this out of the way, Angelina."

"Yes, Señor August, whatever you say."

"Your breasts are magnificent."

"You are so nice, Señor August."

"However, you can button your shirt again. I'm not here for them."

"You are not?"

"No."

"But." She reached for my mug and took it. Her fingers touched mine. "You can anyway. Now."

"Put your breasts away, Angelina. So I can focus."

"I do not understand."

"Not every man you meet will require your body. I am such a man. Hopefully. All I want is information," I said.

"You want to talk?"

"Just talk."

"You don't like me?"

"I like you fine. And they're truly *magnífica*. But I'm in love with someone else and I want to talk. Button up. Sooner the better."

Her look of fear returned. I wasn't someone she could turn with her body. A man uninterested in her offer. An alien.

She fastened one button.

"Talk on the couch," she said.

"In the kitchen." I took the mug back, went to the kitchen, and set the mug down.

"What do you want?"

"Only two people could've spiked the pill bottles and the cigarettes."

"Spiked?"

"Poisoned," I said.

"It was not me!" Eyes widening, hands thrown my direction. "You think I did it! But I do not know poison! It was Barry!"

"It's not Barry."

"How do you know?"

"He was nowhere near those cigarettes," I said.

"Oh."

"Where were you last night?"

"Last night? I was home. Why?" she said.

"Were you with anyone?"

"With anyone?"

"Yes, were you with anyone?"

"No, I was here. Alone," she said.

"What about your husband?"

"My husband?"

"Yes, Angelina, your husband. Calm down. Slow your breathing. You're not under arrest. Where's your husband?"

"I..."

"On social media. you claim to have a husband. A little white guy," I said.

"He...he is away."

"You're not married," I said. This question and answer session felt like a weird scene from *Chinatown* or *The Long Goodbye*, a detective grilling people. I wasn't trying to emulate Philip Marlowe but I liked it, felt like I should be smoking a cigarette. "And that's okay."

"That's okay?"

Angelina was Costa Rican and she might not be here legally—I needed to verify—and claiming to have a husband was probably what she thought she should do early on.

I said, "When did you come to America? That's a hard transition and it's a hard life, and I don't care if you're married. But I need to make sure of it."

"My husband...he left. I am not married."

"Were you ever?" I said.

"No. We were...how do you say it...engagement."

I said, "You were alone yesterday."

"Yes."

"Walter and Liz, the other two inspectors? They were both attacked last night."

"No! It was not me!" she said. She said it with hard earnestness, straining at the syllables to make me believe.

"If you tried to poison Roland, or if you hit someone last night, it's better to admit it than get caught."

"But I...no! I did not! I was here!"

I felt dirty. Scaring the hell out of Angelina to see if she'd make a mistake, even though evidence suggested it was Zeus, was part of the job. Interrogation came with the license. Detectives did it all day long. But I didn't like it.

I said, "I'm giving you options, Angelina, in case you did something. Confessing makes everything go better."

"My neighbor! I spoke to the neighbor last night." She grabbed my hand with hers. "You ask him. Across the street. I like his dog and I walk and I saw him."

"You have an alibi for last night?"

"Yes! Alibi."

"What time?"

"The time as the sun goes down. I saw him then and we talked," she said.

"Which house?"

She released my hand to point through the little kitchen window. Directly across the street, a brick ranch, well tended, replete with garden gnomes and an American flag.

"I'll talk to him," I said. And I would, even though I already believed her. Trust but verify.

"Good. I was here last night. I did not hurt Walter or the girl."

My phone rang, Liz calling. Angelina, worry creasing her forehead, watched me answer. In my ear, Liz said, "Zeus didn't come into work today. Roland called to tell me."

"*Heyo!*"

"Stop saying *heyo*. My head already hurts."

"How's your face?"

"I just told you. It hurts," she said. "Zeus might be going on the run. Roland doesn't know where he lives. Neither does Walter."

"I do."

"I thought you might," said Liz and I puffed up. She was proud of me. Understandable.

"I'll chase him down," I said.

"It's been an eventful few days. Things are heating up. Looks like you were right, Mackenzie. If you put pressure on, people sweat and make mistakes."

"Similar to playing poker. Bluffing with five bucks is easy. Bluffing with five thousand is very different. Pressure changes everything," I said.

"I think it's about to hit the fan."

"Me too."

"Keep me updated."

We disconnected.

Just me and Angelina again. Alone in her kitchen. Somehow that third button had come loose again. She said, "I did not attack anyone last night."

"I believe you. Maybe."

"Maybe?"

"I'll talk to your neighbor."

"Yes. *Bien*. Does Rolly think I hurt him?" she said.

"Roland doesn't know what to think. He wants to live. Before I go, I'm checking your house for poison."

"Yes. You can. But you believe me?" she said.

"Maybe I do."

"Then why do you look for poison?"

"It never hurts to be sure."

"Okay, *sí*." With evident embarrassment she said, "Señor August...thank you."

"For?"

"For not doing..." She indicated herself. "For not..."

"You're welcome. Though it's a blow to the ego to have an attractive women thankful she didn't have to."

She smiled. "You are not my type."

"Handsome, virtuous, possessing the strength of ten men, great hair, not your type?"

"You are not handsome," she said.

"That's...conflicting with my worldview."

"Your friend, the Hispanic man? The police officer? He is handsome."

"Manny is a coward with the heart of a sheep," I said.

"But he is single?"

"I'm going to look for poison now and I hope I find some."

"There is none."

"We'll see," I said.

"You can do anything, yes. Look. Go anywhere."

"Angelina," I said. "You might feel better about yourself if you said that less often to guys."

29

I knew where Zeus lived. The others didn't, but I did because I was industrious and prescient and Angelina was wrong; her taste in men was deplorable. But her house held no poison and her alibi checked out—man across the street said he saw her last night. Unless she was boinking him so he'd play along, but I didn't get that impression. Also he was elderly and a boinking might kill him.

Zeus lived in north Roanoke City. Washington Park, on Rockland. The residents of Rockland didn't take pride in their homes, mostly rentals I'd guess. The paint was chipped, the lawns patchy and overgrown, the shrubs untended. The houses were little income producing units for people who didn't live there and nothing was cared for or replaced until necessary. All the houses except for Zeus's. That lawn was trimmed. No trash near the stairs. No forgotten pile of rusty refuse in the side yard. The drive needed paving and the foundation would give up the ghost before long, but everything that the families could improve they did.

I parked there and got out and three kids ran up, shouting in Spanish. Smiling faces.

"Donde esta tu papá?" I said. "Zeus."

"Eres la policia?" they said.

Are you the police?

"A little. Un poco."

"Tienes un arma?" they said.

Do you have a gun?

"No." I smiled, winsome, and held up my arms. I'd left my gun in the car on purpose. "No gun."

"Estás enojado? Desconocido. Por qué estás aquí?"

You're a stranger. Why are you here? Are you angry?

"Zeus. Quiero hablar. Zeus, por favor."

I want to talk to Zeus. Please.

The littlest girl shouted, "Papá," and the kids ran back to the house. Two disappeared through the front door and one went around the side.

I waited by my car and a woman emerged. I'd seen her before. She'd brought Zeus a beer in his backyard before he cooked chicken and peppers that afternoon. You didn't survive as an immigrant if you weren't hard, and she was. Strong hands and arms, a face that'd seen too much and it showed in the flat eyes, the set mouth.

She planted herself like a shield between me and the house. Crossed her arms.

"Good morning," I said.

"I speak English. Why do you want my husband?"

Her accent was more pronounced than Angelina's. She pronounced speak like *ehspeak*. My fondness for Manny had imparted within me a predilection for that accent. She wore jeans a little too loose and a zip-up hoodie, and she was barefoot.

"He didn't show for work."

"Why is that your business?"

"I'm an investigator. I investigate," I said.

A lame answer. I wish something better had fallen out.

She said, "Are you a police officer?"

"I work for Roland Wallace."

"My husband did go to work."

"Is he there now?"

"The owner of the house. Roland. He has been good to us. Today he shouted at Jesus. He said Jesus tried to kill him."

"Oh." Dammit Roland.

"Oh?" She said it like I should have damn well known. "Oh?"

I rubbed a hand over my face and scratched my chin and I sighed. The international sign of frustration and embarrassment.

"I wasn't told that part."

"Jesus does not kill people. He is a good man."

"I'm not here to arrest him," I said.

"Why are you here?"

"Because I'm lost in this and flailing about like a nincompoop."

She frowned. "What?"

"I want to talk to Zeus. Just talk. Then I'll leave. Zeus might go back to work tomorrow if we talk."

Her eyes were shining with emotion. Resolve and fear.

"Jesus is a good man."

"Okay," I said.

"Our family. We need him." She turned and strode inside. I waited, leaning against the Honda spaceship.

Zeus came out wearing his jeans and a thin plaid shirt and his straw hat.

"I see you at Roland's," he said. "I did nothing wrong."

"What did Roland tell you?"

"Nothing. I see you and police and Roland tells me nothing. Someone is hurting him? But he tells me nothing. I did not know." His accent was less strong, his words forceful. He was angry at me. "I work hard and I don't hurt people. You can not arrest me."

"Today, what did he say?"

"Roland say I hurt him. Poison. And I hit someone with my shovel," said Zeus.

"Last night, two people were attacked."

"I did not."

"Where were you?"

"Last night?" he said.

"Where were you last night?"

"I drank at El Rodeo and I came home."

"Drank at El Rodeo? The Mexican restaurant on Williamson?" I said.

"Yes. They have football. I do not, our house."

"*Fútbol.*"

"Yes," he said.

"How late where you there?"

"It closes at ten."

Ten. Gave him plenty of time to attack both Liz and Walter.

Rats. I didn't want Zeus to be guilty of anything. But he kept acting like he might be.

I said, "Where you with anyone?"

"No."

"No friends?"

"No. People there but not my friends."

"The bartender know you?" I said.

"Maybe." He waffled his hand. "We did not talk but maybe."

"I'll ask the bartender, see if he remembers you there."

"Why?"

"Someone wants Roland dead, Zeus. He's been poisoned, or almost poisoned, and two of my friends got beat up last night. Someone did it. I want to know if it's you."

"*Señor. Amigo*. It's not me. My daughter, *mija*, she has bad teeth." He pointed at his mouth. "Bad teeth? We need to pull them and I am saving. My wife, she works in gardens. Flowers and weeds and caterpillars. People give her money but not much money. Roland and Roland's friends, his... neighborhood, they give me good money. I do not hurt them. I do not hurt people."

"You poison rats at Roland's?"

"Poison rats?"

"Yeah," I said. "You do that?"

"*Sí*, but for mice. In the traps. Mice get in the wood piles."

"You work for Roland and two others?"

"Yes, Roland and Jettie and the Smiths."

"You use poison for them?" I said.

"Yes. Mice."

"A lot of poison?"

"Maybe a lot."

"Little poison pellets? Like this big?" I held up my finger and thumb close together.

"*Sí*. Little little."

"Do you buy the poison?"

"Yes."

"Where do you buy it?"

"The store. When I need it. When I get fertilizer," he said.

"How do you buy it?"

"Roland. His credit card. He gave it to me but I only use

it at that store. I do not use it anywhere else and I do not hurt people."

"Where do you keep the poison?"

"With his tools."

"In the shed?" I said.

"Yes."

"Does he keep his shed locked?"

"No. Just a latch on his shed."

Deep breath. "Okay, Zeus."

"Okay?"

"I'll talk to the bartender. Until then, stay away from Roland."

"What will you say to the bartender? It is a woman."

I said, "If she says you were there all evening, then I know you didn't hurt anyone."

"I did not!" He shouted it, fists clenched. He had a scar at the corner of his mouth that tugged. "I do not hurt people."

"Don't run. Okay? That make sense?"

"Don't run?"

"Don't leave Roanoke. If you're guilty, if you're innocent, either way it'll look bad if you run," I said.

"I did not do it and I will not run."

"Then you have nothing to worry about."

"Yes I do."

"You do?" I said.

"I am here from Mexico. I wait on a work visa. I worry. All the time I worry. And now this."

That made my heart hurt, this man with a girl who had cavities and no money, worrying all day. Jiminy Christmas I wanted him to be innocent.

"Don't go anywhere," I said.

He didn't respond. Made a sniffing noise, furious. He went back inside and I got into my car. Closed the door.

"Dammit," I said.

Why'd the little girl have to have cavities? Guilty or innocent, I decided, I would pay for her dentist visit myself. If I told Ronnie about her, Ronnie would buy her a mouthful of porcelain veneers.

It was still early. El Rodeo wouldn't be open yet.

Please don't be guilty, Zeus.

I left Rockland and circled around to the next street over and parked in the same spot as previously I did, spying on Zeus. I retrieved my binoculars from the glove compartment.

I'd learn nothing from spying on Zeus's family. But I wanted to kill time before El Rodeo opened in two hours for lunch. And if Zeus took off, I could follow.

I looked through the binoculars at his backyard...

My heart sank.

The first thing I saw was a shovel. Black and bright orange, a Fiskars shovel, the same equipment I'd seen Zeus using at Roland's. The shovel was propped next to the ramshackle shed in the back. I wouldn't have seen it from the front yard.

I lowered the glasses and sighed, a blast of air at the ceiling of my car.

"Not looking good, Zeus."

30

Liz parked behind me and got into my passenger seat and closed the door. She took my binoculars and zeroed in.

"How about that," she said, talking into my window. "There it is. I recognize the shovel's brand, the same at Roland's house."

"Yep."

"Zeus and his family would have cheaper lawn equipment if it belonged to them," she said.

"Might have Walter's DNA along the blade."

She lowered the glasses. "Well done, Mackenzie."

"I'm not happy about it."

She looked my way and smiled and patted my leg. I remained calm. "You're too good a man for this job."

"His little girl needs her cavities filled. Or her teeth pulled."

"That's not your problem," she said.

"Now it is. My heart hurts."

"How does killing Roland solve his financial problems?"

"It doesn't," I said. "I am confounded by the whole thing. Poleaxed. Befuddled."

"You like Zeus."

"I do."

"I'm surprised you don't have more callouses, Mackenzie. You've seen it all."

"But I can still be amused. And heartbroken."

She said, "I'll get the shovel."

"Wait until the kids go inside."

"You don't want me to scare them."

"And they'll run tell their parents and Zeus will come out. If he's guilty, we'll have a mess. Better to examine the shovel without a fight," I said.

Her eye and cheek were purple and swollen, and her shoulder looked like the shoulder of a football player, scrapped and bruised.

"You look bad," I said.

"Thank you Mackenzie."

"Did you hit your attacker?"

"A few times."

"Where?"

"The side of his head. I hit him solid, at least twice. Bruised my knuckles," she said, with some pride.

"Then your attacker should look bad too. But Zeus didn't look like he'd been in a fight last night."

Liz shrugged in her leather jacket. "Not sure. Maybe I got him above the hair line."

"Someone could plant the shovel. Let's say someone else attacked Walter. Alan Anderson, for example. He could chop Walter and leave the shovel here as evidence," I said.

"Why would Alan do that in the first place?"

"I don't know. I don't know anything," I said. "I am stupefied and amazed. Dumbfounded. Astonished. Poleaxed."

"You already said poleaxed. Why are you so talky?"

"I'm compensating for not catching the killer yet. I do it through diction," I said.

"Compensating? You feel bad about the case?"

"I'm shrinking in my own eyes."

She grinned and turned her attention back to Zeus's yard. "You're always interesting, Mackenzie. You're literate and intelligent, and you can't fake that."

We stayed another hour, waiting for the kids to go inside. But they didn't. In fact, Zeus came out and sat in a chair to watch them play, his shirt rolled up at the sleeves.

I said, "Can't fake that."

"What?"

"Something you said earlier. It's got me thinking. You hit your attacker and did some damage. You can't fake that, can't cover it up. Zeus's skull should be bruised, maybe the skin broken."

"Should we wander down there and demand to investigate his skull?"

"Not yet. I'll check his alibi first," I said. "If someone planted the shovel, that someone will have a banged up face. And he or she can't hide it."

"If indeed I hit them in a place that will show damage."

"I want to look at Alan," I said. "See if he's purple."

"Why Alan?"

"Because we think your attacker was a guy. And it's not Zeus and it's not Johnny. We're trying to narrow down suspects. That hasn't worked before but maybe it will now."

"Okay. I'll stay here and keep an eye on that shovel."

"Get out of my car."

She grinned. "Yes sir. And good luck."

She moved to her car, borrowing my glasses.

I drove to El Rodeo and I called Alan Anderson, en route. I'd never called him directly before and he clearly didn't know it was me. He answered, "Hello, this is Alan Anderson."

"Alan Anderson, meet me at El Rodeo."

"I beg your pardon?"

"The Mexican restaurant on Williamson. Meet me there, pronto," I said.

"Say again?"

"Pronto is Spanish for hurry."

"Yes, I know. Forgive me, but who is this?"

"God."

"Hah hah," he said. With an entire calculator full of uncertainty.

"Wait. You're a mathematician. I'm not God, I'm Pythagorus. Or Pascal or Isaac Newton or whoever you worship. I'm a sexy index fund."

His voice lost a lot of warmth and professionalism. "This is the private detective, isn't it. The man who *lied* to me about being Roland's nephew."

"Aw shucks," I said. "You got me."

"I'm not amused, Mr. August. You committed identity *theft*. I could file a complaint with the police."

"You absolutely could."

"I know I absolutely could," he said.

"We're in agreement. Hooray!"

"This isn't a joke."

"File a complaint, Alan. I'll get a slap on the wrist but no worse because Roland won't press charges. He was in on the gig. We used a different name on the power of attorney note and you can nail me there, however there's no victim. You're threatening me because you're embarrassed. Here's what I think. I think maybe you and I don't start poking each other about using fake names."

"What's that supposed to mean?" he said.

A pause on my end.

I didn't want to tip my hand yet. I knew he'd used a fake name on his nonprofit charity, Erik Foreman. Or if it wasn't a fake name, it was at least dubious. But I didn't want to wrangle with him on that yet. There was too much I didn't know. Like everything.

I said, "Meet me at El Rodeo."

"Why?"

"I need to ask you a question."

"Fine. I'm listening. For *Roland's* sake, I'll listen."

"I need to ask face to face," I said.

"No you don't."

"Yes huh."

"Tell me why."

I said, "It's...complicated. You wouldn't understand."

"Why wouldn't I understand?"

"It's a private detective machination and you are merely the lay public. You wouldn't get it."

"You're *not* as funny as you tell yourself you are," he said.

"You're right. Not because I'm not funny. But because of how generous I am to myself. Meet me at El Rodeo."

He made a supercilious noise that I tried not to take personal. "I can be there in half an hour."

"Great. Won't take long."

I just need to look at your face, which isn't as good as you tell yourself, Alan.

~

THIRTY MINUTES later I was in the parking lot at El Rodeo. A busy spot on a busy street; the restaurant was surrounded by an auto shop, Trinity Lutheran Church, a USA Auto Sales lot, Breckenridge Middle School, a laundromat, a shop for sex toys, and the convenience store Zeus shopped at. Lots of traffic, cars and pedestrians.

Fifteen minutes later, I was still waiting. He was late. The restaurant would open soon, so that was good. I wanted a margarita and I wanted to get the name of last night's bartender.

I checked in with Liz via text and she was still waiting on the backyard to clear. The shovel remained in view, untouched.

Alan finally arrived in his blue Acura sedan. He parked next to me and rolled down his window. I didn't roll down my window. I got out. Williamson Road was loud with utility, cars whizzing by.

I came around. Said, "Get out, let's talk."

Inside his car, "Mr. August, it's a *busy* day for me. I'm stalling with a client so you can ask your question face to face. I don't have time for lunch."

"Who said anything about lunch? You wish I'd eat lunch with you."

"Then ask away. I'm here, I'll listen. For *Roland's* sake."

"Get out of the car," I said.

"*Honestly*, what is your problem?"

I bent down to his window. Squinted and peered in. He leaned away from me.

"I'm here! Ask!" he shouted.

I heard a noise. A pop pop sound over the traffic.

My car thudded twice, pops and thuds happening simultaneously. I was focused on Alan's face, which I couldn't see well, and didn't register the noises. Background noise mingling in with background noise. But I should have noted these.

A third pop and my car window shattered, directly behind me. Most of the glass went into my car, some of it sprinkling against me. Mackenzie August is not caught off guard often, but this was a doozy.

Someone was shooting. Bullets. At us.

Or me.

Alan cried, "Holy *shit*. Your window just—"

I smacked my hand on the roof of his car. "Go! Drive, move," and I ducked.

I had no sense orientation. No clue where the bullets came from. My gun still in the car where I'd left it.

Crouching between the cars. Looking both ways.

Alan was frozen.

Based on the window impact, I'd guess…the shooter was north? Firing over Alan's windshield? Elevated?

Another round screamed in. The dull thump reached my ears an instant before the hiss of air. My poor Honda had been hit again, in the trunk.

"It's a gun! We're being *shot*!" he screamed

Not north then. Maybe…east? The echo came from all directions.

A family on the sidewalk nearby, confused by the noises and broken glass, hurried the other direction. They didn't know they were hearing gunshots over the traffic. A few pops and broken glass weren't enough to startle them but Alan's screaming had.

I pounded his door with my fist. "Go, you dork, *go*," and I crouch-walked back to my door. Slid into the driver seat, staying low.

Another pop from somewhere. I heard it hiss and snap off the pavement. Missed me, missed my car, missed Alan. My whole body tense, afraid of impact.

Alan dropped into reverse and screeched out of the parking spot, his Acura making the noise so distinctive to

Honda motors. Shifted into drive and surged into traffic. Screaming of brakes, a collision barely avoided.

I had to get the hell out of here. I was useless against an opponent who could be anywhere, firing from a superior position.

Cranked the engine. Put the car in drive and gunned it, forward. In case the shooter was expecting me to reverse. I cut the wheel, up on the curb, nearly hit the restaurant wall, and swung back into the parking lot. Another thud into my car and I ducked. The trunk again, sounded like.

From *where?*

Peeking over the dash, I mashed the accelerator and fled. In my ear, I could hear Roland telling me real men don't flee.

My heart was still in a drumroll when I reached Liz. I parked behind her and got out on shaky legs. Instead of walking to her, I walked away and I dialed Alan.

He answered quickly, "Holy shit, August, I can't believe that just happened. I peed in my pants, Mr. August, I literally *peed* in my pants. Those were gun shots and they almost *hit* me! Right? Holy shit, holy shit."

"You're not hurt?" I said.

"No! Thank God. But—"

"Good, talk later." I disconnected. He called back but I ignored it.

Being shot at is the worst. Bent over, hands on my knees, I tried not to vomit in the grass.

Liz got out of her car.

"Mackenzie? Are you...what happened to your window?"

“My car absorbed some gunfire. Five rounds, maybe six.”

“Someone *shot* at you?” She stopped at my Honda, giving me space. To breathe or throw up, either worked. “I see a bullet hole here. And here, in the trunk. Was it Alan?”

“No. Alan almost got hit. So scared he peed his pants.”

“Where is he?”

“Not sure. Safe.”

“Someone knew you’d be there?” she said.

“I assume I was followed.” I stood up, lightheaded, still breathing deep. “Did Zeus leave in his truck?”

“No.”

“I thought it might be him.”

“He’s been in his backyard this whole time. See for yourself.”

I didn’t. I took her word for it.

What I did instead was, I sat down and I waited for the tremors to subside.

“Would you like me to call the police?” asked Liz..

“No. Not yet.”

“What do we do?”

“Call Walter,” I said.

She got out her phone. Dialed a number. Asked me, “It’s ringing. Why am I calling Walter?”

“I want to know who’s at the house right now. We’re running out of suspects to blame.”

31

On days when someone tried to shoot me, society kept running unchecked and that felt profane and impersonal. Bullets were fired at me and traffic had barely slowed on Williamson. They'd honked at Alan as he fled, but only because he stalled their progress. Shouldn't the city care? Was my story so small?

Normally I absorbed these philosophical arrows of misfortune without dwelling on them. But today, sitting in the grass, it made me empathetic with Roland—multiple attempts on his life and the world didn't care. No wonder he was furious, wanted to kill someone. Instead of carrying a gun on his hip, he should be wearing a sign.

I'm important. My life matters. I will prove it. There will be a reckoning. Notice me.

"Johnny and the nurse are here," Walter said over speakerphone. Liz sat beside me, phone in the grass. "Why?"

"Johnny and the nurse," I said.

"Why do you ask?"

"Isn't that early for Johnny?" wondered Liz.

"You want me to tell him to leave and come back? What's going on?" said Walter.

I told him. "Someone shot at me and Alan Anderson."

"Bullshit."

"They did."

"No they didn't," he said.

"My car bears the proof."

"Oh shit. Oh man, oh man," said Walter. "This is too much. You don't know who it was?"

"No."

"It's not Johnny or Yakira, we know that. Or Alan. They have alibis," said Liz.

Through the speakerphone, "That leaves...who? Zeus! It's gotta be Zeus!"

"It's not. I had eyes on him," said Liz.

Walter sounded panicky. "There is no one else! Barry? Isn't he just drooling at his mom's house? Oh man."

Liz was picking at grass blades. "Angelina."

"Shooting at Mack? It can't be Angelina. No way," said Walter.

"I just came from her house," I said. "She could have followed. But I agree, Walter. She doesn't strike me as a shooter, like she'd climb into a sniper's position with a gun. Plus she has an alibi for last night. She didn't attack anyone."

"That's everyone." Liz threw up her hands. "Everyone has alibis. So it's nobody. Or someone we don't know about yet."

"Zeus could've asked one of his family to shoot you," said Walter.

I nodded to myself. "Maybe. But I doubt a family of immigrants trying to avoid police attention would risk gunfire around town. But. Maybe."

Walter's voice dropped to a whisper. "Yakira's about to leave. Need me to detain her?"

"What good would that do? It's not her. It's not anyone," said Liz. She was no longer plucking grass, she was beating her fist into the ground at the end of each sentence. "We have to assume the person trying to kill Roland is now trying to kill us, based on last night and this morning. And the culprit has brought in help. Right? Mackenzie?"

I was rubbing my hands together and watching them and listening to the sound they made. Thinking. I nodded. The culprit had help.

She said, "You don't look convinced."

"I'm not. Of anything."

Over the phone Walter said, "I got an idea. Let's quit before we die. How's that idea? Let's go home and Roland can move to Guam. This has been fun and all, but holy shit. I got hit with a shovel last night, and you just got shot at. I mean, come *on*."

"We're close," I said. Watching my hands. "The killer has made mistakes but I don't see them yet."

"Or killers. They could be working together, like you said, Yakira and Alan or some alliance along those lines."

"Maybe. I'm missing something big, I know I am. Maybe that's it," I said.

Liz hit the ground again. "Well, I'm stumped. *Stumped.* What do we do now?"

Walter said, "We quit."

"I need more information."

"How?" she said.

Between the three of us, I was talking the softest. "Yakira and Johnny aren't home. I'm going to search their place."

"Why?" said Walter.

"I need more. I need to think. We're close."

"Don't do that. What if you get caught? Or dead? I'm freaked out, Mack," he said.

I stood. Brushed my hands on my pants.

"I'm going."

"Fine. I'll get that shovel," said Liz.

"Great, just great." Walter made a groaning sound. "I'll just be here. Getting killed."

~

I WENT to Johnny's first because chances were Yakira had a full day of clients; she'd come home much later.

Johnny lived on Day Avenue, near the YMCA. He and Angelina and Zeus lived within two miles of one another. A clue?

Doubtful. Over fifty-thousand people lived in the same area.

As Walter said, Johnny wasn't home. Nor were his neighbors. Revitalization or gentrification hadn't reached this street, a road full of similar two-story houses built a hundred years ago. Although it hadn't rained, the street looked damp.

An old pit bull lay in the back of Johnny's yard, inside the chain fence. So old it lifted its head at me to make a woofing sound but nothing else. His door was locked but the window wasn't. I lifted it and ducked in off the porch.

The house might have good bones—built with thick wooden beams like were used back when men were men and they used real trees—but termites and age and neglect had done their work. The house would have to be gutted or demolished after Johnny left. The wooden floor was spongy where it didn't creak. The ceilings were yellow from nicotine and sagging from water damage. The overhead lights were inoperable but he'd set lamps on the floor. I smelled mold or rot or both. There was a couch and a chair that stank of smoke.

Guys came home from war changed. Johnny was doing better than most tunnel rats—he was still alive. But his home provided insight into his mind and it was an untidy, unhappy place. Based on his fridge, he ate a lot of sandwiches. Based on the trash can, he drank PBR beer but not to excess.

Upstairs there was a room essentially being used as a greenhouse, a corner room with a lot of light. Several types of plants, including marijuana. Hard to blame him, looking for peace. Getting high on marijuana was probably better than living as a drunk.

I took photos of the plants I didn't know. They looked similar to marijuana but they weren't, the leaves a little too big and waxy and the seeds were different.

His bedroom was a memorial to his past. A wooden M1 carbine was held on the wall like a trophy, the weapon's stock and barrel polished. The trigger was removed—it was for display only. Dog tags hung from a hook next to military paraphernalia, including a medal. Old photographs were push-pinned into the wall, faded orange and curling at the edges. A man I barely recognized as young Johnny, shirtless, grinning and holding an assault rifle with military pals. Young Johnny dressed in battle fatigues, posing with a tank. Young Johnny shirtless again on a beach with buddies and Vietnamese women. Young Johnny with various women on various beaches. Some of the women were Hispanic, maybe from his post-war visit to Mexico where he'd bought a shack, he said. There were too many photos to examine them all. Dozens, maybe over a hundred. His best memories, confabulated into a past that he could live with, surrounding him at night as he slept on top a mattress set directly on the floor.

Johnny's bathroom was a dysgenic nightmare of hygiene. I didn't stay long.

I searched the unfinished basement too. An old sink, paint cans, tattered boxes, lumber, spiders, roaches.

No ammunition, no strychnine.

I was standing in the basement when my phone buzzed, startling me. Liz was texting me and Walter.

>> **I got the shovel.**

>> **I'm looking at it under a good light but I don't see any blood or hair.**

Walter texted then.

>> **hey mack**

>> **johnny left. said he was going home**

>> **r u in his house? if not don't go**

>> **ull get caught**

>> **im still alive, thx for asking**

I left through the same window. The old dog watched me without interest. He knew I'd found nothing. That I was no threat.

~

Yakira's apartment building was active, the first home for young adults and housing students at VT's med school. After Johnny's, it felt obscenely vivacious. You needed a key to enter the lobby but I arrived as a group came out and they held the door for me. The mailboxes had names and numbers and I found hers. She and a roommate shared 403.

I took the stairs and caught my breath—embarrassing after only four floors—and knocked. A voice inside called, "It's open."

It was.

A girl sat at the kitchen counter, eating Fruit Loops from a bowl. Not a girl, a woman. Women under twenty-five looked younger and younger every year. She saw me and sat up straighter and wiped her mouth. Swallowed and said, "You're not Richie."

"Hi, I'm Jeff."

"Sorry, I thought you were my boyfriend. Um. Help you?"

She was still in her pajamas. Plaid shorts and a crop top sweatshirt that said Radford University.

"I'm Jeff?" I said again.

Polite smile, though she didn't care. "And?"

"Did Yakira tell you I was coming? She was supposed to."

"Yakira tells me nothing," said the girl.

"Sorry. I'm Jeff with At Home Nursing. She left a box here."

"Ah. Yeah, Jeff, sorry, she doesn't talk to me."

"Okay, I get it. She's quiet. And when she's not, she's yelling. At me, usually," I said.

A nod. "Sounds like her." Another bite of cereal.

"Do you know where she left it? The box?" I said.

"Nope. Don't know, don't care. But you can check. Just leave the door open, would you."

"Sure. Which is her room?"

"The farthest room. The neat one."

I walked by her.

She said, "Sorry I'm a mess. Just woke up. I worked the late shift."

Yakira would be a natural at the August household; she prized a crisply made bed. Her desk was exact, her closet color coordinated, her shoes lined, her drawers immaculate.

She had one photograph, a framed 4x6, near her laptop, of an older couple, maybe her parents. No television. Books on the nightstand, some in a language I couldn't read. Her bathroom was clean. No scum in the corners. No hair in the sink. A few beauty products neatly placed on the shelf.

I didn't know what I was looking for, other than poison. A smoking gun? A photograph of Roland, being used for knife-throwing practice? Lasers. An evil cat.

Did I feel dirty about the invasion of privacy? Yes. Yes I did.

Did I feel less dirty because someone had recently taken a run at me? Yes. Yes I did.

Nothing insidious under her sink. Or under her bed. Absolutely nothing to cause her embarrassment. Was that a clue? It'd been so long since I'd seen one.

I returned to the kitchen. "Does she ever leave anything in your room?"

"No. Hell no," said the girl eating cereal.

"In the kitchen?"

"Nope. But look for yourself. How big's the box?"

"Not as big as a shoebox. Full of medicine." I looked in a few cabinets and checked the fridge. No strychnine. Which made sense—the killer could get it easily from the shed. "Well. It's not here."

"Sorry Jeff."

"Does she have a storage unit downstairs?"

"She does and she's never used it. I'm telling you, man, she's into that Marie Kondo minimalism crap. She owns nothing," said the girl.

"You two don't get along."

"We don't argue or anything. She's just in her own universe and visitors aren't welcome. Does she get along with people at work?"

"Same thing," I said. "She wants to be left alone."

"Yeah. She told me one thing about herself. Just one. Wanna hear it? She came to America to be a doctor. But she didn't get into med school and now she's a nurse. That's it. That's all I know. So now she hates her life, maybe, I don't know. Me, I like being a nurse," she said.

I went to the door. "Thanks for letting me look."

"You bet. I wish you worked with me. Big guy like you, I could use those arms lifting patients," she said.

"Also someone recently told me I'm literate and intelligent."

"I don't care about those things. Just the muscles."

Well. I could live with that.

"Hope you find what you're looking for," she said.

Some nagging inner alarm told me I already had. I just didn't know it.

32

After dinner, I sat on the front porch with Ronnie and we watched Manny and Noelle Beck shuffle up and down the front walk. Noelle moved slow and gingerly, and her shirt tugged over the bulky bandage around her midsection, and when she gasped Manny would take her hand and hold her steady. Walking used a lot of abdominal power and many of her ab muscles had been cut clean through not three weeks ago. She wouldn't be running for months still. But this was a step in the right direction. A tiny baby step.

Same with Kix on the front lawn. He pushed himself up to stand and wobble and stagger before sitting hard on his butt. He laughed and shouted at us.

This is so easy. And hilarious. Wait until the girls at school see. Girls like guys who got moves like this.

Ronnie made a sigh of contentment. She'd successfully cajoled Noelle Beck's insurance into paying for all medical bills, plus paid leave. Turns out, life was about who you knew. And she knew Ronnie. And Manny. Powerful allies.

She said, "Therapy, Mackenzie. This is therapy. If I sit here long enough, I'll no longer need to pay a professional psychologist. Every day I am struck with gratitude that I was adopted into this. And I'm at peace."

"Are the voices of your past quieted?"

"No. But gratitude makes them quieter. And I think if I do it long enough then they'll fall silent. Or I'll quit caring."

I thought she was right. I'd gone through a similar process, leaving Los Angeles. Starting a new life wasn't for the faint of heart. Had to win the battle every day.

"But you," she said, "are not at peace."

"I'm not."

I stood. Paced the porch. I felt like my brain was on fire.

"Because of your case," she said.

"Because of my case."

"Because you're a highly paid and highly talented sleuth and you're angry with yourself that it's been two weeks."

"Something like that," I said.

"Can you turn your mind off? Relax? Solve the problem tomorrow. I'll massage your shoulders?"

"Easier said than done, on all accounts."

"Or," she said. "I'll massage anything else you like. To help you relax."

Kix heard and made a retching noise and he fell over.

I said, "I accept. But Kix shouldn't watch."

I'm going to be sick.

"Until then, you can't stop thinking about it? Even though you want to."

"Yes, " I said.

"I'll listen if you want to talk."

"By now the killer has made a mistake. I should see it. But I don't," I said.

"Would it help to plead the case against each?"

"No. But I will."

"Start with Barry, the poor boy shot by his uncle. Did I

tell you the Commonwealth is leaning against arresting Roland? That's nice, isn't it? I threatened to get involved. But anyway, how do you know the killer isn't Barry?"

"He has no financial motive. He was nowhere near the poisoned cigarettes. He does have a history of violence and he did have the gun. But. It's not him," I said.

"Could he be working with someone else?"

"Possibly. But it's not him."

"What about the nurse?" said Ronnie. "How do you know it's not her?"

"I don't. It could be Yakira. Except that she has no financial motive. She's strong and determined, but she couldn't be Walter's attacker. She was upstairs with Roland when he got hit with the shovel. She did return to work after Roland verbally abused her, which is shocking. So it might be her, but it couldn't be her."

"What about the finance guy, Alan What's-it's?"

"Anderson. He does have a financial motive. He may or may not have had access to the cigarettes but he did not tamper with the bottle of poisoned aspirin. And," I said, "he got shot at today, a solid indication he wasn't the shooter."

"Johnny?"

"He can't be Walter's attacker and he can't be Lizzy's attacker and he had an alibi during today's shooting. He's around that house a lot, though, and I worry his mind is unsound."

"Angelina?" she said.

"Angelina has an alibi for last night. She had plenty of access to all poisoned items. But she does not benefit from Walter's death."

"Zeus?"

"He had an alibi during today's shooting. And last night he was watching soccer at a restaurant—I checked with the bartender. But he's got access to strychnine and the shovel was at his house," I said.

"That's all of them," she said.

"That's all of them."

"They're all suspicious, but none of them could do it. At least not alone. So it has to be two of them in cahoots?"

I grinned. "Cahoots."

"I was hoping you'd enjoy it."

"Two of the suspects teaming up is possible. But everyone has alibis. Sometimes even on video," I said. "I'm missing it. I feel the void where an answer should be. I searched their homes. I watched them on video. I grilled them. Liz has investigated their backgrounds and their finances. I have enough evidence. Plenty of it. And yet."

Guys! A squirrel! Dad! Robbie! Look at the squirrel! Robbie!

I sat back down. And stewed. Maybe more of a simmer.

Manny and Beck came up our front walk. An inch at a time.

Manny holding Beck's elbow. "It's unAmerican how slow she is."

Ronnie laughed. "She took a katana to the stomach yet she remains perfect and beautiful. Let's allow her more time before renouncing her citizenship."

"I'm going to die on the front steps." Beck was sweating freely, her left arm pressed tight to her stomach. "They've never looked so tall."

"You can do it," said Manny.

"I know I can do it," she said. "And I will. It'll kill me but I will."

"Bien." Manny scooped her under the legs and lifted. She gasped and grabbed him harder with her right hand until he set her down on the porch, bypassing the steps.

"That hurt, Sinatra." Gritted teeth.

"Hurt's good for you."

"I said I could do them."

"You knew you could. That's what matters, Beck. You were willing. But you already did enough. Next time you can," said Manny.

I got the door and she shuffled through.

Manny made a dramatic sigh, nodding at Noelle. "Takes a village."

"Someone get me a stiff drink. Of water," said Beck.

I closed the door and sat back down with Ronnie.

Those two, said Kix. *They should just get it over with.*

I leaned back in my chair.

And then I jumped out of it.

"Jiminy Christmas."

"What?" said Ronnie.

"Jiminy Flipping Christmas."

She made a laughing sound. "The mouth on you, my husband. What happened?"

"That's it. That's *it*."

"Did you crack your case?"

"I cracked it. I think. Pretty sure."

She smiled and the trees sighed in response. "I knew you would. My faith in you is complete."

I sat down. Missed the chair and sat on the porch instead. Grabbed at my hair and thought it through.

Scenes from the previous two weeks flew at me. Words, faces. I saw it begin. I saw it happen. More puzzle pieces fell into place, each like being hit over the head. My inner critic was humiliated.

"I can't believe I missed it. I can't believe I didn't see it. I am mortified. And I almost got shot because of it. Good grief."

Ronnie looked with animated curiosity at Kix and then

through the window at Manny and Beck. "What happened, oh detective whom I love? This is exciting to watch. Was there just a clue?" Her voice, that melodious chorus of an angels' choir, sounded even better with the sun breaking between my ears.

"I took things for granted, Ronnie. I accepted things as true which weren't."

She leaned forward in her chair, far forward, and kissed my forehead. "Your first mistake. How darling."

I grinned, drunk on life and good fortune and epiphanies. I pulled out my phone. Dialed Liz.

She answered.

I said, "I got it."

"You got it?"

"Cracked the case, worth every penny. And here's what we're gonna do."

33

The next morning, Liz and I sat in her car. Her nervousness manifested in her hands and she alternated between plucking at invisible threads on her jeans and pressing at a spot on her forehead.

"In the DEA," she said, "when we arrested someone, we took twenty agents. Overwhelming force. I was an agent but my speciality was analysis, not apprehension."

I wouldn't insult her by insisting she relax. This would be a fight. Adrenaline was beneficial.

"Now it's just the two of us," she said. "How often do you do something like this?"

"It happens occasionally. We need organic reactions in realtime. We require strife and hot emotions to make it work."

We watched from Jettie Frizzell's drive, one house over, until Yakira left. She drove off in the little red Nissan and I said, "Ready?"

"No. But also, hell yes. Let's do it."

We left the car at Jettie's, who wasn't home from her travels, and we walked across the wide wet lawns to Roland's.

We went up the rear staircase, out of sight from the driveway. I peeked through the window and saw Walter lounging on the couch, playing on his phone, and Roland sitting in the overstuffed recliner in front of the television, which wasn't on. He stared at nothing. I sat down on the rear porch beside Liz and we didn't speak. We watched the drizzle fall, glazing the hilltop neighborhood. Zeus, as I instructed him, was taking the day off.

Angelina arrived on time, today being her day to cook and clean. We heard her car, heard her humming as she walked to the front door, and we detected the sounds she made inside the kitchen.

Still Liz didn't speak.

Johnny and Alan arrived together, Alan in his blue Acura and Johnny in his rattling pickup. We stood. I grabbed the doorknob and waited. Johnny and Alan walked through the front, and I opened the rear french doors and we entered. Because of the open floor plan, everyone saw everyone at the same time.

Showdown at high noon.

At ten in the morning.

Roland maintained his stare into nothing, holding tight to the overstuffed armrests. Walter jerked up, looking with confusion at me and Liz and then at Johnny and Alan Anderson. Johnny and Alan gaped at us. Alan had two bags with him—a document case and a laptop case. Angelina had been chopping veggies in the kitchen but her knife was frozen in place, taking it all in.

For a long moment, silence reigned. I loved it.

Alan Anderson cleared his throat. "Roland, is everything okay?"

"I'll ask the questions," I said.

Alan appeared affronted. "What do you mean?"

"Just kidding. But I thought it might ease the tension." Liz and I came in and I closed the rear doors.

"What's the deal, ol' buddy?" asked Johnny. "You said I should come at ten?"

Alan said, "He called me too. Something important about his will. Roland, what is this?"

Roland didn't respond.

Walter slipped his feet into his slippers. He kept staring at his phone, but his thumbs weren't moving.

I said, "I asked Roland to call you. He hired us to determine the identity of the person or persons poisoning him. We're about to solve the case. And everyone in this room is invited to the big reveal."

Angelina dropped the knife, a loud clatter that startled us.

"Roland," said Alan Anderson. He swallowed. "I demand you tell me what's going on."

"I don't know a damn thing," said Roland, looking out the window. "He didn't tell me. I...I don't know."

"Have a seat, everyone," I said.

"I will not," said Alan. "I had a busy morning that I postponed because Roland is one of my faithful clients. I don't have time for games."

Liz walked around the room to the front door, which was still open. She closed it with a boom.

"I'm afraid I insist, Mr. Anderson."

"Rolly? You got me spooked, Rolly," said Johnny, but he came in and sat on a chair.

In response, Roland lit a cigarette with shaking fingers. He held it to Johnny, who stood to take it and he sat back down, and Roland lit another for himself.

Again Roland said, "I don't know. They didn't tell me."

Angelina, from the kitchen, "Do I stay?"

"Yes please." Liz smiled. She was relaxing, I could tell, falling into the moment.

Angelina sat beside Walter, the far end of the couch, barely perched on the edge of the cushion. I took a chair for me and a chair for Liz and a chair for Alan from the big table near the kitchen and I placed them along the circle with the couches and overstuffed chairs. I sat. Liz sat. Alan remained standing behind his.

"This is a *farce*," said Alan.

Liz, as though remembering, stood and drew her pistol. Alan's face went white and he said, "Good God, *really*?" and he sat.

"Sorry." Liz said it but she didn't look it. "That appeared threatening but it wasn't. The gun's for Roland."

She placed the pistol, a Glock 22, on the little table near Roland's chair, within his reach. She sat again. Everyone stared at the gun.

I said, "Roland, I'd like to solve the mystery for you."

"Good." He snapped a nod, looking at the gun. "I'm ready to be done with this. Tell me."

"Wait a minute," said Alan.

"I'm close," I said. "I don't have every detail. Some of it we can prove, some of it we can't."

"I'm leaving."

Liz said, "No you're not, Mr. Anderson."

"That is preposterous. I'm a *hostage*? You think you can keep me here?" he said.

"Yes. I do."

"I'll call the police."

"Do it," she said.

"What's your objection, Alan?" I said. "No one has implicated you for anything."

He pulled out his phone. "I'll dial 911."

"No police," growled Roland.

"To begin, I'll regale the room with a story, starting in Vietnam," I said. "You go there during the war, Roland. You build roads and infrastructure, and your life is never in danger or not much of it. You even get married to a Vietnamese woman. Afterward you return home and pretend to be a war hero. Which you shouldn't have done, but that's not germane. Eventually she divorces you, concluding that chapter of your life. Johnny, on the other hand, goes through hell in Vietnam and he comes home a villain. He's told not to speak a word about it, and the hell in Vietnam has followed him. He came home with a little cash, no wife, and a lot of PTSD. So he goes to Mexico with his war money, which isn't much, and tries to pretend he isn't a wreck. While there, he buys a house. It's a grand two months, at the end of which he has to return home because he's broke."

Johnny, staring at the cigarette he's holding, gives a jerky nod.

I continue. "So he's home in Roanoke. You're home in Roanoke. You two meet. Roland, you're doing well. He's not. You're making a lot of money. He's having nightmares and can't hold down a job. You become friends. You help him. And that's great. Johnny returns to Mexico as often as he can, using his disability money. It's only once every few years. So far, you know all this. Right?"

"I don't agree with all the words you're using, but keep going."

"Here are some things you don't know. I can't prove them, yet, but we could in a hurry if we need to." My audience was rapt. Even I was interested in what I was saying. "Johnny wasn't going to Mexico. He was going to Costa Rica. I saw a flag in one of his photos," I said.

Roland shifted in his chair.

"I didn't know that. But what's the damn difference?" he said.

"That's the point. For you, there's none. I bet he told you Costa Rica, but you started calling it Mexico and he didn't correct you. In your mind, it's the same place. But it isn't. And here's the next thing you don't know. While in Costa Rica, he fathered a child. Maybe he got married, but I don't know for sure."

"Oh." He looked with interest at Johnny. "Is that true? You have a family?"

Johnny didn't respond.

Liz, beside me, said, "Put the puzzle pieces together, Roland. Johnny fathered a child in Costa Rica. And that's where Angelina is from, and now here she is."

Roland's mouth opened but he produced no sound. He looked at Liz and at Johnny and at Angelina. Johnny continued to examine the cigarette, Angelina the floor.

"That's not true. Is it?" said Roland.

I said, "Based on the timeline, I bet a DNA test will reveal that Angelina is Johnny's granddaughter. That's why Johnny was so revolted when you admitted you hit on her years ago and she let you."

Walter, crack detective on the couch, said, "Good Lord. I didn't know that. None of it." He turned off his phone and put it away. Crossed his arms over his big belly. Stared at the ceiling.

"Angelina wanted to come to America and her grandfather is American. So he helped her get settled into the land of opportunity. It was great for him, having some family. But he's broke, can barely take care of himself. She's broke too, but Johnny helped her find work. With his old pal Rolly."

Ten seconds of silence and Roland nodded in his chair. "That's it. You're right. Johnny recommended her."

"Nobody here is denying it, so that fact is settled," I said. "The story progresses and everything is fine except Johnny and Angelina are still broke. She's tried marrying into some money but it didn't work. Sure would be nice to have cash and Rolly's got bunches of the stuff."

Angelina began to quietly cry.

"Enter Alan Anderson. Roland, as you know, you're giving away millions to charities. Three of them caught my eye, the three getting the most money," I said.

Roland had been slowly nodding this whole time. "We talked about this. I remember."

Alan stood up, arms stiff. "This is absurd. I won't listen to slander. Roland, you selected the charities. Remember? Not a dime is going somewhere you didn't approve. Look over the will yourself. You know all of it."

Roland said, "That's true, I do. I signed off on them."

"So don't draw me into your pathetic machinations, detective." The way Alan said detective, I hated it.

"He may have signed the paper, Alan, but you deceived them."

"Them?" said Roland, surprised. "Them who?"

"Alan tricked you. And Johnny and Angelina."

Liz pointed at the chair. "Sit down, Mr. Anderson."

He did, mumbling about suing us for defamation.

"I'm confused," said Roland. "Johnny and Angelina aren't in my will."

"They are. Or they think they are," I said.

"How?"

"I'll continue and you'll get it."

"Okay," said Roland. "Okay. I just don't understand..."

"The story goes on. You decided to make a will within the past few years. Or at least, amend your will. I'd guess it happened around the time of your brother's death," I said.

"It did, yes."

"So you get Alan to help. That's not really his job, but he's your financial advisor and you trust him. He advises you on the numbers and he arranges for the lawyer in the office adjacent to his to help. Easy peasy. However, Alan can't help but notice you're leaving precious little money to your family. Most of it is going to charity. And the love of money begins to eat at him."

"Outrageous. *Outrageous*. I've never been so insulted," said Alan.

"It turns out, nonprofits only take a few months to set up. And so he does. He sets up three and he advises you bequeath significant funds to them. You trust him. You didn't know the nonprofits are brand new, and it's child's play to influence your altruism. You feel good about it, your money staying in Roanoke. Ten million dollars going to the parents of kids of special needs, and to veterans, and to Alan's own financial literacy nonprofit. What could be better."

Roland blinked. Blinked again, thinking it through. Asked Alan, "You set those three charities up…yourself? When?"

Alan tried to reply but paused.

I said, "Good question, Roland. Because Alan can lie about a lot but he can't change the federal record. The dates on those three nonprofits are fixed in stone. They were set up simultaneously and they coincide with your amended will. You can see for yourself online. I confess I didn't notice the first time I checked."

"Okay." Alan was red in the face. "Okay sure. My personal charity benefits and I set it up as an avenue for Roland's funds. I won't deny it. But I *do* charitable work in the city!"

"Twice a year," I said. "Hardly worth four million dollars."

"That's not *your* concern. I plan to expand."

"What about the other two?" said Roland. "About the veterans and the kids with special needs."

"I'm not on those boards!" shouted Alan.

"But you are Barry's conservator upon Roland's death. A neat trick, creating a charity to benefit kids with special needs and you just so happen to be set up as a guardian of one."

"That's...I wouldn't keep all that money for myself. It would benefit Barry, of course."

"I got suspicious when those nonprofits wouldn't return my calls. You know who's presiding over them? Retired guys who left their clients to Alan. They're real people but officers in name only, because Alan handles their portfolio. He's the de facto manager of all three. He controls the purse strings."

"I...just because I manage them..." said Alan. "That doesn't mean I committed a crime. I fully intend to honor Roland with his disbursements. His memory will live on in his charitable causes."

Roland was having trouble keeping up. "But...the charities won't benefit veterans and the parents of kids with special needs?"

"Of *course* they will, Roland. Don't listen to him."

"Mackenzie researched all three, Roland, extensively," said Liz. "They do nothing. They're just bank accounts, waiting for you to die and dump ten million divested dollars into them."

"So..." Roland waved a hand at Alan. "He wants me dead."

"No! Roland! Please don't listen to them."

Liz smiled. "The story isn't over, Roland. It's only now getting interesting."

"Okay. Keep going."

Johnny made a noise of protest but it didn't amount to much.

I said, "This part is a guess. But as Alan was setting up a charity for himself, and as he was setting up a charity to provide himself with *more* money when he became Barry's conservator, he decided to include Johnny and Angelina in his scheme."

"Bull*shit*," said Alan. "There is no scheme. I broke no law."

"Alan saw that Johnny and Angelina were broke and he approached them. Let them in on the details. Told them he had a way to make them rich. To get you, Roland, to fund an account earmarked for veterans upon your death. And Johnny and Angelina would get it all."

"But you said Alan is getting all the money," said Roland.

"I did. I bet this is the first time Johnny and Angelina are learning that the fake veteran's nonprofit is controlled by Alan. They don't get the money, he does. And now they're wondering if he intends to share. Quite a shock for them."

"That charity will benefit veterans, Roland. Don't listen."

Roland said, "You lost me, August. Why would Alan tell Johnny and Angelina he'd make them rich?"

"This is hearsay and conjecture! You can't prove *anything*!" shouted Alan, standing again.

Roland ignored him. "If what you're saying is true, why wouldn't Alan keep it all? Why would he help them and lie to me about it?"

"Because," said Liz. "Alan and Angelina are lovers."

A sudden silence. Alan's legs surrendered and he sat heavily down, and the chair squeaked.

Roland, gobsmacked. "They...Alan and Angelina...they..."

I said, "Angelina was with another man at the time, based on her photos online. My guess, Alan used the prospect of money to win her over. And it worked."

Walter, arms still crossed over his big belly, still staring at the ceiling, said, "I didn't know that. Didn't know they were dating."

"That..." said Alan. He swallowed, his knobby Adam's apple bobbing. "That doesn't matter."

Angelina had been quietly crying and she released a louder sob.

Walter shook his head. "Honest to God. Didn't see that coming."

"I bet you didn't," said Liz.

I continued my story. "Alan had been watching Angelina for a long time and he wanted her and he offered her millions. So the three of them set everything up. It was set. You die, Roland, and they inherit a fortune. Or, at least, their charities will inherit a fortune and they'll pay themselves extravagant salaries. The only problem is, Roland, you're in great shape. You just keep on living. By the looks of it, you'll outlive Johnny by a decade."

Roland had been looking back and forth around the room, growing more and more surprised. Now, though, the implications settled in. His shoulders slumped and a cloud descended. Misery and betrayal.

"They needed me to die," he said, barely audible. "If I'm alive, they don't get anything. They needed me...dead. It was...it was them."

"Rolly." Johnny took a drag with shaky fingers but the cigarette was out. "Don't listen to 'em, buddy. I didn't...I never—"

"I was right." Roland said it so soft that Liz leaned forward to hear. "I was right. Follow the money, I said. I was..."

"I don't know who came up with the idea of killing you, Roland," I said. "Alan had promised Angelina a fortune and he wasn't delivering, so it might be him. It might be Johnny. I found a castor bean plant in his house. Those are used to produce ricin, a poison probably used to spike the water bottle that killed the birds several weeks ago."

"You were in my house?" said Johnny, talking in a soft rattle.

"I was," I said.

"That's a rotten, disrespectful thing to do," he mumbled. "I'm a veteran."

"This is ludicrous, all of it," said Alan. "You can't prove anything."

I said, "Another guess—Angelina has been using the strychnine. It's in the shed out back and she's no pro at it. She bought the aspirin bottle and thought she'd give it a try. I think she also took the gun out of your room and put it in Barry's. She cleans both rooms so it was easy. It was Alan who attacked Liz in the cemetery. He took pains so I couldn't see his head, but I bet we'll find a purple spot where Liz hit him. Point is, Roland, it wasn't one killer. It was three. It took a village."

"Good hell."

"Walter," I said. "You were correct, in your office. You said it might be Hickam's dictum. Remember? There was more than one cause."

On the couch, he sniffed. Not a laugh but kinda.

Tears dotted the floor near Angelina's feet, where she was bent over, crying. I hadn't seen her face in several minutes.

"This..." said Roland. "I...I can't believe this. This is damned— This is...this is outrageous."

"And untrue. None of this is true, Roland. These sonofabitch detectives have nothing and they're lying to cover it up." Alan stood up again. I lost track of how many times he'd done that. He pointed at me. "You're just guessing! You're throwing around accusations with no evidence. It's... dangerous and destructive. Yes, I set up charities but Roland approved of them. Yes, Angelina and I are...we're together. But none of the rest is true. You have no proof. We have alibis. We have alibis for everything!"

"Alan," I said. "Alan, you poor bastard. It's about to get worse."

"What in the hell does that mean?"

"Were you waiting for Roland to die before marrying Angelina?"

"I...no. No we're not waiting for anything. We just..."

"You have a status in the city to protect. Is that it? All your prosperous clients would see you marry a girl from Costa Rica. They'd see her Instagram photos. They wouldn't blame you. In fact they'd envy you. But it'd make you look... eager. Immature. Unprofessional. They wouldn't know if they could trust you with their money. Is that it?"

Angelina cried louder again.

"You can go to hell, August." Alan's face was white. "Ang and I are in love. We simply haven't gone public yet."

"Maybe. Maybe not," I said. I didn't feel good about this part.

"What's that mean?"

I said, "We should have caught on quicker, Alan. It drove me nuts that I couldn't figure it out. But, looking back on it, the cards were stacked against us."

Although he didn't want to hear anymore, Roland asked, "How?"

I answered him. "Alan had help. They all did."

"Help?" said Roland. "There's more? There are others?"

"One more. They had an inside man. A way to feed us fake alibis. And I never saw it. That's why it took so long."

"Never saw *what*?"

"Walter," I said. Nodded at the guy on the couch who didn't even flinch at the revelation. He'd known. "Walter Lowe betrayed us. He moved in and fell for Angelina. He even told me he did, but I didn't listen. He's the one who discovered the bottle of strychnine and Angelina realized she had to prevent that from happening again. So she seduced him. She used sex and got her way."

"Holy..." Roland stiffened. "Holy God."

Walter, arms crossed, stared at the ceiling.

"That's not true," said Alan. "She didn't seduce him. Right? Angelina? You didn't use..."

I said, "That's why Walter started requesting days off. Looking back on it, they coincided with Angelina's off days. I even found him once with his pants undone after she left but I didn't understand. To quote my son, they needed to get a room. Somewhere other than this house."

Alan was still standing, but he looked small. "That's not...not true. You don't know anything. Right? Angelina?"

"The cameras started going off. They weren't malfunctioning—he was flipping a switch. But I didn't pick up on it. He did it so he and Angelina could talk and fool around. Make plans to meet outside the house."

Angelina's head was down. Still crying.

"Ang...did you...?" said Alan.

Roland twisted in his chair to address Liz. He was a mess

of emotion. Outrage and hurt. "You brought a traitor into my house."

"More like, I brought an imbecile. A horny one. I apologize. I had no idea he would start fooling around with your killer."

"They did *not* fool around!" Alan was going hoarse. "Right, Ang? Walter?"

Walter sighed. He took out his phone. Turned it on. Turned it off. Set it down. Picked it up again. Looked miserable.

"You have no proof," said Alan. He dropped into the chair again. "No evidence. And Angelina wouldn't."

"Alan," said Liz. She sounded sympathetic. "How did you and Angelina get together?"

"What do you mean? We fell in love."

"You were seduced. She's gorgeous. No offense, Alan, but why would she want to be with a skinny white guy twenty years older than her? Because you held the promise of wealth. She needed your services."

"No. *No.* We...we love each other. Sure, I provide financial security and she—"

"Not yet you don't. She seduced you. And she seduced Walter. She's a survivor and she's good at it, I'm sure, just look at her," said Liz.

"Yeah." Another long sigh out of Walter and he spoke with a breathy, sad voice. "I'm sorry, Mack. Sorry, Lizzy. It didn't take much."

"No," said Alan. "*No.* What do you mean?"

"What do you think I mean?"

"No," Alan said again. "She wouldn't."

Angelina raised her head up. Her eyes were puffy and she stared defiantly out of the windows.

"If it helps," said Walter, "I didn't know she was the

killer. She promised. I thought we were hiding our...*relationship.* Not covering for attempted murder. Johnny told me that night, on the porch. Said they needed my help. And by then...well, I knew I'd screwed it up and I didn't want to get busted. Hand to God, you guys, I didn't know. They didn't tell me about the cemetery and the gunshots until after they happened."

Angelina did an eye roll and a scoff.

"You...you're..." Alan blustered. "What, you couldn't keep your dick in your pants?"

"Well, I had help getting it out, Alan, so back off."

"I'm confused." Roland, the poor guy, had tears. "Who attacked Walter with a shovel?"

I said, "Nobody. I bet it was even Walter's idea. He asked Johnny to whack him with a shovel and hide it at Zeus's so we wouldn't suspect him. And it worked. Yesterday Walter lied to us, told me Johnny was here at this house. But he wasn't. He met Alan to get a gun and take shots at me. That's why Alan was late and why he refused to get out of the car. He was afraid he might be hit. They arranged it."

Walter said, "I'm sorry, Mack. Really. I feel horrible about it. Honest to God..."

"But me? You...you fat bastard, they could kill *me* and that was okay?" said Roland.

"No. No it wasn't and I'm sorry. I was getting laid for the first time in a long time and I wasn't thinking straight until it was too late. They used me. Manipulated me. I suck at my job, what can I say." He mumbled it all.

Liz said, "So there you are, Roland. It wasn't one person. It was three, plus an accomplice."

"You can prove nothing," said Alan. He was talking to us, but watching Angelina and his future crumble. "This is still...still a farce."

Johnny hadn't spoken in a while but now he stood. He looked like a shell of a human, no lights on. I hated this most of all for him. War had left him unsound, his life ruined.

"I'm leaving," he said.

"Johnny, not yet."

"Why not? Are you gonna attack an old man?"

"I'd rather not," I said. Although no one looked at it, all the attention in the room latched onto my holster. Everyone looked at it without looking at it. "We're waiting on Alan and we're waiting on Roland."

Roland said, "Waiting on Alan? What for?"

"He has a gun in the bag he brought. He's reached for it a few times but stopped. I bet ballistics will match it to the bullets fired at me yesterday. I'm wondering if he'll go for it. I hope so. He attacked a woman in a cemetery with a flashlight and I'm angry at him. His perfect world is crumbling. It's been ordered and codified for years until the last few days, and desperation makes us do stupid things, and I'm hoping he'll try."

Liz was surprised. "You're hoping he will?"

"Yes."

"Why?"

"It'll give me reason to hurt him."

"That won't heal my eye," she said.

"But still."

Liz shot both me and Alan with a withering glare, like a teacher with angry students. "There doesn't have to be violence."

"There often is."

Johnny sat back down. Watching Alan.

Alan dropped his gaze to his hands; he couldn't bear to

look anywhere else. "I'm...I'm not going for my gun. I have nothing to hide."

Walter, arms still crossed, nodded at Roland. "What do you mean, we're waiting on Roland? The case is closed."

"Remember why we hired me?" said Liz. "Why he hired us? He wanted names. He wants to kill someone."

Roland, on cue, leaned forward and picked up Liz's Glock. He stood stiffly.

34

Angelina issued a strangled cry and she got up. She backed against the wall, made a thump.

"Rolly! *Ay dios mio*, no! I'm sorry, Rolly!"

"Careful, there's one in the chamber," said Liz.

"Rolly, buddy." Johnny held his hands up like shields. "Easy with that pistol. You shot one person already. Maybe you give it to me?"

Roland's hands were shaking and so was the barrel of the Glock.

"*You*." He cried the word. "You three. Tried to kill me." He waved the gun at Walter. Walter winced and ducked. "You four."

"I think," I said, "that Walter never tried to kill you. He aided and abetted. Often unwittingly."

Alan standing again. "No! Roland! Put the gun *down*. This is *madness*. You can't kill us! Nothing is proven! They can't prove anything!"

"Don't be asinine, Alan," I said. "Yes we can. It'll be simple for the police to get your phone records. You can delete this history off your phones, but not from your permanent call log. I bet you three call and text. A lot. Besides, Walter's already confessed, and how quickly do you think Angelina will turn on you?" I snapped my fingers. Everyone jumped. "Like that. She's a survivor. So is Johnny. I bet they say it was all your idea. And maybe even that you did the poisoning."

Angelina, crying, at the wall, nodded. "He did. It was Alan."

"Hey! *No!* She's lying!"

"Shut up!" Roland shouted. "All of you! You tried to kill me. Kill *me*."

"Rolly." Johnny's hands still raised. "Now, calm down, buddy."

"I helped you, Johnny. I'm the only guy in the world who's taken care of you! Who understands what you went through!"

Johnny shook his head. "You understand nothing. You never did. And that's the whole problem."

Roland raised the gun. Angelina screamed. He aimed it at the ceiling and fired three blasts. Rocked our ear drums. "Enough!"

Walter, on his feet, moving behind the couch, face white. "Why the *hell* did you give him a loaded gun?"

"That's why he hired us," said Liz. She and I were the only ones sitting.

"He thinks it'll help," I said. "To kill his killers."

"It doesn't. It doesn't, Rolly old buddy. Trust me, it doesn't."

Roland pointed the gun at Alan. "Pick it up."

"Pick what up?" Alan's whole body shook.

"Your weapon. Like a man."

"I...I don't have one."

"Yes you do. A pistol in your bag," I said.

"But I won't pick it up."

"Do it! Coward!" Fired twice more at ceiling. Hard echoes off the walls. Our ears throbbed and cartridges tinkled on the hardwood.

"You have six more bullets, Roland," said Liz, talking loud.

"I wouldn't though," I said. "You still got at least a good decade left. Spend it free. But that's up to you."

"Rolly, please," said Johnny. "Put it down."

"Shut up. Shut up Johnny." Roland said it and he spit on the floor. "You. All of you. Just...stop talking. You lie. You all lied. I don't want to hear your voices anymore."

No one spoke. Everyone behind the couch. Angelina hid behind Alan for protection.

"Don't say a word. Bastards. Because you mean nothing to me. Not a damn thing. You're worth *nothing*. And I could kill you. I could. Right now." Roland released the pistol and it landed on the chair next to him. "But I won't. You're not worth it. I won't go to jail for you."

Nobody moved. Like if they did he'd change his mind.

Roland took a few shaky breaths. The pungency of burnt gunpowder—nitroglycerin—was strong in the air.

Without looking at me, he said, "Did I pass your test, inspector?"

I said, "Did you pass your own?"

"I don't know. I feel old. An old man who doesn't have what it takes to kill a man."

"That's the problem, Roland," I said. "You see that as a weakness. It takes more strength to be merciful."

With slow steps, Roland went for the lonely stairs. Started crying again. His slippers scuffing. He ascended, gripping the rail for support, bent over. Finally gone.

Liz moved first. She retrieved her fallen pistol and slipped it into her holster.

Walter, behind the couch. "I can't believe you gave that maniac a loaded gun."

"Look at the ceiling, you idiot. You see any holes?"

"What?" Walter looked up.

"I loaded it with blanks," she said.

"Then why the shit did you give it to him? I think I almost had a heart attack. Like a real one," said Walter.

"He had to know," I said. "Had to have the chance. Or the illusion of it."

"Why?"

"That's why he hired us. And sometimes," I said, "you define yourself by what you don't do. Or won't do. He'll be a new person now, based on what he refused to do. Hopefully."

I got to my feet. Walked toward Alan and he backed up.

"Don't," he said.

I reached into his bag and took his gun. "A Springfield. Good for you, Alan. Think I'll sell this to a pawn shop, pay for the repair to my car."

"We can go," said Alan. "Right? We *can*. You can't prove it. I'll deny everything. So will they. They were just *scared*. Nobody will admit it."

"Maybe." Liz smiled, as if there wasn't gun smoke drifting in the room. "But Sheriff Stackhouse is waiting for you four in her office and she's already offering reduced charges to whoever confesses first."

"That's..." Alan looked nervously at Angelina and Johnny. "No. We're—"

"I'll go," said Walter. "I screwed up. I own it. I feel bad about it. Let's go, I'll tell the police."

Alan said, "No! You fat idiot, we stick together."

"I'll go too," said Johnny.

Angelina, wiping her eyes. "It was Alan's idea. And he did the poisoning. Right?"

"Bullshit!" Alan was spitting with his words. "I didn't do any of the poison. *You* assholes did it all! I have the texts to prove it!"

The three of them shouted at each other, filling the house with noise. Walter took out his phone.

I grinned. Liz grinned.

"Those sound like confessions," I told her. "Lucky my iPhone's recording everything. How convenient."

"Nice job, Mackenzie."

"You too, detective."

"I'm glad I hired you," she said.

"Obviously."

35

Liz and I finally got out of the police station at 1:30 in the afternoon, having deposited four would-be killers and two hours of testimony. Detective Green didn't say it, but I could tell he thought I was the cat's pajamas.

The two of us met Ronnie downtown at Sidecar for lunch. Liz drove; my car was in the shop, being treated for gun-related injures. Liz stayed on the sidewalk, talking on the phone to Roland's niece, telling her she and Barry should move into Roland's house because they could all use the company and support. I wouldn't blame Barry if he balked, however. That house might no longer be salutary.

I walked into the restaurant and Ronnie took my face with her hands and kissed me.

"Mackenzie," she said. "It went well?"

"According to plan."

"But you are melancholy."

"I am. Johnny's life has been a disaster since Vietnam and Angelina was trying her best. It doesn't excuse their crimes, but it explains them. Walter and Alan, they fell for a beautiful woman and it made them do stupid things," I said.

"Can you relate?"

"I can. I would do stupid things for you, if you asked."

"As I would for you, Mackenzie." She kissed me again. We sat and ordered drinks.

Liz joined us and the waiter made recommendations and we took them. Liz asked for a to-go meal and explained, "For my husband. I've been missing him the past few days. He's a little jealous of Mackenzie."

"Hard to blame him," I said.

"You should see him work, Ronnie, your husband. Mackenzie's cool under pressure like I can't believe. He had it all lined up, orchestrating the conversation."

Ronnie beamed and the waiter, refilling our waters, paused to enjoy it. She said, "I've seen him in action a few times. It's breathtaking. He'd make a great attorney."

"Except," I said. "I have a soul."

"One of us should. What will you do now, Liz?"

"Take a few days off. Roland paid us well and I need a vacation." Liz smiled and reclined in her chair. "That confrontation really took it out of me. So stressful. How about you, Mackenzie?"

"Nothing a day of golf and a good book won't fix. Superman doesn't take extended vacations."

"I need to ask this crazy-ass question. Get it off my chest," said Liz. "Are you two married or engaged or what? Because for a long time everyone knew you two were fooling around. But then, Ron, I see you're always at his place. What's the deal? Can I know?"

"Of course you can." Ronnie leaned my way to rest her head on my shoulder. "We're engaged. And married. And I'm so happy I could die."

"You're both?"

I nodded. "We throw off the shackles of society and do things out of order."

"It's confusing. We're legally married but we haven't exchanged vows yet. Until then, I keep him around using my sexual wiles," said Ronnie. "Tell everyone."

"About your sexual wiles?"

"Yes please, and that they are being plied on one man for the rest of my life."

Liz said, "Gotta be careful with those wiles. I just left a police station where a woman got in trouble doing that."

"Perhaps," said Ronnie, "she plied them to a lesser man."

"Speaking of, you're not going to say it?" asked Liz. "Mackenzie? You told me *not* to hire Walter. You won't remind me of that fact?"

"Some things," I said, "you have to learn on your own. Like, Mackenzie August is all the man you need."

"Did he ever flirt with you?" said Ronnie. "I told him he could."

Liz grinned. "He didn't. Matter fact, he insulted me. A lot."

My phone rang. As a rule, I don't answer phones on dates with sun goddesses. But it was Kix's school calling. I showed Ronnie the screen and she said, "Answer it."

I did.

The nice lady on the other end said, "Good afternoon, Mr. August. I know pickup isn't for another hour, but I thought you might like to come early? He's fine, he's *fine*, but your son had an accident. He's fine, really. Kix was walking and he tripped outside, and he hit his head on the playground equipment. He's fine! But he bled and he's upset and if you—"

"I'll get him early." I hung up.

"What?" Ronnie's eyes were wider than usual. "What is it? What happened?"

"Kix sustained a head injury."

Ronnie stood and her chair fell backward.

"Those bitches," she said. Her face lost some color. "I'll kill them."

"He's okay."

"I'm going."

"Drinks and appetizers first?"

"We're suing, Mackenzie. I will bury them under a lawsuit so thick they'll have to flee the country."

"Maybe," I said, "Maybe you wait here so you don't scare the faculty."

"My baby's hurt, Mackenzie."

I nodded. "You're my ride anyway."

Liz made a shooing motion at us. "Go. I'll pay. Or rather, Roland will pay."

I tried to get behind the wheel but Ronnie boxed me out. She drove to the Montessori school and she obeyed not one traffic law. She beat me through the front doors.

Kix was there, waiting in the arms of the dean, a woman trying to preempt litigation by smiling a lot. Kix had two bandaids on his forehead.

Ronnie stopped at the sight and covered her mouth and her eyes welled. Protective instincts engaged. But, as on the first day of school, she stayed back. Like she didn't belong yet, an outsider.

Kix had his emotions under control until seeing us and it spilled out again. He raised his arms and cried.

The woman talked over him, "He's fine. He *really* is! The poor thing. It happens."

I nodded. "We know. It's okay." I went to get him.

His arms reaching, mouth turning down, lip jutting. The saddest, most beautiful, most pathetic boy alive. He cried, "Momma!"

I stopped.

He wasn't holding his arms to me. He was holding them up to Ronnie.

She made a gasp. I thought her knees might give out.

He shouted again. "Momma!"

Mom! I hit my head and it hurts and the girls laughed! Mommmmm!

He wanted his mom and he knew her when he saw her. My knees might give out too. I could barely stand.

She dropped her car keys, a shattering crash on the tile. Collected Kix from the dean. Gripped him tight and he gripped her tight and I ached with joy. Physical pain, watching them, mother and child.

"Did you hear, Mackenzie? He called me..." Ronnie falling apart, laughing, crying. "He knows I'm... He called me mom."

Kix wept into her shirt, a blouse I knew cost three hundred dollars, and she didn't care. She left the lobby, retreating outside because she was crying harder than the injured boy she carried.

I wiped my eyes and signed him out on the log.

The dean, the poor creature, was confused.

"Mr. August, I am *so* sorry Kix hit his head. He was outside playing and..."

"We get it. These things happen. I'm surprised he's lived this long."

She looked past me. "Is your wife...I mean, is his mother...I mean, do you think Ms. Summers is okay?

"Yes." I smiled and turned to go. "His mother, my wife, is

fine. In fact, despite appearances, this could be the happiest we've ever been."

THE END

Dear Reader,

I CRIED SOME, writing the final chapter. If you didn't get a little emotional then you are a monster. Or else I failed you.

A few fun notes about the Mackenzie August journey.

The first August book (*Last Teacher*) was published in 2015. The next, (*August Origins*, originally titled *Sophomore Slump*) was released in 2017.

Last Teacher sold a few dozen copies.

During the first month, *August Origins* and *The Second Secret* each moved a few hundred.

TO GIVE you an idea of how Mackenzie's readership is growing, the latest August book, *These Mortals*, has sold over 10,000 so far (including Kindle Unlimited reads).

Progress.

I wanted to be writer since sitting in detention in the 9th grade and picking up a novel out of boredom. That novel soon led to Mickey Spillane and Alistair MacLean, then to Tom Clancy and Robert Parker.

I came home from soccer practice and tennis practice and I read, homework forgotten. To graduate with an English degree from college, I had to write a senior thesis. My professor returned the thesis, and along the top she'd scrawled, *This is so bad, I cannot believe you're a college senior.* She later apologized and admitted she'd been drinking, which, I thought, was hurtful.

But all is well that ends well. A senior thesis is no place for a mystery writer.

I hope you'll stick with me. I'm having too much fun to stop.

Mackenzie and Ronnie and Kix and Manny are only getting started.

Made in the USA
Middletown, DE
20 May 2024

54597522R00163